# Shrine of the Ancients

## By

## Terry L Shaffer

# ACKNOWLEDGEMENTS

This is my thirteenth published novel. The more I write, the more people I owe for their generosity and loyalty. Writing is a lonely, arduous endeavor and I, for one am grateful for all the help and encouragement given me by a very special group of folks who have also become good friends. Barbara and Len Eaton, Becky Geroux, Mike Early, Jean Batchelder, David Graves and Colleen Bretches all generously gave of their time and expertise to make this novel better. No one person can proofread a 92,000-word manuscript and catch all the errors and inconsistencies contained therein. I only hope that one day I'll be able to reciprocate.

Other books by this author, found on Amazon and Kindle:

*Legacy of a Primitive*

*Caballo Gold*

*Treachery Island*

*Charlie Perkins*

*Charlie Perkins: Challenges*

*Charlie Perkins: Resolutions*

*Charlie Perkins: Conclusions*

*Coronado's Deceit*

*The Charlie Bell Sting*

*The Imam's Evil*

*Theft of Lives*

*Four and a Half Days*

# CHAPTER 1

The go-fast Mustang in front of him was being driven erratically, speeding up, slowing down suddenly, then speeding up again and swerving across the center line and fog line. It looked like a sure DUII to Santa Fe (New Mexico) Deputy Bob Connelly and he duly reported it as such before he flicked on his overhead lights, hit his high beams, take-down lights and waited for a reaction. The driver, and apparently sole occupant of the car, immediately stomped on the brakes making Bob brake hard to avoid a collision.

The Mustang, cut abruptly to the right and almost went into the borrow ditch before the driver got it stopped part way in the traffic lane. Bob quickly called in the plate number before he got out of his car. He stood by his door, watching the driver and waited for dispatch to tell him the car's status. It came back clear, so he approached the driver's side, being careful not to silhouette himself in front of his spotlight beam. He arrived just behind the driver's door post and shined his flashlight into the car noting that both the driver's hands were on the wheel.

"Good evening, Sir," Bob said, loudly over the growl of the Mustang's exhaust.

"I stopped you because you seem to be having trouble keeping your car in your lane."

The driver looked at Bob through bleary eyes and slurred, "I'm drunk, Officer, take me to jail." With that, the driver struggled to unbuckle his seat belt and open his door. Bob caught the edge of the door when it opened and held it for the driver as he clumsily slid from behind the wheel and stood up, leaning heavily on the car in a cloud of alcoholic vapors.

"Let's walk to the back of your car so we're safely out of traffic," Bob suggested. He took hold of the driver's arm and guided him back to the space between the two cars. "Why don't you put your the hands on the trunk of your car to steady yourself and pull your legs back away from the car?" The driver sloppily complied but remained leaning against the Mustang's bumper.

*Too drunk for sobriety tests.* Bob tucked his flashlight in a hip pocket then reached out and grabbed the driver's left wrist and pulled it behind the man's back in order to handcuff him. As he told the driver to put his right hand behind his back, the man jerked away from Bob and shouldered the deputy in the chest. The blow drove Bob backward where he lost his balance and fell butt first into the borrow ditch. The driver staggered back to his car and took off, spraying gravel over Bob's patrol car and Bob. Bob scrambled back up the ditch bank to his car and, as he buckled in, he was on the radio reporting that the traffic stop had become a pursuit. He shifted the high performance Dodge Charger into gear and accelerated after the Mustang. He could see its weaving tail lights ahead on the straight-as-a-string stretch of highway and settled in for the chase. The Mustang's driver pushed the car up over one hundred twenty

2

miles an hour until the straight away ended, then began to slow dramatically to clumsily negotiate the curves as they entered a canyon. The driver started riding the brakes to slow the car until the brakes got hot and began to lose their effectiveness. Bob had meantime approached within a few car lengths and was content on this stretch of road to just maintain his distance until such time as cover could join him and they could employ spike strips or he could effect a PIT (Precision Immobilization Technique) maneuver to throw the Mustang out of control and get it stopped. He needed low speed and a fairly straight section of road to tap the rear corner of the car, throwing it's geometry off, and bringing it to a halt, hopefully, not after it rolled!

The Mustang had slowed sufficiently for the PIT but the road through the canyon was too curvy; he would risk rolling the car into the canyon. Bob maintained a steady distance behind the Mustang, keeping the pressure on the driver and hoping no oncoming traffic would appear since the Mustang was all over the road. The suspect had sideswiped two parked cars already, then clipped a couple of power pole guy wires, but managed to keep going.

They finally emerged from the canyon onto a flatter plain but before Bob could set up for the PIT, the driver made a sharp turn onto a side road, fishtailing badly. It was gravel surfaced and Bob knew it was a dead end since it wound around back into the canyon they had just traversed. The Mustang slowed down due to the gravel and the curves and Bob closed up, now knowing how this pursuit was going to end.

Within a quarter mile, the gravel road became a cul-de-sac with a railroad tie

barricade blocking the way forward. The Mustang skidded to a stop almost nudging the barricade and Bob eased up behind it so that his push bars were pressed against the back of the Mustang. The driver of the Mustang suddenly put the car in reverse in an attempt to escape and only succeeded in spinning gravel beneath his car and out to the sides. Finally the driver gave that up and appeared to be sitting in the car thinking. Bob could see that the man was taking pulls off a bottle of something.

Bob keyed his PA microphone and informed the driver that Bob was with the Sheriff's Office and that the driver was under arrest. He ordered the driver to get out of the car and lay down on the ground with his arms spread-eagled away from his body; he would not be harmed.

The driver just sat there in the Mustang. Bob waited behind the open door of his patrol car, his service weapon at the ready. Time was on his side. As soon as cover arrived, they could deal tactically with this guy. In the meantime, Bob was content to just keep him in the car.

The driver wasn't thinking along the same lines. Suddenly the driver's door lurched open and the driver struggled out. "You ain't arresting me, you son-of-a-bitch!" screamed the driver as he straightened up and faced the bright wall of light that was all he could see.

Bob could see a handgun in the driver's right hand; he yelled over the PA for the driver to drop the weapon and back away from it. It was if the driver didn't hear him. He started for the patrol car and started shooting. His walk became a staggering run and he kept screaming obscenities and firing at Bob, hitting the patrol car's windshield once and peppering Bob with broken glass as another round struck the driver's door window frame. The driver almost made it to the back of the Mustang before Bob fired two rounds into the suspect's center mass, hitting him both times in the chest. The driver stopped suddenly and looked down at his chest before collapsing to the gravel.

For a short while, Bob remained by his door, looking for movement from the suspect. After he was satisfied the man would not get up and continue firing, Bob approached him with gun still drawn. He kicked the weapon away from the man's hand then knelt to check for a carotid pulse. He found nothing. He saw that the suspect was only a teenager – Native American by his looks – and it devastated Bob. He had enough presence of mind to ensure there was no one else in the Mustang then holstered his weapon and began to shake. In twenty-six years, this was Bob Connelly's first life-threatening confrontation.

Ten minutes later the first cover officer arrived and found Bob leaning against the front fender of his patrol car staring at the body.

***** 

5

The next two weeks proved to be the absolute worst of Bob's career and it was because of what transpired during that time he was convinced that there was no longer a place for a man such as him at the Santa Fe County Sheriff's Office, or in any other facet of law enforcement. There seemed no end to the plethora of criminal investigators, administrative investigators, civil investigators all wanting to talk directly with him with, he insisted, his attorney present. With few exceptions they all appeared to be self-absorbed with the objective of meeting the protocols laid out by the Department of Justice and the International Association of Chiefs of Police. They really didn't seem to care what Bob's answers were, only that they asked all the right questions. It was driving Bob nuts.

The only person who seemed to really give a damn about how Bob was doing was the veteran sergeant running the actual shooting investigation, Chuck Eversole. He didn't seem to give much of a damn what all the suits thought. He and Bob went back a ways and had been partners once upon a time.

"We've been getting pretty lucky in our investigation," he told Bob. "The kid stole the car from his uncle who didn't know the car was gone when you stopped it. The .380 auto he shot at you came from his dad's collection so Dad is sweating bullets, excuse the pun. We found a couple who lived across the wash from the barricade. Your PA woke them up and they could hear everything you said to the suspect. They couldn't make out what the suspect was screaming but knew right away when the shooting started, first with a bunch of pops then with two booms. They'll be excellent corroborating witnesses if it comes to that.

"Don't let all the pinheads get to you, Bob. None have a clue how it feels to be where you are now and that's why they're so damned impersonal about how they go about talking to you. To them it's another academic exercise and then they go home. I don't much like all the lawyers involved but the county is sweating this out big time mainly because it's the first Officer Involved Shooting (OIS) fatality in eight years. Most of them were still in school during the last one. Anyway, I'll keep you up-to-date as the investigation progresses."

"Thanks, Chuck, you don't know how much better that makes me feel."

"Yeah, I probably do. I've been where you are, and if it wasn't for an old salty veteran running the show, I might well have bailed. Is that on your mind?"

"Yeah. I think I've had enough. When the time comes, where it doesn't look like I'm retiring because I have something to hide, I think I'll pull the plug. Financially I'm in good shape and I can see now that there's more to life than putting up with all this bullshit," Bob finally admitted to himself as he spoke the words.

"I only had about fifteen years on when it happened to me, and they were no more understanding in the investigation at that time. I couldn't really retire, and to quit and go somewhere else

7

would seem like what you said, I was hiding something," said Chuck.

"It's a lousy way to end a career that I loved, and it leaves a bad taste in my mouth," Bob admitted.

"My advice?" said Chuck, "make it a different life than the one you're living now. It should be left in the past."

"I've thought of that, but I don't think I'll ever get over the memories of seeing that kid bleeding out in the gravel."

"Give it time, it'll scab over Bob," said Chuck. "Find yourself a distraction, something to get your mind off it and onto something else. I know that's easy for me to say to you now, but there was a time when I was where you are and felt just as much pain and remorse as you're feeling now. Time is the great equalizer."

"You should have been a counselor or a therapist!"

Chuck grinned. "Couldn't put up with all the bullshit red tape and the whiny-ass boobs that would be most of my patients! Gotta go, talk to you soon."

Bob felt his spirits rise dramatically after his talk with Chuck. He tended to take responsibility for problems even when they weren't really his, and he knew that was a shortcoming he was paying for now.

After two weeks of administrative leave and administrative duty, Bob was released to full duty and went back to graveyard where his interrogators were scarce. Even so, he could tell that his comrades were treading lightly around him, afraid they'd touch a nerve.   In that environment he found it hard to be his old irrepressible self and took to staying within himself.  A month later he had had enough and put in his papers to retire.  There was a half-hearted attempt at a farewell party but Bob was glad to see it end.

Almost immediately, he set out to create a new life for himself.  He bought a fancy new Dodge diesel pickup that he had lusted after for years.  He became more accessible to his neighbors and discovered a few of them were actually worth knowing.  He decided he didn't have enough time left on earth to bother with the deadbeats, and discovered that he was actually beginning to enjoy his retirement.

He still often thought about Darby, his late wife.  She had been the love of his life; they had been inseparable since college until pancreatic cancer took her fifteen years ago.  He vowed then that there would never be another woman in his life since no one could ever take her place.  Now, with time on his hands and a whole lot less people to talk to, he felt her absence more than ever.  Lately he found himself looking at his life and thinking that a companion wasn't such a repugnant idea.  Bob knew he was a long way from becoming attached to another woman but perhaps he was thawing?

At fifty years of age, he didn't feel like he was over the hill. He kept himself in shape with long walks nearly every morning and a thirty-minute kick/punch session with the heavy bag in his garage. To an outsider, he was attractive enough, with chestnut-colored hair starting to show a little gray at the temples, hazel eyes and the beginnings of laugh lines around his eyes.  He only wore glasses to

9

read, never smoked or did drugs and imbibed in alcohol in extreme moderation.

In short, Bob felt good, but restless and tried to put his finger on why. There were no chronic problems around the house that needed his attention and little demand on his time. He found himself joining a small group of retirees for coffee once or twice a week at a local, favored café just for the intellectual stimulation.

One day the topic of conversation around the table was travel. Some of the participants owned recreational vehicles and told endless stories about their adventures on the highways of America. They talked about the places they had visited and the interesting people they had met and suddenly it crystallized in Bob's head: *Road trip.* One of the participants told of a recent trip to the Mojave Desert and Bob sort of tuned it out until there was mention of Monument Valley, Bryce Canyon and Zion National Parks. He did not realize that the Mojave Desert extended all the way up into southwest Utah.

Bob didn't want to go all the way up to Moab though there was much to see. The man who had been talking about the Mojave Desert had mentioned how beautiful it was around Moab but how crowded and expensive it had become! Bob decided that if he ever went that far north into Utah, it would be during off-season months – whenever they might be. He started doing some investigating of the southeast corner of Utah and the northeast corner of Arizona around the Four Corners area and decided that was where he wanted to go.

He found lots of information online about the area and settled into to doing some serious studying.

The more he dug, the more he found and the more eager he was to see it for himself. He found that if he went soon, he would be heading into the monsoon season but didn't worry about that; he didn't want to wait until sometime in September.

He had plotted all his objectives on a large-scale map centered around Bluff, Utah. Bears Ears National Monument, Monument Valley, Comb Ridge, Valley of the Gods, Natural Bridges, Edge of the Cedars State Park, Goosenecks State Park, Muley Point, Moki Dugway, Twin Rocks, Sand Island Petroglyphs, Bluff Fort, Cedar Mesa and myriad Ancestral Puebloan ruins that permeated the area were all places he wanted to visit and, for the first time, felt a twinge thinking he would be doing it alone.

The day of departure dawned sunny with bright blue sky. It would be in the mid-eighties here in seven-thousand-foot Santa Fe but a bit warmer down below. Bob left with an edge of excitement and a twinge of apprehension. As he drove, he settled into the routine, taking his time and enjoying the scenery as he got farther away from Santa Fe. In less than four hours he was in Farmington and stopped for lunch and topped off his fuel. As he departed westward toward Shiprock, he saw heavy cumulo-nimbus clouds forming ahead of him. Undeterred, Bob pressed on, confident that his new truck could handle anything the coming thunderstorm clouds could throw at him.

He was partly right.

# CHAPTER 2

Fast-moving, roiling black monsoon clouds quickly blotted out the setting sun and the rain began, first a light drizzle, then soon, a deluge. The windshield wipers couldn't keep up. Bob had to slow down as waves of water coursed across the pavement in the sudden wind, the pickup's tires hydroplaning. His high beams were of no use since the torrential rain limited his forward vision to no more than a car length.

He had slowed to a crawl before sensing something on the road ahead. A darker mass suddenly blocked out the fog line; Bob instinctively cut the wheel hard to the left, just missing a body walking along the pavement on the narrow shoulder. It took little braking power to stop the creeping pickup.

Bob rolled down the passenger window and called to the person, "Get in before you drown." Without a word, the person obeyed, and as he crawled onto the front seat, Bob could see that it was a young, rangy teenager of no more than seventeen. His dark windbreaker was soaked through to his t-shirt, as were his jeans and tennis shoes. His long, dark hair was tied back in a bedraggled pony tail that reached to his shoulder blades. He appeared to be of Native American descent, probably Navajo, since this section of the road was on the Navajo Nation. The similarity between this boy and the one he had shot was not lost on Bob.

"There's a blanket folded up on the back seat. You can wrap yourself up in it until you get warm." The boy didn't say a word, just twisted around until he could see in the back seat. He retrieved the blanket, shook it out and wrapped himself in it.

"You would warm up faster if you shucked your clothes and let them dry away from your body."

The boy took Bob in at a glance, then said, "I have a knife, Mister, and I don't go in for none of that homo sex stuff."

Taken aback, Bob chuckled and said, "Neither do I. I was just trying to keep you from catching cold or pneumonia."

The boy pulled the blanket closer around him, and stared out the seemingly submerged windshield, saying nothing more.

Bob shifted back into gear and eased forward. He didn't dare go faster than a brisk walk for fear of hitting something or going off the pavement. He turned on his emergency flashers to accompany his head and taillights then turned the temperature in the cab up to as high as it would go.

The boy seemed content just to sit there and stare out the windshield. That wasn't going to work for Bob. He wanted to know who this boy was and where he was going. Was he a runaway, had he just committed a crime, was he destitute with nowhere to go?

He gave the kid about five minutes to break the silence, but in the end, Bob had to do it himself, "Where are you headed?"

The boy just sat there staring out the window seemingly mesmerized by the deluge on the other side of the glass. It was as if he hadn't heard the question. Bob knew he could hear, the little shit

13

heard well enough when he told him to get in and about the blanket. *Maybe he's dreaming up a good story to tell me.*

Bob let it go about another ten minutes, until he saw a wide shoulder next to the road and pulled over. "Listen, bud, I'm not trying to be a hard ass but I asked you a question and I expect an answer. If you choose not to answer, that's your option; but my option is to kick your ass out of the truck right now and don't forget to leave the blanket."

There was silence except for the rain pummeling the roof of the truck. The young man continued to stare out the windshield as if weighing his options. Finally, he looked over at Bob and said, "I'm sorry, I don't mean to be a jerk. I guess I was lost in my own little world and wasn't paying attention." He sounded genuinely contrite.

"My name is Abe Redwolf. I'm from Shiprock. I've been walking to Mexican Hat ever since my mom died two days ago and my uncle kicked me out of the house. My grandfather lives somewhere around Mexican Hat, and I'm hoping he'll let me stay with him. He is an *Hatáli,* a Singer. He is called Carlos Grey Hawk."

Now, Bob felt like the jerk! "Sorry, Abe. I had no way of knowing."

"Nothing to be sorry for; if anyone should be apologizing, it should be me. Anyway, I really appreciate your picking me up. For a while there, I wasn't sure I was going to make it."

"Where does your grandfather live?"

"I'm not really sure. I know he's a well-known Singer, but I don't think he lives with anyone, just in the mountains by himself."

"He'll be hard for us to find," Bob commented.

"Us?"

"I can't leave you out here all by yourself, can I? Look at the shape you're in after two days. Do you have any money?"

"I have a little."

"A little isn't going to get you very far when you're hungry. After two days, I'm assuming you haven't eaten much?"

"Not really, I've just been walking."

"No one stopped to offer a ride?"

"A few, but not since it's been raining so hard."

"Do you know where you are?"

"I'm not sure if Highway 64 has turned into Highway 160 yet, but I know I'm west of *Teec Nos Pos* and, hopefully, heading toward Red Mesa

"Well, at least you're not lost, but it has to be another sixty or more miles to Mexican Hat. What do you say we find us rooms in Bluff, get something to eat, and you can dry out properly and sleep in a bed out of the rain?"

"Sounds great but I can't afford that," said Abe apologetically.

"Abe, I just retired from the Santa Fe Police Department. I have promised myself a backroads trip through the red rock country for years, and now I'm taking it. I have decided you've just become part of the adventure. If I couldn't afford it, I wouldn't have offered;

15

but I don't want you to feel like I'm pressuring you. After all, you have a knife … ." The last part Bob said with a grin and saw that Abe got it right away and returned the grin.

The rain had started to taper off by the time Bob pulled back onto the highway. Water was still standing on the pavement and running across in small torrents but their forward visibility had improved immeasurably.

"Had your mother been ill?" Bob asked.

Abe's countenance darkened. "Yes, they said she died of 'complications related to Co-Vid 19.' She got it a long time ago, and never got better. She got weaker and weaker until she just couldn't fight it anymore."

"Abe, I have to ask though I hope I already know the answer. Are you running from anything? I mean, like the law? Have you committed any crimes?"

"Not like you're asking," Abe replied. "I have never stolen anything, broken into anyone's home or anything like that. Right now, the only thing the law might want me for is running away from my uncle and I *really* doubt he'd ever report me. We don't get along at all and now that Mom is gone, there's nothing stopping him from doing whatever he wants with me and that's why I left." He took in a deep breath and finally let it out. "He wouldn't even let me get my stuff before he pushed me out the door and told me to never come back."

Bob decided he was venturing into personal affairs that the boy might not want to divulge, so he changed the subject, "We'll need to get you some clothes but I don't know of any shops in Mexican Hat. I'd bet the trading post at Twin Rocks in Bluff has some clothes. We'll stop there first, and get you changed into something dry before we eat."

Less than an hour later they passed Sand Island State Park and its famed petroglyphs as they neared Bluff. Bob had been on Highway 191 before, but by the way he was gawking around him, this was Abe's first time. When Bob parked in front of the trading post, Abe stared at twin illuminated rock spires towering above them and the accompanying red rock formations as far as he could see.

"Wow, it's impressive. There isn't much like this around Shiprock, except for the Shiprock."

"Can you see why I've wanted to make a trip through the red rock country?"

"No doubt."

They walked inside the building and as Abe made a beeline for the clothes, Bob approached the young Native American girl behind the register. She was pretty, with big dark eyes and glossy black hair that was braided down almost to her waist. He drew out his wallet, extracted a Visa credit card, then told the girl, "My companion needs to buy some clothes and accessories. Charge it all to this card, within reason." The girl smiled, nodded and accepted the card.

"He might need some help if you can spare the time," Bob added. The store wasn't busy and the girl went right over to Abe and soon they were chatting as if old friends. They quickly picked

17

out an outfit and Abe disappeared into a dressing room. Minutes later he came out dressed in jeans and a western shirt that was a little too big for him. His wet clothes were in a plastic bag.

Bob walked over with a grin on his face. "Probably ought to buy everything a little big. You'll grow into them in no time."

Abe nodded. "Yeah, I didn't have many clothes at home that fit."

Three complete sets of outer clothing, a denim jacket, underclothes, a cowboy hat and a pair of cowboy boots later, Abe was set. He put it all, less what he was wearing, in a backpack and thanked the girl. Abe ran the clothes out to Bob's pickup while Bob got them a table in the dining room.

After half an hour and two coffee refills, Bob decided he'd better go try to round up his charge. He had a pretty good idea where Abe was and, sure enough, he found the with girl from the register. When Bob walked up, Abe stood tall and looked a little guilty.

"Hungry?" Bob asked, already knowing that the boy was starving, but had opted to chat up the pretty girl instead of eat!

"Uh, yeah. We'd better go find a table," stuttered Abe, his eyes never leaving the girl. "Um, Bob, this is Meredith Twin Feather. Meredith, this is Bob Connelly, the guy I was telling you about." Meredith offered her hand and Bob shook it gently.

Then Bob had an inspiration. "Meredith, what time do you go off the clock?"

She hesitated for a moment, looked at the clock which read a minute after seven. "I'm off now," she blurted, then covered a shy smile with the palm of her hand.

"Might that mean you could join us for dinner?" asked Bob, raising his eyebrows at Abe who nodded vigorously in response.

"I usually get dinner after my shift is over, I guess I could join you," she replied.

"Okay. Well, do whatever you need to do to close out, then come find us in the dining room."

As she turned to close out her money drawer, Bob gently pulled Abe with him back to the table.

As they sat down, Abe started to apologize, "Geez, Bob, I lost track of time, I'm sorry I made you wait …."

Bob held up his hand to silence his companion. "She's pretty and she obviously liked talking with you, what's the problem?"

"She's more than just good looks!" Abe exclaimed. "She's a straight A Honor Society student like me and is going to the University of Arizona next fall. We had so many things in common, time just flew by."

Just then their waitress appeared to take their orders. Abe quickly scanned the menu then ordered a double cheeseburger with bacon, and fries. After Abe rounded off his order with a chocolate milk shake, Bob ordered something for himself, then told the waitress to be prepared to double Abe's order. She smiled knowingly and said, "I understand, I have two growing teenagers at home."

As the waitress turned to leave, Meredith appeared and sat down in one of the empty chairs at the table for four. She smiled and said that their orders would be ready at about the same time as hers.

"So, Meredith, you're off to Tucson for college this fall?"

"Yes!" she gushed. "My grades got me a full scholarship and I plan on getting at least a Bachelor's degree in Sociology and then maybe go for my Masters. I want to work for Navajo Strong to find ways to improve my people's quality of life."

"What about you, Abe?" asked Bob.

"I graduated early, and I want to join the tribal police. I figure that's the cutting edge of a lot of Navajo problems and the attitude of the cops needs to become far less apathetic and more proactive in keeping kids out of trouble so Meredith here can work with them."

"I didn't know you graduated early!" Meredith exclaimed. "How did you manage that?"

Abe looked kind of sheepish. "Oh, they gave me a bunch of tests then had me in a lot of advanced and college level classes and I guess I did okay."

"The tribal police requires you to be twenty-one before they hire you, right?" asked Bob.

"Yeah, I figure I have just enough time to get a degree in police administration before I can be hired. I was late getting my applications into the local schools and haven't heard back."

"With your academic record, you are sure to be snapped up by one of the universities," said Meredith.

"Yeah, well I hope it's the University of Arizona," Abe cracked with a smile.

"Meredith, are you from around this area?" asked Bob, an idea popping into his head.

"No, my family is in the Many Farms area, I'm staying with an aunt in Montezuma Creek while I work here and save up some money for school."

Bob looked at Abe and said, "You might ask her if she knows or has heard of your grandfather, after all, we're not that far from Mexican Hat."

Abe looked back at Meredith and asked, "Have you ever heard of a Singer called Carlos Grey Hawk? He is my grandfather; the last I heard he lived in the Mexican Hat area."

Meredith stared back at Abe for a moment before replying, "The name sounds familiar. What kind of sings?"

"I don't know, I've never met him, but I know he is old, well-known and is supposed to be living somewhere up on Cedar Mesa."

"I've only been here for about two months," she said, "let me go ask the trading post manager, he knows everyone."

Before they could respond, Meredith popped out of her seat and went into the back. She was back in less than a minute with a man about Bob's age in tow. He was average height, heavily built, clearly Native American but had a European haircut combed back from his forehead. Bob's cop sense started flashing in his head the

21

moment he laid eyes on the man. Something about the manager told Bob he was trouble.

The manager walked up to the table as Meredith sat back down. He turned on a thousand-watt smile. "Hello," he said, "I'm Robert Begay, I'm the manager here. You were asking about Carlos Grey Hawk?"

Bob took the lead. "I'm Bob Connelly and this is Abe Red Wolf. I'm from Santa Fe and Abe is from Shiprock. The answer is yes, we're trying to locate Mr. Grey Hawk" At the last minute, Bob decided not to inform Mr. Begay of the relationship between Abe and the missing Singer.

"I've heard of Carlos Grey Hawk, he's a Singer, right?"

Abe nodded his head eagerly.

"As a matter of fact, we've been trying to find him too. A member of the staff is in need of his services. The woman is very ill but insists that all she needs is a sing."

"What's wrong with her?" asked Bob.

"She won't say, insists that it's a matter between her and the healer."

"Do you have any information regarding where we can find Mr. Grey Hawk?" asked Bob.

"Only that he lives independently on Cedar Mesa. A few people have seen him up there, above the Moki Dugway and Muley Point but no one knows where he lives – we've been asking all over. If you find him and can put us in contact with him, I would really be grateful."

"Do you have a card in case we run across Mr. Grey Hawk, Mr. Begay?" asked Bob. He had a strong gut feeling that Begay was lying about why he was looking for the old man, but kept that to himself.

Begay retrieved a card case from his breast pocket and gave one to Bob and one to Abe. "That phone number is the trading post switch board, they know where I am at all times.

"Well! I'll let you get back to your meal," said Begay with another dazzling smile. "Nice to have met you both, and I hope to hear from you."

Begay walked away after pausing for a few words with Bob and Abe's waitress.

The trio was pretty much silent as they ate their dinner. At Bob's urging, Abe was tempted to order another burger but decided against it. He was more interested in continuing his conversation with Meredith.

"Are you going to stay in one of the dorms? At least for your first semester?" Abe asked.

Meredith nodded. "I'll look the sororities over but I'm not going to be hasty. From what I hear, most of them are pretty conservative until it comes party time. I'm not into that nor is my attitude likely to change. I've watched alcohol and drugs ruin too many fine people to get caught up in something like that."

"I know what you mean," said Abe. "My uncle is an alcoholic. Even though he has a good job working for the tribe, I don't know how my aunt has managed to make ends meet. He's

23

always out late and is known as a hell raiser. I don't want to be anything like him."

Ten minutes later a beautiful, slender Native American woman in a gorgeous Navajo-patterned wool coat appeared at the entrance. "Oops, that's my aunt, come to fetch me home," said Meredith. "It's been really nice talking to you both; maybe we'll see each other again." Her words seemed directed to both of them but her eyes were only for Abe.

After she left, Bob and Abe walked up to the register. Their waitress was there and smiled at them but didn't give them a check. Bob smiled back and waited but she didn't produce a check.

"Did I miss your bringing our check to the table?" Bob asked.

"No," she said, "Mr. Begay comped your meals."

Bob handed her a ten dollar bill as a tip and she accepted it with thanks. "Is that something he does often?"

"No, only when he wants something. He can be very persuasive, but a word of advice, don't let your guard down around him." She said nothing more, gathered up two menus and went to meet a couple who had just walked in.

"Well, that was interesting," said Abe as they walked down the steps and headed toward Bob's pickup. It was full dark and the parking lot was only illuminated by the lights from the trading post. Bob felt a tingling at the back of his neck, like someone was watching them, but shrugged it off as they entered the vehicle.

"As I recall," said Bob, "there's a newer decent motel at the west end of town. I vote we bunk there and head to Mexican Hat after breakfast."

"Yeah," Abe mumbled, "it's getting pretty sleepy in here."

# CHAPTER 3

Bob didn't expect Abe up much before nine or ten but he came bouncing out of his motel room at eight o'clock the next morning and knocked on Bob's door. Luckily Bob was an early riser and had already consumed the in-room coffee waiting for the boy. Abe looked wide awake and fresh out of the shower. Bob envied his youthful energy and vowed not to slow him down.

"Have you had breakfast yet?" Abe asked. When Bob replied that he had not, Abe suggested they go back to the trading post to eat.

"Why don't we try one of the other places in town, or even wait until we get to Mexican Hat?" asked Bob, just to get a rise out of his young friend.

Abe looked crestfallen. "Okay," he said slowly, "if you want."

"Yeah, that little place on the right as we came close to the motel, the one, with the old pickup in front, looked like it might serve breakfast."

They gathered up their gear and set off back toward Bluff. Bob drove right by the little restaurant he had suggested and drove straight to the Twin Rocks Trading Post. Abe looked at him questioningly, then blushed when Bob said, "Let it not be said that I stood in the way of true love."

Much to Abe's disappointment, Meredith didn't come to work until noon. They ate more or less in silence, Bob paid the bill and they headed for Mexican Hat.

"What are Moki Dugway and Muley Point?" asked Abe.

"Both are on the Trail of the Ancients in the Bear's Ears National Monument," said Bob. "Back in the fifties, a mining company cut a helluva road into the cliffs up from the base of Cedar Mesa to the top so they could haul uranium ore to a processing plant near Mexican Hat. They cut the road through sides of a series of canyons creating an amazing gravel road with lots of switchbacks that climbed twelve hundred feet on an eleven percent grade in just three miles. The eleven percent grade is frightening to some, exhilarating to others and scenic to all. It's called the Moki Dugway.

"Muley Point is an overlook at the top of the Moki Dugway with fantastic views a thousand feet above the goosenecks in the San Juan River, and two thousand feet above the surface of the river. Monument Valley is also in view as are some of the mesas and canyons of canyon country.

"Gooseneck State Park, sort of at the base of Cedar Mesa, is a vantage point from where you can see five miles of the San Juan River crammed into a mile and a half of terrain not unlike a small intestine. We'll make a point of visiting these places before we're done looking for your grandfather."

"Man, that's a lot of scenery to take in."

"That's just part of what's in the area," Bob explained. "There are hundreds, if not thousands of Ancestral Puebloan ruins all over the area. So many, in fact, I wonder if they've all been explored."

"Cool. Do you think we'll see anything like that on, what was it, Cedar Mesa?"

"I would be amazed if we didn't. Your grandfather has picked a huge area to live in – over four hundred square miles. I'm sure he's capable of taking care of himself but there are inherent dangers for a person alone in wild, untamed country.

"I've been giving some thought on how to find him. We'll ask around town, of course, and if we're really lucky we might find someone who takes supplies out to him periodically. How long since you last saw him?" Bob asked.

"I've never met him. Mom always said he was tall for a Navajo but she couldn't give me much more of a description since she hadn't seen him for years either."

"How old was your mother when she died?"

"She was thirty-six," said Abe.

"That probably puts *her* father in his fifties or sixties. That seems a little advanced to be roughing it in an area like Cedar Mesa but I understand Singers are an independent lot who go their own way."

"That's what Mom used to say," Abe observed with a sigh. "Every once in a while she'd talk about how nice it would be to have her father living close by, even if it was in a hogan near the house. She always said he would be a good influence on me."

"Well, it has been my experience that older men either shy away from kids or embrace them. I wonder if he even knows you're around.

"What about your dad?" asked Bob.

"Don't know much about him. He was killed in Afghanistan in 2010 – I was only five. All I have – *had* – of him was his Bronze Star and his Purple Heart."

Bob suddenly changed the subject by pointing ahead and to the left. "Now you know why Mexican Hat was named Mexican Hat," he said. Abe saw that he was pointing at a curious rock formation consisting of a large round flat rock perched atop a much smaller rock. The two formed what looked like an upside down Mexican sombrero.

"Wow," was all Abe could say.

"I read somewhere that the 'brim' of the 'hat' is about sixty feet in diameter," said Bob, slowing so that Abe could get a good look.

"I've never even *heard* of anything like that around Shiprock," said Abe.

"It's quite a landmark," said Bob, as they passed the formation and neared the small settlement of Mexican Hat. "It's probably a long shot, but I thought we'd try the post office first. Your grandfather probably doesn't get much mail but you never know unless you ask."

They pulled up in front of the post office and both of them went in. They found that their luck was holding since the operation was only open from 10 AM to 1 PM and it had just turned 11 AM.

There was no one in line and they walked right up to the counter. The middle-aged woman behind the counter looked up and smiled.

"Hello," said Bob, "we're trying to find a man named Carlos Grey Hawk. Have you ever heard the name or maybe know who he is?"

The woman's smile disappeared, replaced by a distinct frown. "I've already told you people the Post Office has no record of a Carlos Grey Hawk," she said crossly. "He doesn't get mail at General Delivery nor does he have or ever had a post office box."

"Uh, okay, thank you, sorry to bother you," said Bob and he turned and left the building followed by Abe.

"*That* was interesting," said Abe, as they climbed back into Bob's pickup.

"Yeah. I wonder why the attitude?"

"Maybe she was just having a bad morning. Where to next?"

"Probably a grocery store if there is one. There's a convenience store in the Exxon station, we can try that," said Bob.

He pulled up in front of the store. The clerk was a middle-aged Native American who looked up as they approached. "Hello, can I help you?" he asked.

"We're," said Bob, motioning to Abe, "looking for a Navajo man probably in his fifties or sixties by the name of Carlos Grey Hawk. Have you ever heard of him?"

The man instantly became surly. "Jeez, don't you guys ever give up? I've already told you I don't know any Carlos Grey Hawk so please just move along."

They complied immediately and returned to the pickup. "What the *hell?*" growled Bob.

Their third try was at the San Juan Inn, tucked away against the bank of the San Juan River at the bridge. The clerk was an older Navajo man and he too became testy when they inquired about Carlos Grey Hawk.

Bob was again taken aback by the attitude until an idea popped into his head. "Sir, we are *not* part of the group that has been asking around town about Mr. Grey Hawk. This," Bob said, motioning at Abe, "is his grandson. His mother, Mr. Grey Hawk's daughter, died recently, and the young man is trying to reach his grandfather."

The clerk's demeanor changed a hundred eighty degrees. "Well, why didn't you say so? Those assholes were in town all last week – two of them – demanding information on your grandfather," he said, looking at Abe. "They were pushy and threatening and downright rude and I don't think they got any help from anyone in town. Sure, I know Carlos, he's been a fixture in this area for a long time. He's a typical Singer, though, he never stays too long in one spot so I can't tell you where he's laying his head these days. He's a

31

nice old man – lots of dignity – and, like I said, he's been around a long time."

"How do people reach him when they need a sing?" asked Abe.

"Word of mouth. There are a couple of Navajos who haul him supplies once in a while, if they get word where he is, but he spends a lot of time up on the Mesa by himself."

"Could you give me the names of those men?" asked Abe.

"Adrian Tso works down the road at the Exxon station, he's a part-time mechanic. Adam Benally works on one of the ranches in the area, but he can usually be found here at the trading post when he's not working."

"Is he here today," Abe asked eagerly.

"I don't think so, I heard they're starting to round up cattle."

"If I left a phone number, could you give it to him and ask him to call me?" asked Bob.

"Sure, anything to keep ol' Carlos away from those jerks."

"Did they say what they wanted him for?"

"Oh, some lame excuse about one of their fathers needed a sing to cure his failing liver," said the counterman.

"I think we'll drive down to the Exxon station and see if we can talk to Mr. Tso," said Bob. "Thank you for your help. Oh, is there anyone else here in town who might know Mr. Grey Eagle?"

"Marge Deschene down at the Seven Eleven at the Shell station saves the deli stuff they can't sell and gives it to Carlos if he gets here in time."

Surprising Bob, Abe walked over to the desk man and shook his hand as he thanked him profusely.

\*\*\*\*\*

The phone rang six times before it went to Robert Begay's voice mail. He never answered this phone. It was for people to call in information and he was above talking to the source. If he was in, Begay would listen as the message was left but he didn't want to get tangled up with dealing with the riff raff who always needed something. If the information was worthwhile, he would reward the caller through a lieutenant but never personally. When he wasn't in, Begay had a sophisticated system only he could access on which the message was recorded.

"Yeah, uh, Mr. Begay, this is Ernesto Lapahie. One of your men that was here in Mexican Hat told me to keep my ears open and report in if I heard anything about Carlos Grey Hawk. There have been two guys, one young and one older, who have been asking around about Grey Hawk. The younger one is Diné but the other one is an Anglo. Oh … yeah," said Lapahie, as Begay could hear someone prompting him, "the younger one is saying he's Grey Hawk's grandson. Uh, that's all. Your man said you would make it worth my while if I reported something useful. I, uh, hope you can use this. Goodbye."

33

Lapahie wasn't telling Robert Begay anything he didn't already know until he got to the last part. *A grandson?* How could he use that? Perhaps in the near future he could use the kid as leverage against the old man – if it was true. He'd look into it a little more. Abe Red Hawk came from Shiprock. He'd send a couple of men over there to see what they could turn up.

*****

Bob and Abe returned to the Exxon station but, avoiding the store, walked into the service bay. There were two men under the hood of a dusty but newer Ford pickup and they were arguing about what was wrong with it.

"Dammit," one said to the other, "it has to be electrical. It's getting gas but it's not kicking over with the starter."

"Can't be, Adrian, these newer rigs have electronic ignitions, there's no points or condenser. There's a rotor and a distributor cap and that's all."

"I *know* that!" said the first man angrily as he stopped reaching under the hood long enough to look at his companion. "There could be a busted wire or a bad coil wire or a dozen other electrical things causing the damned thing not to turn over. Hell, for all we know, it might be a neutral safety switch!"

Bob eased up near the men and directed his attention at the angry man whom he concluded was Adrian Tso. During the uneasy silence, he said, "Excuse me, are you Adrian Tso?"

"Yeah, who's askin'?"

"That's not important, though my name is Bob Connelly. My friend and I have a problem we're hoping you could help us with."

"Can't you see I'm already elbow-deep in a *problem?*"

"Our problem doesn't involve mechanical expertise. We only have a couple of questions and then we'll be out of your way."

Tso pulled back from the pickup, turned and looked full on Bob and Abe. "Okay," he said, "what's your problem?"

"We're trying to find Carlos Grey Hawk – before you get all fired up, we're not with the men who were here last week. This is Carlos's grandson, Abe Red Wolf. He just lost his mother and is hoping to find his grandfather."

Tso scrutinized Abe for several seconds. "I guess you could be related to ol' Carlos, you resemble him and you're tall like he is. What makes you think I can help?"

"We heard that you periodically take supplies up to him on Cedar Mesa and were hoping you could tell us where, better yet, show us."

Tso continued to stare at Abe while he considered Bob's request.

"How do I know you're not working with them other guys?"

Abe spoke up, "There's no way I can prove it to you but, like you said, I look like him."

35

Tso came to a decision. "I haven't heard from Carlos for about ten days, he's about due to get a message to me, needing some more stuff."

"How do you communicate with him?"

"I usually hear from Harley Uskilith. He lives up on the Mesa and either Carlos comes to his house or Harley meets him on the Mesa. He gives Harley a list and Harley brings it to me. I take the stuff up to Harley's place and Carlos comes and gets it."

"You don't know where Carlos is living?" asked Abe.

"Nah. Nobody does. I hear he moves around but stays loosely in touch with some of the residents up there."

"We heard another name who has done what you do for Carlos, Adam Benally. Do you know him?"

"Sure, I know Adam. He hangs around down at San Juan Inn Trading Post. Sometimes he works at a ranch so he isn't there every day. Harley contacts him when he can't find me."

"Why do you suppose Harley doesn't go get the supplies himself?"

"He don't like driving into Kayenta. Most of what Carlos needs you can't find here in Mexican Hat."

"Is there any chance we could go with you when you take your next load up to Carlos?" asked Abe earnestly.

"I'd rather ask Carlos first. How long since you seen him?"

"I've never met him," Abe admitted. "All I know about him is from my mom, that he's a Singer and lives on Cedar Mesa."

"What makes you think he will believe you?"

36

"Just tell him my grandmother, his late wife, was named Chenoa Acothly and that she died just before I was born."

"I'll do that. How can I reach you?"

Bob handed Adrian Tso a card. "That's my cell phone number and I have the damned thing with me all the time."

Tso laughed. "Okay, I'll call you when I know something. Where are you staying?"

"We stayed in Bluff last night," said Bob. "I don't know if we'll be staying there tonight or not." He looked a question at Abe as he spoke. The young man blushed but didn't say anything."

As Tso turned back toward the pickup he was working on, Bob said, "Don't forget that the newer models require your foot on the brake before they'll start."

Both Tso and his companion looked at Bob then at each other. Tso got in the pickup, put his foot on the brake and started the engine. Bob smiled at him as he waved and walked out toward his own pickup with Abe in tow.

"Well, it looks like we're going to hang around here for at least a few days," said Bob, a mischievous glint in his eye. "We might as well get settled in a motel then maybe do some sightseeing?"

"Jeez, this is getting expensive!" Abe remarked. "Why don't you drop me off somewhere and be on your way? I don't want to be a burden. I'll manage."

"Yeah, you're a real pain in the butt alright," Bob said with a grin. "Hell, you'd die of starvation in a week or be road kill. Nah, I think I'd better stick around.  Besides, I was looking for adventure and we may find it yet!

"Why don't we go find Mr. Adam Benally and see what he has to say?"

Benally was substantially less suspicious of Abe than Adrian Tso.  He pretty much reiterated the communication pipeline and agreed he was more of a back up when Tso wasn't available.  Just in case, Bob gave him a card too.  He too had been contacted last week by Begay's men and had told them the same thing Tso had – nothing.

"It doesn't seem like there's much of a reason to go back to Bluff," said Bob, hiding a smile.  "We might as well bed down at the San Juan Inn and Trading Post since the guy was so helpful.  What do you think?"

Abe was onto him this time and said, "*You* can sleep here in Mexican Hat if you want to, but *I'm* going back to Bluff, even if I have to sleep under a mesquite tree."

Connelly laughed.  "Okay, okay, we'll go back to Bluff.  I suppose we can't even stop for lunch until we get there?"

"Hey man, *you're* the one who said he wouldn't stand in the way of true love."

"Okay, okay, you win.  But could we make a short side trip or two on the way back?  It'll be worth your time."

"Well … okay.  But just this once," said Abe with a little tease of his own.

"Nope, I changed my mind. I'm too hungry to wait. We'll go back to Bluff, have lunch and either sight see or you can sight see inside the trading post."

About 1:30 PM they pulled into the trading post parking lot. It was nearly empty, the lunch crowd had come and gone. Abe took another long look at the Twin Rocks and surrounding formations before following Bob into the place. Surprising Bob, Abe followed him to the dining room and sat down.

Bob looked at Abe with a question. "I'm hungry. She'll be there after I eat."

# CHAPTER 4

Two Navajo tacos later, Abe was raring to go. As he started to get up, Bob waved him back into the booth. He counted out five twenty-dollar bills and pushed them over to Abe. "You shouldn't be broke, no matter what the circumstances."

He held his hand palm outward toward the young man as Abe started to protest, and said, "No argument. Consider it a long-term loan if you want, but keep it just in case. And wipe the salsa off your chin, it doesn't go with your shirt."

Bob's last comment effectively distracted the young man, and in the time it took him to vigorously rub his chin with a napkin for the non-existent salsa, Bob was up and headed for the cash register. They reached the register at about the same time and Meredith gave them a warm smile.

"Did you have any luck in Mexican Hat?" she asked.

"We contacted a couple of people who know Grandfather, but they weren't in a position to get us connected. It may take a few days," Abe replied. "How have you been?"

"It's been so long since I've seen you, I hardly know where to start," Meredith joked as she made change for Bob. Bob smiled but Abe looked a little flustered.

"Could you keep Abe out of trouble long enough for me to go find us rooms for tonight?" Bob asked Meredith.

Meredith laughed. "I guess I could try. You might try the Posada Pintada. It's just down the road on Seventh and I hear it's very nice. And it's close," she added, looking at Abe.

"I'll take a look. In the meantime, keep him out of the hands of the law, okay?"

Meredith laughed again and nodded as Bob left.

Bob drove directly to the Posada Pintada and liked its looks immediately. He walked up to the desk in the lobby and made arrangements for him and Abe to stay for a week. He explained that he didn't know how long they'd be there for sure. The desk clerk was very accommodating and left the reservation open. Bob accepted keys to adjoining rooms and hauled his and Abe's luggage into his room. It was early afternoon and he debated taking a short nap to afford the kids a little more time together but decided Abe and Meredith could find their own time.

As Bob re-entered the trading post, Robert Begay appeared from a door marked "Private," spotted Bob and walked over to him. "How went the search for the boy's grandfather?" Begay asked.

Bob wasn't surprised that Begay had been informed of the relationship between Carlos Grey Hawk and his grandson, the Navajo news pipeline was well-known. He and Abe had certainly not kept it a secret or asked anyone to keep it quiet. He assumed the gossip pipeline in Mexican Hat was every bit as efficient as anywhere else.

"We didn't have much luck, but we did discover that the folks you sent are none too popular there. Every time we asked about Carlos Grey Hawk we were met with hostility and suspicion until we explained about Abe's relationship to the old man, and even then some people didn't believe us, assuming we were working with your men."

"That's not good to hear," said Begay, looking none too concerned. "I'll have a word with them and see if the next time they're in Mexican Hat they can do better."

The double *entendre* wasn't lost on Bob and only made him more suspicious and careful around Begay. "By the way," Bob said, "thank you for dinner last night, that was very generous and thoughtful." Begay waved it away as a king would wave away a small boon to a peasant.

"So what's your next step?" asked the trading post manager.

"I guess we'll go up to Cedar Mesa, talk to whomever we meet, and see if we get lucky," Bob said with a shrug. "I don't know what else we can do. People told us they see him up there on occasion, but no one knew where he was living." *At least the last part of that is true!*

As Bob looked over to see if Abe was at the register - he was - Begay said, "Looks like Abe and Meredith have hit it off. Between you and me, a little social interaction is good for the girl, she's too shy. As long as it doesn't interfere with her work."

"Will her having dinner with us present a problem?"

"Nope. She's off the clock then and can do what she wants, at least until her aunt comes to collect her."

"I'll see that Abe doesn't abuse the privilege. I'm going to take him out and show him some the sights around the area this afternoon since it's too late to go up on the Mesa. Any suggestions?"

"The petroglyphs at Sand Island are always a good place to start," said Begay as he headed toward the door marked "Private."

Bob walked over to the young people. Abe's first question was, "Am I getting her in trouble by hanging around?"

"No, as long as you don't interfere with her work and I don't think Meredith would allow that."

Meredith smiled as she nodded. Bob looked at her and said, "I'm taking Abe out to see some of the sights. Have you been here long enough to have seen what you think you want to see?"

"Oh, not really. I'm only here when I'm working; otherwise I'm in Montezuma Creek."

"Maybe, with your aunt's permission we can take you along on one of your days off. We'll save some of the neat stuff for when you're with us. Perhaps you could meet us for dinner tonight after you get off work then introduce us when she comes to pick you up?"

"I don't think my aunt would object once she gets to know you. I'll tell her you're a retired police officer and that will help. As far as dinner goes, Abe and I already made a date for that and you, of course, are invited."

"You get off at 6 PM, right?" asked Bob.

She nodded.

"We'll be waiting at a table for you then. Meanwhile, I should take Abe away and introduce him to a little of his culture."

Abe followed after Bob as they headed for the exit. He managed to wave to Meredith before he stepped through the door.

As they got in the pickup, Abe said, "Thanks, Bob."

"For what"

"For being gentle and kind with her and giving us some space. I really like her but she is painfully shy about the world outside the Res. You're probably one of the few *Bilagaana* [white person] she's ever met. She's eager to learn and looking forward to college but she has misgivings too."

"Then you'd better treat her right or I'll kick your ass," Bob said simply but emphatically.

Abe was silent but out of the corner of his eye, Bob could see he was smiling.

"Okay, at Mr. Begay's recommendation, our first stop on our tour will be Sand Island State Park to see the petroglyphs. These are deemed by 'experts' to be Ancestral Puebloan, and three hundred to three thousand years old."

Bob pulled into the entrance and drove around near the petroglyph panels. They got out and gazed at the rocks covered by ancient pecked and scratched drawings. Some were recognizable as people, animals and even the sun, but others were a question mark. "You probably won't find any relatives here, but you can't help but wonder what the messages were they left behind," said Bob.

Abe seemed wholly absorbed in his examination of the rock art. "This is fascinating. To think these were made probably long before the Navajo existed."

"I'm not sure about that," said Bob. "I just don't know; but I'm sure if you wanted to do the research, you'd find lots of answers and not all of them would agree."

"Wow, this is very sobering. Every Navajo should have a chance to see this."

They finally got back in the pickup and headed more or less west. Bob called Abe's attention to the Comb Ridge, a prominent monocline that Bob explained extended from Kayenta to the Abajo Mountains, a distance of some eighty miles. "As I understand it, Comb Ridge is rife with Puebloan ruins and petroglyphs. I suspect we'd need a more basic mode of transportation and a lot of time if we wanted to see it close up."

When the sign appeared for the Valley of the Gods, Bob turned off and they soon were on a gravel/dirt road that opened into a large valley populated with monoliths reminiscent of the better known Monument Valley in Arizona. "As I understand it," said Bob, "this is a very, very holy place for your people. Each monolith is named and symbolizes a facet of the Navajo religion. I'm no expert on that stuff but I find the Valley serene and beautiful."

They drove the whole loop until they connected with Highway 261. At the T intersection, Bob pointed to the right and said, "That's where we'll go tomorrow, up the Moki Dugway onto Cedar Mesa." He turned left and drove Highway 261 back toward

Mexican Hat. He abruptly turned right onto Highway 316 and drove several miles to Goosenecks State Park where Abe was able to witness the enormous switchbacks of the San Juan River as it flowed a thousand feet below the Goosenecks overlook.

Abe seemed at a loss for words. He had never seen anything like the enormity of what lay before him. "No throwing rocks," said Bob. "People raft that river all the time and I don't reckon they'd appreciate a missile from above."

He turned back toward the northwest and pointed at a distant cliff. "That's Muley Point. We'll be stopping by the view point after we ascend the Moki Dugway. It's a thousand feet higher than this valley floor and another thousand feet higher than the San Juan River. God's sculpture at His finest."

"I wish I had a camera for all this," said Abe, his arms sweeping wide before him.

"It is pretty impressive and it never gets less impressive unless, perhaps, you see it every day," Bob agreed. "And a picture, no matter how well set up, doesn't do it justice. Still, it's nice to have a photographic memory if you can't get back here now and again."

"Yeah, I can see what you mean. Then maybe I don't have to take pictures since I'll be coming back … often! I wonder if Meredith has ever been here."

"Montezuma Creek is a ways away. Maybe she hasn't. Speaking of Meredith, we'd probably ought to get headed back. I don't imagine she'd be pleased if we were late."

"I can sure see why my grandfather lives here."

As they drove back, Abe looked over at Bob. "Thank you for showing me this stuff, I understand now why you call it part of my culture."

"It's always good not to forget where you came from, Abe."

They made it back to Bluff in plenty of time and were seated at the same table when Meredith appeared. She smiled widely and took a seat next to Abe. "Well?" she asked, "did you get cultured?"

"Unless you've been there before …" She shook her head no. "… you have some real sightseeing to do!" Abe exclaimed.

"Well, that tells me how your day went," she said. "It was busier today than usual for me but I don't know why. All I know is the day went by really fast and it was my Friday."

"Those are the best kind," said Abe. "Do you think your aunt will let you go with us tomorrow … or do you have something else planned?"

"No, nothing else going on," said Meredith.

The same waitress came and took their orders. Abe again ordered two Navajo tacos which amused Meredith to no end. She giggled, then said, "Guys your age *never* get enough to eat."

Abe took on a mildly pained expression. "I'm a growing boy, I need sustenance."

Bob smiled then asked Meredith, "Do you think your aunt will let you go with us tomorrow?"

"I don't know why not. Oh! Can I ask her to go with us? I know she's been on Cedar Mesa before but I don't know if she has seen everything you saw today. Please?"

Abe nodded eagerly and Bob smiled. "Sure, why not? There's plenty of room in the pickup. We can pick you up in Montezuma Creek – it's only a twenty-minute drive."

"That would be perfect. She doesn't socialize much and I think it would be very good for her to get away, even for a day. She's a widow, you know, and doesn't do much except work and weave."

"What kind of work does she do?" asked Abe.

"She teaches at the elementary school and takes care of what tribal paperwork is required in Montezuma Creek. I guess you could say she's the Navajo Nation representative. It's not too demanding, and allows her time to weave blankets and rugs. She's pretty well known among the trading posts on the Res but not really famous in the blanket and rug weaving world."

Their orders came and conversation dwindled around the table as they dug in. Abe finished first, debated having a piece of pie, but decided that would be too much. Meredith just shook her head.

When Meredith's aunt entered the trading post, Meredith stood and waved her over. Both males stood as she approached. She was tall for a Navajo woman at about five feet nine inches and, simply put, as beautiful as her niece, with a long braid down her back and dressed in a traditional Navajo dress and a white cotton blouse. "Aunt Rita Makespeace, these are the guys I was telling you about. This is Bob Connelly," Meredith said, gesturing toward Bob. "And this is Abe Red Wolf," she said smiling at Abe.

She shook hands with both of them and Bob suggested she join them. Rita sat in the unoccupied seat and looked around her.

"Aunt Rita, have you eaten?" asked her niece.

Rita nodded but spoke up, "I could do with a glass of iced tea though, it's hot outside."

Their waitress arrived moments later and cleared the dishes. Bob ordered iced tea for Rita Makespeace and the waitress came back and refreshed all their drinks.

"Mr. Connelly is a retired police officer from Santa Fe. Abe graduated early from Shiprock High School and is seeking admission to one of the universities in the southwest," said Meredith.

"What do you plan to major in, Abe," Rita asked.

"Administration of Justice though the first two years will be mostly general studies," Abe replied.

"How long have you been retired, Mr. Connelly?"

"Only about four months, and please call me Bob."

"You must have had an interesting career, Bob," said Rita.

Bob nodded. "It had its moments but I never regretted it as my profession."

"Congratulations. Not many can say that these days," Rita said.

"How long have you and Abe been together?" she asked.

Bob chuckled. "Not long. I almost ran over him during that big rainstorm a couple of days ago. He was walking from Shiprock to Mexican Hat and I just couldn't let him drown."

"Abe's mother died of CoVid recently and his uncle made him leave – permanently. He was very, very lucky to run into Mr. Connelly," Meredith chimed in.

"So you two are not connected in any other way?" asked Rita.

"Not really. I see it as a sort of an informal uncle/nephew relationship at this point."

"Aunt Rita, the guys are going out tomorrow in search of Abe's grandfather. He is a Singer and lives somewhere on Cedar Mesa. They have some feelers out, and maybe some clues, but nothing concrete. They have invited us to join them and offered to show me some of the more significant scenic and cultural sights on the way. They've invited you too."

"I wouldn't want us to be in your way, gentlemen ...." Rita began.

"Quite the contrary, Ms. Makespeace," Bob interrupted. "Abe has never been in this area and me only as a tourist. I promised myself a tour of the red rock country and maybe a little adventure and this fills the bill. I assume you know the country better than we do."

"Adventure?" Rita asked.

"Well, someone else is looking for Abe's grandfather and we think he's lying about the reason. For the old man's sake, we want to get there first."

"Is it dangerous?"

"I doubt it. Carlos Grey Hawk is a pretty old man and I can't imagine him being involved in something dangerous."

"Please, Aunt Rita? It would be like taking two very interested students on a field trip!"

Rita Makespeace appeared to be debating the idea in her head. She had already decided in the affirmative but didn't want to seem too eager. She liked the looks of these two and Meredith was clearly taken with the younger one.

"Sure, why not?" she said finally.

"We thought to pick you up at about eight, stop for breakfast then head west," said Bob.

"How about we meet you here at 8 AM?" Rita countered.

*She's not ready for us to know where she lives, prudent.*

"That works but there is so much to see, we won't be able to do much except see it and go on to the next, but that will get us up on the Mesa before noon and we can drive around and maybe talk to a few people."

"I doubt you'd have much luck by yourself, Bob, but with a car full Navajos, you might get lucky. The natives up on the Mesa are even more close-mouthed than those on the general Res and they don't like talking to strangers, especially white ones. I don't mean to sound racist but that's the fact of the matter."

51

"Yeah, I assumed that, and frankly I don't blame them for feeling that way toward whites. I just figured we'd give it a shot with Abe here doing most of the talking; maybe someone would feel sorry for him."

"Navajos are very sensitive to young/elder relationships and that might be a deciding factor," said Rita. She stood up. "Okay, 8:00 AM, we'll be here. There are no services in the Bears Ears National Monument so I'll pack a lunch."

"That'd be great! See you tomorrow morning," Bob exclaimed.

# CHAPTER 5

The next morning, after they finished breakfast and had piled into Bob's pickup, Abe lobbied for a stop at the Sand Island Petroglyphs. "I still don't see how they can date those carvings but they say some of them might be up to three thousand years old," said Abe. He was obviously fascinated by the carvings and Bob wondered if this was the beginning of a change in college majors before the fact.

When they arrived at the park, Abe took Meredith's hand and led her over to the panel. "See?" he said excitedly, "you can actually imagine the hunt for the big horn sheep and they weren't on horseback! Horses came with the Spanish in the 1500s. That makes it clear the hunt occurred before, say, 1500. It's almost as if we're looking back in a time machine over five *hundred* years!" As he excitedly pointed out more images, Bob noticed that Abe hadn't let loose of the girl's hand.

"To see something like this through the eyes of youth," Rita said. "Abe seems very interested in the petroglyphs, I wonder if it will affect his thinking about his major."

Bob chuckled. "I was thinking the same thing earlier. He's awfully young to be etching his future in stone at his age."

After fifteen minutes or so, Bob tapped the horn and the two teenagers returned to the pickup. "Ready for scene two?" Bob asked.

"Wow!" said Meredith, "that's going to be a tough act to follow."

"Oh, don't worry about that," said Abe. "This country has all kinds of things to see. What's next, Bob? Valley of the Gods?"

Bob nodded as they drove through the cut in Comb Ridge as Abe enthusiastically explained to Meredith the significance of the monocline. As they neared the turn off to the Valley of the Gods Abe asked Meredith, "Have you ever been through Monument Valley?"

Meredith shook her head no. "Neither have I," said Abe, "but Bob says the Valley of the Gods is a mini-Monument Valley. Seeing it makes me want to see the big one."

Rita said, "We don't have time for me to tell you about each of the monuments and their significance, that will have to come on another field trip."

When they finished the loop through the Valley of the Gods and reached Highway 261, Bob turned right instead of left like he had done last time. It was a short distance to where the road turned to gravel and began a series of dizzying, vertigo-inducing switchbacks on the steep road up to Cedar Mesa.

Before they started the climb, Bob turned to the young people in the back seat, "If you are afraid of heights, keep your eyes averted from the road." He knew well enough that neither teen would do that but at least they couldn't say they weren't warned!

The series of switchbacks up the road were sharp and sometimes they were on the inside near the rock. Other times it seemed like they were crawling along the outside edge. Bob drove very slowly both out of consideration for his passengers, and because he simply couldn't go fast.

Though only about three and a half miles long, it took them the better part of a half hour to drive the intimidating road between slowing down for sharp curves and stopping momentarily to gawk and for Rita and Meredith to shoot pictures with their phones. There was a wide parking area at the top and Bob pulled in then looked into the back seat. Meredith was wide-eyed and Abe was grinning like the proverbial Cheshire cat.

"Everyone okay?" Bob asked with a smile.

Both kids nodded. Rita said, "From this viewpoint you can see Shiprock to the east and Monument Valley to the south, not to mention the Valley of the Gods just below us."

Everyone got out and wandered along the edge of the viewpoint seeking the best places to employ their phones. "Just doesn't do it justice," Meredith murmured as she looked at several photos she had taken, including a few selfies with Abe.

When they were satisfied, they got back into the pickup and Bob made a left turn onto an unimproved gravel/dirt road. "This will take us out to Muley Point," he said, "keep your cameras handy."

It had not rained for some time, so the road was easily passable but Bob took it easy. Abe started to protest when Bob passed a spectacular viewpoint but stifled it when he stopped at an overlook that afforded a one hundred eighty degree view. Easily identifiable were Monument Valley, Goosenecks State Park, much of the Navajo Nation and the twisting San Juan River, not to mention a vast array of red rock canyons.

Little was said until they got back into the pickup. Even less was said after Bob said, "I'm pretty sure we're being followed. I noticed a 60s or 70s Ford HiBoy 4x4 pickup, green and white, in the parking lot where we had breakfast. It had two men in it and they seemed very interested in our departure. Later, I saw the same rig parked along the side of the road outside of Sand Island. It waited until we were half a mile or so ahead then pulled out and followed. It was parked at the bed and breakfast just outside the Valley of the Gods when we drove by and I saw it behind us on the road up the Moki Dugway."

"Who is it? What should we do?" asked Abe, alarmed.

"Well, we're not going to try to lose them," said Bob. "My guess is it's the men hired by Robert Begay to find your grandfather, Abe. As to what we should do, I'll open the floor for comments and votes."

"Do you think there's any danger?" asked Rita, involuntarily looking back through the rear window.

"I would say that as long as we *don't* find Mr. Grey Hawk, we're fine. They're letting us do their work for them, and I'd bet they'll be content to let us look. If we find him, the game might change dramatically, and not for the better. That's when things might get dicey and that's when I'd rather you ladies were at home. Since no one is supposed to be living in the Bear's Ears National Monument, I suspect we can drive around all afternoon unmolested."

"Singers are not social people. They eschew the trappings of civilization and pursue *Hózhǫ*, the state in which all living things are ordered, in balance, and walking in beauty – unless they're called upon for a sing," said Rita.

"That's what Mom used to say," said Abe. "Grandfather would disappear for days or weeks with no one knowing where he was or if he was okay. It used to worry Mom, but she finally came to grips with it after she got sick. I vote we drive around for a while and get the lay of the land."

"Meredith?" asked Bob.

"If they don't bother us, it seems okay to drive around for a while."

"Rita?"

"This all makes me very nervous, especially with the kids here. But I guess I can handle driving around for a while as long as we don't talk to anyone. That defeats our purpose up here though, so maybe it's better if we go back."

"I wish we knew why they wanted Abe's grandfather," Bob muttered. "Seems to me they'd try something a little more assertive if they thought we knew where he was. If they are convinced we know, I can see them grabbing Abe as leverage and then things will probably get rough."

"Rough?" asked Rita.

"Me taking aggressive steps to get him back," Bob answered.

"As in violence?"

"Whatever it takes," Bob said simply. "But not now. I move we take the long way home, Highway 95, Blanding and on to Bluff."

The motion carried and Bob headed the pickup north along Highway 261. "If we see ruins, we'll stop, but we won't make any detours so our escorts won't get their undies in a bunch."

They marveled at the vast variety of landscape as they regained the pavement and headed north. Forests of piñyon pine and juniper were interspersed with open desert and assorted rock formations. It would be the perfect place to go to find *Hózhǫ́*. At four hundred square miles, it was also impossible to seek someone out unless the seeker too knew the terrain.

No one spotted the Ford pickup emerging from the Moki Dugway, but Bob was confident the two men would catch up to make sure their target didn't take a side road. Sure enough, less than two miles up Highway 261, the pickup hove into view for a moment then dropped back out of sight.

"Are they still back there?" asked Abe, trying to look through the convex outside mirror of Bob's pickup.

"Yup, they just slowed down to get out of sight," Bob replied, watching his inside rear view mirror. "How about we quit worrying about those two and direct our attention to the scenery?"

"I wonder where Grandfather is?" mused Abe, "I hope he's okay."

"Hopefully Adrian Tso has convinced him to meet you. It will take time to get the communication back and forth so we have to be patient. Adrian is our best chance of connecting with your grandfather without Begay's people poking their nose in. You, Abe, might give some thought to what you're going to say to him. Considering his lifestyle, I can't see you living with him, especially if you plan on going to school."

"Bob's right," said Rita. "I think you're a little too old to become an apprentice Singer anyway, so where does that leave you with regard to living accommodations?"

"Pretty much the same place as when Bob picked me up," Abe said glumly.

"Not necessarily, if you can cook and clean, you can stay with me," Bob said with a sly look at Rita. She caught on right away.

"There you go," she said with a grin, "your problem is solved."

If possible, Abe looked more woebegone than ever. He looked out his window but said nothing.

"They're messing with you, Abe," said Meredith, smiling at the young man sitting beside her.

Abe looked at Bob through the inside rear view mirror and caught him in a smile.

"Okay," said Bob, "so maybe it won't be that bad. As a matter of fact, I have a very nice and very capable lady who comes in twice a month and does all that stuff for me. Mrs. Lopez is wonderful and has been with me for just over four years."

Abe sat there feeling sorry for himself for several miles. Finally Meredith nudged him with her elbow and told him, "Lighten up, they're only kidding."

Bob was serious now. "Maybe a little bit, but Abe you *can* stay with me for as long as you need to. At the very least until you find housing at a university or fraternity."

Abe looked at Bob through the mirror and Bob winked.

Abe smiled slightly then looked back out the window at the scenery that was passing by. Finally, he looked around him, and said, "I'm hungry."

Bob turned into a rest stop just past the intersection of Hightway 261 and Highway 95. "No sense wasting a good lunch," he said as he unbuckled his seat belt.

"Hey you guys," said Abe. "I'm sorry to be such a drag but so much has happened to turn my life upside down, I don't know which way is up."

Meredith leaned over and kissed him on the cheek. "It's okay, Abe. Just don't forget you have friends."

He nodded through the tears in his eyes and tried to smile. He covered it by jumping out of the pickup and looking around. "Jeez, it's pretty up here."

Bob and Abe got the basket and the cooler out of the back of the pickup and set them on a nearby picnic table. As Rita and Meredith set out the picnic, Bob said, "Our friends in their Ford pickup should be along pretty soon. It'll be interesting to see how they handle overshooting us."

As if on a racetrack, within ten minutes the green and white Hi-Boy came roaring around the first curve past the intersection. The driver immediately spotted Bob's pickup and let off the accelerator which was a sure tell. He put his foot back on the gas and pulled away and out of sight in the next curve at a more moderate pace. They heard the revs from the pickup drop off immediately as the driver frantically tried to find a place to hide where he could watch for them.

The foursome ate their lunch and said no more about the pickup. "Are there any state universities in Santa Fe?" asked Meredith.

"Probably nothing that would interest Abe," said Bob. "But Albuquerque is only an hour away and there are lots of educational institutions there for him to look at."

"I suppose being Navajo and out-of-state would really hurt my chances of going to the University of Arizona," Abe speculated, looking at Meredith.

"On the contrary," said Rita. "State universities are always trying to fill minority positions and with your grades, and the fact that you graduated a year early, you might have a pretty good shot, but you must get the applications in."

"I know," said Abe with a grimace. "Things were so confused at home with Mom being so sick, the paperwork fell by the wayside. I did get the applications in but later than my advisor suggested. Now I'm hoping to get a response, but I don't know how I'll get them since I don't have a home anymore."

Bob was silent for quite a while as the discussion continued about Abe's school applications. Finally he said, "You know, Abe it might be worth our while to make a run up to Shiprock, timing it to arrive when your uncle is elsewhere. Is there anyone at the house who would let you in to get your stuff?"

Abe pondered the idea for a moment then said, "Anyone but my uncle would let me in, as long as he wouldn't find out about it."

"Are there predictable times when he wouldn't be there?"

"He's a custodian at the school district and has been for years. He usually works at the high school and the last I knew he was working noon to 8:30 PM. I could find out easy enough by calling for him at the school to see when he's at work." It was clear that the idea of getting his belongings back had excited Abe. "I don't have much," Abe continued, "and mostly I care about my dad's medals and the correspondence from the schools I applied to."

Rita was mulling the idea around in her head too. "If Abe's uncle came home unexpectedly …."

"We'd take all precautions we can to minimize that happening. I wouldn't want a confrontation any more than Abe would," said Bob, "but I'm certainly not going to stand by and let the uncle manhandle a seventeen-year-old. We can drive it in a day, it's only about an hour and a half from Bluff to Shiprock. Let's think about it for a while and we'll discuss it again when we get back to Bluff."

They gathered up their equipment and trash and set off for Blanding. They didn't see the Ford pickup but felt the eyes of the men on them. Bob drove nonstop to Blanding where he topped off his fuel then headed south on Highway 191 to Bluff. Bob pulled into the trading post parking lot next to Rita's Toyota Highlander. He shifted into park and shut off the engine.

"Okay. Everyone gets to voice an opinion, starting with Meredith," said Bob, looking into the back seat at the two teenagers.

"I don't want anyone to get hurt," Meredith began. "I can appreciate Abe's need to get his stuff from his uncle's house but, again, is it worth violence?"

"Abe?" asked Bob.

"You all know I need my correspondence from the schools to which I sent applications and I feel like I'm entitled to get my personal property back from the house – if it's still there. I wouldn't be surprised if he burned everything when I left, he was so angry."

"I abhor violence under any circumstances," Rita declared. "If there's *any* chance your uncle would be home, I'm against your trying to regain your property. There's the matter of a *biligaana*

63

involving himself in a Navajo matter. Tribal police take a dim view of that and if something were to happen, I could see the authorities holding you, Bob."

"I don't want that to happen for a variety of reasons," Bob said, "but I feel Abe has been wronged, and I'm inclined to make things right if reasonably possible."

The look of gratitude Abe shot Bob's way made Bob feel like he was doing the right thing for the right reason. "But let's not rush into this with self-righteous guns blazing. We need to take every precaution that Abe's uncle is at work when we go to the house."

"So you're going to do it?" asked Rita.

"The ultimate decision rests with Abe, but I'm going to reserve veto power if the circumstances are not in our favor," Bob replied.

All eyes went to Abe who nodded. "I'd really like to get my stuff back if it's possible."

"Then it's settled. Abe, is there a day of the week most suited for something like this?"

Abe pondered the question for a moment. "My two cousins go to school Monday through Thursday. They catch the bus at the corner at 7:35 and are dropped off by the bus at 3:45 in the afternoon. The only one there would be my Aunt Beulah, who is most likely to help me get my stuff. Sometimes she goes across the street to the neighbor's for coffee in the morning but usually she stays home because Uncle Raymond is home until just before he has to report to work. He doesn't like his job but it pays well so he keeps going to work."

"Can you remember the last time he didn't go to work at the regular time?" asked Bob.

"It was back when Co-Vid was so bad, no one but emergency workers were allowed out even to go to work. Since then he has gone to work every day that I can remember."

"So, if we showed up at the house at, oh, 2:00 in the afternoon, he'd probably be at work and the cousins in school?"

Abe appeared to give the question careful thought before he answered, "Yes, that would be the normal schedule."

"Okay, then we'll make a trip to Shiprock next Tuesday," said Bob. He looked at the two females and said, "That's assuming neither one of you turn us in." He said it with a laugh but there was a serious request there as well.

"Don't worry, Bob," said Rita, "we won't mention your plan to anyone. Will we dear?" She reached into the back seat and patted Meredith's hand. She nodded in agreement. "Well," said Rita, "It's time we headed for home, Meredith, and let these two nefarious individuals make their plans." Once again it was said jokingly but there was a thread of seriousness.

Bob and Rita exchanged business cards and the women gathered up their possessions and drove away but not before both Bob and Abe thanked them for coming and bringing a lunch. As Rita started to back up, she rolled down the window. "Today was a good day, you two, let's not make it the last one, okay?" Both guys nodded as Rita drove away.

"Well, I'm no expert," said Bob, "but I'd say that was Auntie's approval."

# CHAPTER 6

For the next few days – until Tuesday – Bob and Abe did more sightseeing including a long, nearly whole day, trip to Monument Valley and Kayenta. Bob noted the ever present tail but didn't mention it to Abe. During their trips, Abe spoke often of the upcoming "raid" – as he called it, with mounting enthusiasm. They hashed out every little detail they could think of several times over until they were satisfied. The plan was actually very simple. They would drive to the house at the appointed day and time. Bob would stay in the pickup and Abe would make contact with his aunt. He was confident she would let him in and help him gather his few possessions together. Bob, by staying in the pickup, parked on the street, would avoid a trespassing accusation should a confrontation occur. The only reason he would get out of the pickup was if Raymond Tsinajine showed up and looked like he was going to start something.

One morning they drove to Mexican Hat to confer with Adrian Tso but no one, including Adam Benally, knew where he was … or at least they weren't saying. Abe saw that as a positive sign; hopefully Tso was in Kayenta picking up supplies for Carlos Grey Hawk.

They were followed wherever they went and twice got close enough to get a license plate number and a good look at their shadows. Both were rough-looking Navajos in their mid-thirties and Bob didn't doubt for a moment they were armed. He, on the other hand, was not. Despite his police ID, he was on Navajo land where possession of a firearm by a *biligaana* was prohibited.

Finally the day for the "raid" arrived. They were both up early and had their customary breakfast at the trading post before setting off for Shiprock. Ironically, they drove right through Montezuma Creek on the way!

An hour and a half later, they entered Shiprock. Abe was very quiet, but observant, keeping an eye for their shadows and his uncle. Bob followed Abe's directions to his aunt and uncle's house which was situated right in town. He pulled to the curb in front of the house and put the transmission in park. "Okay, bud, here we are, do what you gotta do; I'll be right here."

Abe offered a weak smile, took a deep breath then walked up to the front door. He couldn't see or hear anyone around and knocked on the door. It sounded like a cannon had gone off to Abe! He heard no stirring in the house and knocked again with the same results. He looked back at Bob, held out his hands in front of him and shrugged his shoulders. Abe walked over to the driver's side of Bob's pickup as Bob rolled the window down.

"It looks like no one is home," said Abe, sounding just a tad relieved.

"Does your aunt have a car?"

"No, just Uncle Raymond's pickup."

"Who does she go visit in the neighborhood?"

"Usually Mrs. Etsiddy across the street," Abe replied, pointing around behind him.

"Do you want to go knock on her door to see if your aunt is there?"

Abe sighed deeply, then said, "Okay."

Abe walked over to another of the cookie cutter houses across the street and knocked on the door. This time a woman opened the door and she and Abe spoke for a few seconds. Suddenly another woman appeared at the door and gathered Abe in an embrace. Bob could not hear the conversation but it looked like the second woman was very glad to see Abe.

The woman nodded her head vigorously and the two of them came down the steps and headed for the Tsinajine home. The other woman shook her head and slammed the door.

The woman was talking animatedly to Abe as they crossed the street in front of Bob's pickup. They walked to the front door and the woman didn't hesitate to open the unlocked door and lead Abe into the house. She shut the door behind him. Bob waited in his pickup, not seeing anything else to do.

"Abe, I'm *so* glad to see that you're alright!" said Beaulah Tsinajine. "I've been so worried and I think Raymond has been too, but he'll never admit it. I don't expect him home, but let's get your things gathered up right away just in case."

"Has there been any mail from the universities for me?" asked Abe.

"Yes," said Beulah. "Raymond just threw them in the trash but I retrieved them and saved them for you." She handed him four envelopes addressed to him from different universities to which he had applied – including one from the University of Arizona. She scurried around grabbing a plastic grocery bag then taking the envelopes back and stuffing them in the bag.

"Raymond already got rid of your clothes and things but I was able to save your father's medals." She reached into a drawer and pulled them out. Abe's eyes glistened.

"I'm afraid there isn't …." She was interrupted by the squeal of tires in front of the house. Beulah dashed to the front window in time to see her husband skid to a stop behind Bob's pickup. Raymond glanced at Bob's vehicle as he stormed toward the house.

Recognizing the situation immediately, Abe stuffed his mail and the medals in his jacket pockets and made for the front door. He and Raymond arrived at the front porch at the same time. As he tried to move around his uncle, the man grabbed Abe by the collar of his jacket and said, "Beulah, call the cops, maybe a few nights in jail will convince this
cabrón that he's not welcome here."

"Raymond!" Beulah screeched, "let him go! He's leaving and won't be back, let him go."

"You go in and call the cops right now or you'll regret it!" snarled Raymond.

A strange male voice said, "Let the boy go, Raymond. He's leaving and won't be back."

With Abe's jacket still bunched in his hand, Raymond half turned and spotted Bob at the foot of the steps. He held nothing in his hands but had the easy, relaxed posture of one ready for a fight.

"Who are you? Get the hell off my property or you'll go to jail too!" Raymond bellowed, incensed that a *biligaana* was ordering him around, much less on his own property.

Bob stepped up onto the porch, no more than an arm's length from Raymond. "Last chance, asshole," he said softly.

Raymond saw the steely determination in Bob's eyes and knew the man wasn't kidding. He let loose of Abe with a shove. "Go get in the pickup and lock the doors," Bob ordered, glancing at Abe. Saying nothing, the young man immediately complied.

Just then two Tribal Police units arrived, and parked, blocking Bob's pickup in front. Both officers got out of their cars and joined the group near the front porch of the Tsinajine home. The neighbor across the street came running over, "That's him in the *biligaana's* truck!" Abe stayed rooted where he was.

Almost simultaneous with the neighbor's arrival, Bob's old friend, the green and white Ford Hi-Boy rolled up and its two occupants got out and joined the fray. "We saw everything!" exclaimed the driver. "The *biligaana* shoved the man holding the suspect so hard he had to let go of the kid to keep his balance. The suspect ran and got into the *biligaana's* pickup."

"That right?" the senior officer asked Raymond.

"Y ... yeah, that's what happened."

"Why were you holding on to the kid?"

71

"He's my nephew and I made him leave recently and now he's back to cause trouble. I told my wife to call the co - you, and I was holding onto him until you got here."

"That's not true," said Beulah indignantly. "Abe just came to get what personal possessions of his still existed. He wasn't causing any trouble then Raymond showed up."

The second cop walked over to Bob's pickup and Abe rolled down the window part way. "What's going on?" the cop asked.

"My uncle threw me out of the house for no reason after my mom died about a week ago. He wouldn't let me take any of my stuff. I came back today to see if my aunt would let me get some mail and my dad's medals."

"Where's your dad?"

"He died in Afghanistan. My aunt was at the neighbor's so I contacted her there and she took me home and we got my stuff. Then my uncle showed up, grabbed me and told Aunt Beulah to call the police."

Meanwhile, the first officer was handcuffing Bob. "Sir," said the officer, "you're under arrest for trespassing." He then advised Bob of his Miranda rights.

The first officer looked at Raymond and asked, "No one got hurt, no one punched anyone?"

"Nnno." stuttered Raymond.

"Sir," the first officer asked Bob, "did you shove this man?" indicating Raymond with a nod of his head.

"No, Officer, I didn't touch him."

72

"Then why were you on his porch?"

"He was starting to manhandle the boy and I wasn't going to let that happen," Bob replied.

"What were you going to do?"

"Whatever needed to be done to prevent this man from assaulting the boy."

"Okay," said the first officer. "I've heard enough. The boy was invited onto the premises by his aunt so there's no charge against him. This man," indicating Bob, "is under arrest for trespassing and will be dealt with appropriately."

The first officer walked Bob to his patrol truck and helped him sit down in the back seat. The second officer came over and relayed what Abe had told him. "Okay, I got this," said the first officer. "Go ahead and clear us both but don't say we have one in custody."

"Why not?"

"Raymond Tsinajine is a trouble making asshole and if he wasn't such a coward, he would have gotten his ass kicked today. I'm not going to arrest someone, even a *biligaana,* for protecting a kid from a jerk like that. I'll go tell the kid to follow me out of town then I'll turn my prisoner loose. No harm, no foul."

The first officer walked over to Bob's pickup and spoke to Abe, "follow me away from here - don't ask any questions – and do what I say, okay?"

The first officer returned to his patrol car, got in and drove off with Abe following closely behind. They drove through

73

Shiprock to an abandoned mill where the first officer pulled in and got out of his car. Abe pulled in behind him.

As he opened the back door, the officer said, "That was probably the lamest trespass complaint I've ever handled, and you sure don't need to get into the legal system because of it. I assume you're not from around here and I suggest you not stay around here unless you want trouble." With that he unlocked Bob's handcuffs and told him he was free to go.

Bob rubbed his wrists then looked at the officer. "Thank you, it's a breath of fresh air to know that police officers other than myself can read bullshit when they see it." He handed the officer a card showing his retired status from Santa Fe PD.

"I owe you one," he said and offered his hand. The officer smiled and shook it.

As they drove away from Shiprock, Bob turned to Abe and asked, "Did you get what you were after?"

Abe nodded. "Uncle Raymond threw out everything of mine including my cell phone, but Aunt Beulah retrieved the letters from the universities and Dad's medals, so I got what I really wanted. How do I say thank you for helping me?"

"Did you get a letter from the University of Arizona?"

Abe nodded excitedly.

"Well? Open it, let's see what they have to say."

Abe pulled the wrinkled envelopes from his jacket pocket. "Arizona State University," he murmured as he leafed through the envelopes. "Northern Arizona University, University of Phoenix

[New Mexico] and University of Arizona!" He placed the other envelopes on the seat and opened up the one from the University of Arizona.

Dear Mr. Red Wolf,

Thank you for your impressive application to the U of A. The University is always

on the lookout for promising students who can build on what the University has already

established as excellence in its fields of study.

Your transcripts and academic excellence are commendable and have attracted the

attention of Admissions. If you are interested in matriculating at the U of A, please call

Counselor Ms. Fran Emmons at 520-612-7327 at your earliest convenience.


Sincerely,

Marko Roberts

Dean of Students


Included with the letter were several brochures from the various colleges within

the university and a map of downtown Tucson.

Abe was ecstatic; it was what he had dreamed about since he met Meredith!

He re-read the letter then read it to Bob who congratulated him profusely. All he could talk about all the way back to Bluff was Tucson and the fine university located there.

It was just after noon when they pulled into the parking lot at the trading post. Both were hungry and went inside. First, though, Abe had to share his news with Meredith. When she saw him, her face clouded over until he told her the visit in Shiprock, though not proceeding according to plan, went okay and he got his mail and his father's medals thanks to his aunt - and Bob. More importantly, the University of Arizona was interested in him as a prospective student and he had a name to call for further information. She became as excited as he was, until she had to calm down to ring up a customer. They agreed to meet for dinner then Abe and Bob went in to have lunch.

The matter of the Ford pickup and its occupants showing up in Shiprock came up in conversation. "Why on earth did *they* show up?" Abe wondered aloud.

"Most likely they saw an easy way to separate us, and if I was in jail, they could either snatch you or easily keep track of your movements until they did want to take you," Bob explained. "One thing about it, they tipped their hand and made their plans clear. Either they put hands on your grandfather or you, either way they eventually get what they want which is Carlos."

When Robert Begay appeared to greet customers at the entrance to the trading post, he spotted Abe and Bob in the restaurant and looked shocked to see them together. He did not acknowledge their presence and did not walk over to greet them. Abe thought that was funny but Bob was more circumspect as he tried to anticipate the man's next move.  Bob only wished that he would get a call from Adrian Tso.

Less than an hour later, that's exactly what he got.

"Mr. Connelly," Tso began, "Carlos Grey Hawk wants to see the grandson
he wasn't sure he had.  He told me that he will wait until sun sets tomorrow.  If you cannot make that, you will have to wait until he needs supplies again.  He will wait at Harley Uskilith's, and I am to bring you to him tomorrow.  Can you make it?"

"We will be there, what time do you want us in Mexican Hat?"

"7:00 AM would be good."

"Our only problem is that we are being followed wherever we go.  I'm pretty sure we can lose them but it might make us a little late."

"If you cannot lose them," said Tso, "let them follow you into Mexican Hat.  We will take care of delaying them.  Just call me and let me know your status as soon as you can."

"You'll be the first to know."

"Who was that?  Mr. Tso?"

"Yes, he wants us in Mexican Hat by 7 AM.  I told him about our shadows and he said if we can't lose them, they will."

"So we're going to go see Grandfather?" asked Abe excitedly.

"That's the plan. As I understand it, Mr. Tso will take us up to Cedar Mesa, Harley Uskilith's place, where your grandfather will be waiting."

"But what do I say to him?" asked Abe, coming down off his high a little. "You told me a while back to be thinking of what I should say to him, and I have thought but I don't know what to say."

"I suggest – and this is only a suggestion – that you go up there planning on spending at least a couple of weeks with him. To get to know him, to get a feel for how he lives and to, maybe, figure out where you fit in."

"*Live with him? For two weeks?* But he lives in some of the wildest country in Utah!"

"Yes, he does, and if he can do it, you can do it. No one said it would be easy, but out of respect for your grandfather, I think you should try."

"I don't know. We're coming from such different lifestyles – different worlds. I don't even know if he speaks English!"

"Then you'd better brush up on your Navajo, hadn't you?" said Bob with a smile.

"Jeez, I never thought it would be like this!"

"My advice? Give it a shot, you might be surprised and you're sure to learn a lot about your mother's father."

"I'd better go give Meredith the news," said Abe glumly.

"Abe, I suggest you don't tell anyone what our immediate plans are. That way they won't leak out and something bad happens. I'm not saying you can't trust Meredith – I'm sure you can – but let's play it safe.  Your welfare and your grandfather's might be at stake, okay?   Oh, and let's go look at hiking boots for you. Considering the terrain you'll be in, I don't expect cowboy boots or tennis shoes will hold up very well."

Bob could almost read the mass of "what ifs" flitting through Abe's mind as they went in to pay the bill then to find some boots.

# CHAPTER 7

Bob had been giving a lot of thought to how to avoid their shadow the next morning. It was a tough problem since there was only one highway going in and out of Mexican Hat. His best shot was to leave very early before the shadows took up station. If they saw him, there just wasn't enough turns and side roads from the highway to lose them. He guessed he'd have to turn to Adrian Tso for help.

Bob called Tso at about 8:00 PM, "Adrian, I've wracked my brain trying to come up with a way to ditch those two guys in the Ford pickup and I'm just drawing a blank."

"Don't feel bad, Mr. Connelly, none of us has come up with any idea either except a couple of pocket knives to the rear tires. Just pull into the Exxon station and go in like you're going to buy something. We'll be watching where they pull over, and a couple of our guys will just stop next to them for a minute. Get out, stab the tires and leave."

"They'll know what was done!" Bob protested.

"Yup. But they won't have time to do anything about it. We'll just take the rear license plates off our rigs and the bad guys won't even know what to report."

"Okay," said Bob a little dubiously. "The Exxon station at 7 AM, right?"

"Right. After you see their tires flattened or after I call you, just do a u-turn and head back toward Bluff. Turn left on Highway 261 and that will take you to the Moki Dugway. It's a lot shorter than going through the Valley of the Gods. I'll catch up to you or meet you at the viewpoint at the top. Got that?"

"Is the boy going to stay with his grandfather or just meet with him?" asked Tso.

"He has mixed feelings," Bob said, "but I think I've convinced him to spend at least a couple of weeks with Carlos. Hell, how can you get to know someone in just an hour or two?"

"If we're lucky, we'll find out why Begay and his men want Carlos so badly," Bob added almost as an afterthought.

"Yeah, that'd be nice. Okay, see you tomorrow morning," Tso said and hung up.

Bob thought about knocking on Abe's door just to see how he was faring, but decided not to interrupt the boy's thoughts.

Bob hadn't been in his room long enough to take his wallet and keys out of his pockets before there was a timid knock at the door. He put his wallet back in his pocket and answered the door. It was a forlorn-looking Abe Red Wolf.

"Can we talk?" he asked. "I mean, could I come in?"

Bob pulled the door open wide enough for Abe to walk past him into the room. He could read all that he needed to know in Abe's face. "Feeling a little anxious, huh?" he asked as Abe sat down on a corner of the bed.

Abe smiled ruefully and nodded. "He's a stranger and a lot older than me. We have nothing in common and come from different worlds."

"Nothing in common? What about the fact that he's your mother's father and knew her a lot better than you? For that matter he knows your whole family better than you do even though he's been a recluse since your grandmother died. Without question he knew your father better than you did. I know the Navajo give some of their family lineage when they're formally introduced to another Navajo, what about all he can tell you about that?

"You can learn a great deal from him if you just find a way to bridge the gap between you. Keep in mind he wants to do the same since he wants to see you. Is Beulah your blood aunt or is Raymond your blood uncle?"

"Aunt Beulah is Mom's sister. She married Raymond who has been a jerk from the beginning."

"So, are their other aunts and uncles, cousins and so on?"

"I'm not sure. Mom didn't talk much about her family when I was younger and she wasn't sick. When she got sick, it didn't seem as important to know as getting her well."

"I can understand that," said Bob, "but family is very important to a Navajo and you have a golden opportunity to learn about yours. That's just one thing you two have in common.

"You clearly have an interest in the history of your people and beyond. No one would know the oral history better than your grandfather and I'm sure he'd like to hand the stories down to you. As far as I can see, this is a match made in Heaven."

"You think?"

"Yes, I do. And think what he can teach you about living in the wild, so to speak. You'll never get a better opportunity or a better teacher."

Abe's face brightened. "You mean we're not living in the wild now?" he joked. "Can I borrow your phone long enough to call and leave a message for Ms. Emmons at UA? I don't want her to think I'm not interested. I'll tell her I'm going to be unavailable for the next couple of weeks but then I'll call again."

Bob handed over his phone and Abe made the call. He left a message for Fran Emmons and, with Bob's permission, left Bob's cell phone number too.

As he rose to go back to his own room. He stopped at the doorway, turned and said, "Thank you, Bob. What would have become of me without you?"

Much of his anxiety relieved, Abe fell into a deep sleep and dreamed of soaring high above the Cedar Mesa and the red rock formations that were canyonlands. Below he could see rivers twisting and writhing their way through the maze of thousand-foot deep abysses and thousands of rock panels with petroglyphs and pictographs displaying the history of his people and those who had come before.

In a flash he was back on the ground, surrounded by a copse of pine and juniper. He could see a tall Navajo man walking toward him. When the man came closer, Abe could see that he was older, in at least his sixties, and heavily sun worn with deep squint wrinkles around his eyes and mouth. He was dressed in jeans and a flannel shirt and carried no weapon except for a large hunting knife at his belt.

"Who are you? What is this place?" Abe asked.

The man did not answer but turned and walked back toward the woods. Abe stood rooted to the spot until the man turned and motioned for him to follow. Awkwardly Abe tried to follow before he realized he was struggling to walk in high-heeled cowboy boots. Moments later he was floating after the man but not gaining on him. Meredith's face, smiling sweetly, floated before him for just an instant and then he was back on the ground, this time facing the man near a hogan.

"Why am I here? Who are you?" he asked again but the alarm on the bedside table chose that very second to sound his alarm and he awoke to a blaring clock radio he had set for 5:00 AM, to make sure he wasn't late for their return to Cedar Mesa. Abe lay there trying to sort out the dream but it quickly faded leaving him wondering about it.

He rolled out of bed and headed straight for the shower, hoping the spray would clear his mind. He knew he had had a significant dream, but his brain was not having any part of him remembering it, much to his frustration. He dried off and got dressed, making sure the rest of his possessions were in his backpack since it was likely he would be spending some time on Cedar Mesa. At least now, he sort of looked forward to it.

When he heard Bob stirring next door, he knocked on his door. Bob opened it and Abe walked in. "Good morning," said Bob, "how did you sleep?"

"Like a rock. I had a dream that would make a great screenplay except I can't remember it, only that it was really good."

"Yeah, I know the feeling," said Bob. "I'm glad you're up early. We can get an early start and maybe be gone before our shadows know we're missing. That would simplify things in Mexican Hat a lot."

The restaurant at the trading post wasn't open yet, but Bob promised to stop at a convenience store to pick up some breakfast burritos. More importantly, Bob could get his first cup of coffee. What neither of them anticipated was that there were *no* convenience stores between Bluff and Mexican Hat! A little disgruntled by the realization, Bob sucked it up and drove. He was glad that part of the plan with Tso's men was to go into the Exxon station ostensibly to buy something.

Thirty minutes later, Bob pulled up to the gas pumps at the Exxon station in Mexican Hat. While he went inside, Abe topped off the fuel tank in case they were in for a longer drive than expected. He wasn't inside the store more than fifteen minutes; when he came out, Abe was laughing.

"Two rigs just went by and the passengers gave me a thumbs up and honked. I assume that means 'mission accomplished?'"

85

Bob nodded with a grin as he handed over a bag with burritos and doughnuts in it and put two tall cups of coffee in the cup holders. "Okay, now we meet Adrian at the viewpoint at the top of Moki Dugway."

He started the pickup and headed back the way they came so they could take Highway 261 up the Moki Dugway. A quarter mile from the Exxon station, they spotted the green and white Ford parked in a wide spot off the road. Both rear tires appeared flat and the two occupants were still raging as they kicked the tires and directed obscene gestures at Bob and Abe as they smiled and waved as they drove by.

"I don't imagine we made friends with those two," said Abe with a chuckle.

Bob took his time ascending the sinuous gravel portion of 261 as it climbed higher and higher onto Cedar Mesa. When they reached the viewpoint, Adrian Tso was already there, sitting in his red Dodge Ram drinking coffee. He got out when Bob and Abe approached.

"Everything went as planned," said Tso with a grin.

"Yeah," said Abe, "but you left two hot tamales alongside the road."

"Good for 'em, receiving instead of dishing it out for a change," Tso growled.

"Now what?" asked Bob.

"Just follow me. The road is rough in places but you have high enough ground clearance that there won't be a problem. I'd drink your coffee now, though, before we get to the cut off. Like I said, it's rough in places and you don't need a coffee bath this morning."

Tso walked back to his pickup and slowly pulled out of the parking lot ahead of Bob and Abe. He drove slowly on the pavement until he was sure they were with him then accelerated up to about fifty miles per hour. After the gravel road of the ascent, the paved road was smooth as could be.

"So, if I stay up here for a couple of weeks, what are you going to do?" asked Abe.

"I'll probably head back to Santa Fe to check on things until Adrian lets me know you're ready to come out. I'm sorry we didn't get around to getting you a phone before now. It would prove useful if you have coverage but you probably wouldn't have much of an opportunity to re-charge it for a while. I need to check my mail. I've been able to check my voice mail at home remotely but God knows what kind of junk has come in the snail mail. Is there anything you can think of I can do for you? Other than setting up a guest room for you?"

"You really mean I could stay with you? At least temporarily? That would be awesome!"

"Hell yes! I'm getting used to you hanging around and I'm eager to hear what you see and learn from your grandfather."

Just then Adrian signaled a turn to the left and slowly left the pavement entering a track that wound its way around patches of pine, juniper, creosote bush and some plant life neither of them could identify.  Adrian hadn't been kidding.  It was rough and though both had their seat belts fastened, they were bounced around the cab.

The scenery was constant, but the terrain varied from almost flat ground to infinite washes and canyons.  Those they couldn't cut through, they drove around, seeing the wash from both sides.  Abe marveled at the skill it had taken to cut this trail through the wilderness and wondered who had originally blazed it, and whose equipment had cut it.

Adrian Tso finally stopped his pickup near the head of a particularly densely wooded canyon next to what appeared to be a deserted, derelict mid-fifties International pickup.  In places Abe could see that the pickup had been green but was so oxidized and sun-faded much of the finish appeared to be desert varnish.  Abe could see and hear a trickle of water meandering down the canyon floor.

Adrian got out and motioned Bob and Abe to follow him as he led them deeper into the woods and farther up the canyon.  After a quarter-mile hike, they came to the head of the canyon and saw that it had been walled off with bricks and stones in the fashion of the ancient dwelling structures at Canyon de Chelly or Mesa Verde.  There were two windows in the wall bordering a five-foot high opening that could have been an entrance.  The area in front of the door had been artificially built up so that one was not tumbling down into the canyon after leaving the structure. A natural rock overhang created a roof for the wall and extended out far enough to create a drip line downhill from the structure.

There was a wooden x-frame made of pine poles off to one side used for cutting wood, and a rusty wheelbarrow nearby. A chopping block with a double-bladed axe and a splitting maul buried in it sat next to the x-frame. On the other side was a small fire pit bordered by rocks.

Abe started to walk toward the structure when Adrian stopped him. "You must wait to be invited, it is the old Navajo way."

"But how will he know we're here?" asked Abe.

"He will know," said Tso.

Less than ninety seconds later, a short, wiry Navajo emerged from the structure. He was dressed in jeans, a flannel shirt, a denim jacket and, to Abe's surprise, cowboy boots. He paused for a moment, scanning his visitors, then walked out to greet them. Tso and Harley Uskilith grinned and stepped toward each other, greeting with a handshake and a "Yá'át'ééh."

Tso then introduced Bob who shook hands with Uskilith, then Abe whom he introduced as Carlos Grey Hawk's grandson in Navajo. Abe nodded and said, "Yá'át'ééh." Uskilith returned the greeting and offered Abe his hand which Abe hastened to shake. "Is my *'acheii'* [maternal grandfather] here?" Abe blurted, unable to contain his excitement and nervousness. Almost immediately, he apologized, "I'm sorry, I didn't mean to be rude."

"It's fine," said Uskilith, "and I suggest we speak in English so Mr. Connelly can understand what we're saying. But to answer your question, Abe, yes, he is inside waiting to meet you. I'll go get him."

Uskilith returned to the dwelling's entrance and disappeared inside. He reappeared moments later with a man in tow who made Abe's jaw drop. It was the man from his dream! Carlos Grey Hawk smiled broadly, displaying white, even teeth. He was close to six feet tall and lean but not skinny as Abe had expected for one running around out in the wilderness alone. He was broad shouldered and carried himself with a grace that belied his age. It was his face that drew Abe's attention. Framed by shoulder-length silver hair, dark, intelligent eyes in a sun-wrinkled and very dark face, it was, indeed, the face from his dreams. This was his long sought after grandfather, at last!

"*Shicheii*?" Abe asked. "Are you my *Shicheii*?"

Grey Hawk smiled and nodded. "Yes, I am he, *shicheii* [maternal grandfather or daughter's son]."

"I dreamed about you last night," said Abe in almost a whisper.

"Yes," said Grey Hawk, "and I you."

Abe was nearly overcome with emotion and didn't know what to say. Grey Hawk picked up the slack, "And you …" he said, looking at Bob, "… are the *biligaana* who saved my grandson's life. I dreamed about you and that night of bad rain on the highway. Thank you."

He reached out and took Bob's hand and shook it. "Thank you," he said again, then looked back at his grandson. "Come, we will talk." Grey Hawk led the boy into the dwelling leaving the others a little tongue-tied and shuffling their feet.

Abe discovered that there was a large foyer behind that first wall. It smelled of butchered meat and smoke which was not surprising since there were stretched animal skins and drying meat scattered throughout its length and width. Grey Hawk led Abe past this entry room into the darkened interior of what was a large cave. It was cool and quiet. Grey Hawk pointed to a rough, hand hewn bench and they both sat down.

"First, tell me of my daughter. She died, I know nothing more than that."

Abe took a deep breath and began, "She caught the *Dikos Ntsaaigíí-19* disease which is a lung disease that makes things grow in the lungs and makes them fill up with fluid. Mom fought it for three years until she was too weak to go on and it took her. She suffered much and, toward the end, was on a ventilator and was unable to talk. Before she got that bad, she told me to find you and to get away from Raymond Tsinajine as soon as I could. Aunt Beulah and I got along fine but for some reason I never learned, Uncle Raymond hated me and it got worse as Mom got sicker. After she passed, Raymond and I got into it about a funeral. I guess I was expecting more of a traditional burial but Raymond insisted that a mortuary take her body and cremate it as soon as possible. We

91

argued and he made me leave without even letting get my stuff including Dad's medals and even my birth certificate.

"Mom told me you lived on Cedar Mesa so I decided to walk there from Shiprock. The weather was awful and it started raining so hard I could hardly see. No one was on the road so I could hitchhike until Bob, in his pickup, almost ran over me. He told me to get in and I've been with him ever since. He is an honest, generous man and I owe him a lot. He bought me clothes, a place to sleep inside out of the rain and food to eat. I don't know if I would have survived had he not come along when he did.

"I have so many questions and Bob pointed out that you're probably the only one left who might have the answers and can tell me about Dad."

"All in good time, Abe. I will hide nothing. You are a man now and deserve to know everything I know. Do you have plans beyond finding me on Cedar Mesa?"

"Bob helped me get some letters back from Raymond – Aunt Beulah retrieved them after Raymond threw them in the trash. One of them was from the University of Arizona in Tucson inviting me to go to school there. That's what I want to do and with my grades and academic record, I should be able to get a full ride."

"A full ride?"

"All expenses paid, room, board, books, tuition, the works. I can live in a dorm on campus and not have to worry about Raymond anymore."

"And that's what you want to do? Go to the University of Arizona?"

"Yes. At first I had thought about getting a degree in the police science field but Bob has been showing me, as he puts it, my culture, and now I'm thinking about anthropology or archeology so I can study the history of my own people."

"And the girl?"

"Who told you about her?"

"There is always a woman."

"Well, yes there is, but I hardly know her. I haven't even really been out on a date with her."

"But she will be at the same school?"

"Well, yes ... but ...."

Grey Hawk chuckled. "She is someone special to you, yes?"

Abe blushed, glad that it was darker inside the dwelling. "Yes, she is."

"That is good. She is part of your life and it is good that she is important to you."

Suddenly Grey Hawk changed the subject, "What do you expect here on Cedar Mesa?"

"Well, to get to know you, I guess. You're all the family I have that I know about except for Aunt Beulah and her daughters. Despite Bob being there, before I found you I was feeling pretty lonely in the world."

"Do you think you can adapt to living here after so many years in town?"

"I am determined to try.  I'm grateful that I'm even getting a chance to talk to you what with those other guys looking for you."

# CHAPTER 8

"What other guys?" asked Carlos.

"There is a man, Robert Begay, at the Twin Rocks Trading Post in Bluff, who is very interested in finding you. Bob and I don't know why, but we don't believe it has to do with you doing a sing for one of his employees as he says. He has sent two men to Mexican Hat asking questions about you, and they are not nice men. They have been following us for days hoping we'll lead them to you."

"And you are sure they did not follow you?" asked Grey Hawk.

Abe laughed. "The last we saw of them, they had two flat tires on their pickup and were stranded in Mexican Hat. Boy, were they mad! Didn't you know they were looking for you? Do you know why?"

Grey Hawk was silent for several heartbeats. Finally, he said, "Yes, I believe I know why he wants me; it has nothing to do with a sing. These are bad men, you must be careful around them, better yet, stay away from them."

"Why do they want you?"

"I would tell you except it might put you in danger as I am. Perhaps it is best if you go to Tucson, go to school and get to know the girl. I can avoid them up here and they will never get what they want unless they capture me."

"But why?"

"Perhaps one day I will show you, it is enough now to know that they are not our friends."

"Does that mean you don't want me to stay up here with you, at least for a while?"

"That is for you to decide. Adrian will be back in less than two weeks. If you want to stay that long, you are welcome. After that we will have to decide what is best for you and include Bob in the decision making."

"We sort of thought I could stay with you at least until Mr. Tso comes back," said Abe. "Bob planned on going back to his home in Santa Fe for a while to check on things, then come back out here to wait for Mr. Tso's call. Bob originally was going to do a long tour of the canyon country but now he wants to see this through. He said I could stay with him in Santa Fe until school starts."

"Let us not keep him waiting. You are welcome to stay with me until Adrian comes back. By then, maybe we will know more."

"Well," said Abe, "I want to stay with you if you'll let me."

It was all arranged. Abe would go with Grey Hawk until Adrian or Adam Benally returned with supplies for Abe's grandfather. Adrian would return to Mexican Hat, as usual, and Bob would make a quick run to Santa Fe to make sure all was well. He didn't expect to be gone more than a few days and by then, Abe would have received a good taste of what it was like to live in the Cedar Mesa wilderness.

There was little concern about Begay's men coming across Tso and Connelly when they came out onto Highway 261 from Harley Uskilith's camp. Nevertheless they were cautious and saw no sign of the green and white Ford pickup with new tires on the back.

Feeling a little lonesome, Bob drove back to Bluff for one more night. He saw Meredith when he paid at the cash register and she immediately read Abe's absence. "Is he …?" she asked, her eyes wide.

Bob smiled. "But you can only tell your aunt, okay?" She nodded vigorously, a big grin spreading like a sunrise across her pretty face. "I'm going back to Santa Fe for a few days," said Bob. Hopefully Mr. Begay will assume Abe has gone with me and won't ask any questions. Maybe, if we're really lucky, the men in the Ford pickup will follow me to Santa Fe and I'll be able to introduce them to my old department pals."

Abe watched his grandfather load Abe's little pack with his clothes into a much larger pack containing what looked like a *whole lot* of supplies that looked heavy. He realized that this was not going to be a stroll in the park. Still, he was determined to stay up with his grandfather no matter what. He had checked, and found that the town of Shiprock was slightly higher than most of the Cedar Mesa so getting acclimated to the elevation shouldn't present a problem. He was ten times grateful to Bob for suggesting hiking boots, he could only imagine what kind of shape his feet would be in if he tried this trek in tennis shoes or cowboy boots.

Seeing his grandfather swing a much larger pack onto his shoulders, Abe tried to emulate the move and discovered the pack didn't seem quite so heavy as he originally feared. He tangled his shoulder straps in the process, but managed to get the pack up onto his shoulders. Carlos walked over and adjusted the straps so the load was much more comfortable and it didn't seem to cut into his shoulders quite so deeply.

Without a word, Carlos Grey Hawk set off down the hillside away from Harley Uskilith's dwelling on a narrow game trail Abe had not noticed before. Abe noticed right away he was putting a lot of pressure on his knees as he tried to stay balanced and up with his grandfather on the downhill grade. The effort wasn't overly demanding and Abe was grateful. Soon he wasn't so grateful anymore as they reached the bottom of the wash, and started up the other side. It didn't take Abe long to start puffing but he stayed up with his grandfather's pace which seemed awfully fast for a sixty-something-year-old man.

By Abe's reckoning, they had left Harley's place sometime between eleven o'clock and noon. He was trying to orient his direction and wasn't doing very well since the sun was nearly directly overhead. Finally he gave up and plodded along up and down the washes behind the man ahead of him who seemed inexhaustible. Abe was sweating heavily and working so hard to keep up he barely noticed his surroundings. His gaze rarely strayed from his grandfather's heels. Now he knew how a pack mule felt!

Abe reckoned they had walked for about two hours when his grandfather stopped for a rest and a drink of water at a point of rock that afforded a massive view of the canyon country. Carlos walked up behind Abe who stood there trying to catch his breath, and removed a canteen from a side pocket of Abe's pack and handed it to the boy. "Here. It is important to stay hydrated when it is warm."

*Warm? It feels like it's a hundred ten degrees in the shade!* Abe gratefully accepted the canteen and took a couple of deep swallows. Nothing had ever tasted and felt so good. He wanted to ask Carlos how much farther, but was sure that would make Abe sound weak. "By carrying that pack," said Carlos, "you are saving me an extra trip into Harley's place. Are you making out okay, is it too much?"

"No," said Abe, damned if he was going to admit he was already exhausted. "We can go on whenever you're ready." Immediately he regretted his words as Carlos put the canteen back in Abe's pack and set off down another wash. Grimly Abe followed, he was willing to die before admitting this was too much.

After another two or so hours of climbing up and sliding down on narrow game trails, Carlos stopped. "Do you need water?" the kindly man asked, knowing full well Abe was pushing himself and Carlos was testing him.

"Only if you do," Abe muttered as he looked around him. They had come into a relatively level heavily timbered area that Abe could hardly believe existed among all these washes and canyons. There was tall grass growing among the pines and juniper and, from Abe's perspective, looked like easier walking – at least it wasn't extreme up and down for a change.

"My camp is on the other side of this small forest, no more than a mile," said Carlos.

Abe's heart sank. *Another mile?* Then he remembered his vow to keep up and stood taller. He would be sore for days after this hike, but he knew he could make it to the end, and that gratified him like nothing he had ever done before.

Traversing fairly level terrain made the going easier and Abe wasn't staggering quite so much. He was still puffing like a steam engine but keeping the pace that Carlos set. He noticed that the older man had not broken a sweat nor was he breathing hard.

The mile seemed like it went on forever but eventually Carlos led them to one last steep talus slope. At its apex was a wide ledge walled in with larger rocks than the scree that littered the hillside. Abe couldn't see any way up the talus slope until Carlos started around the left side of the hillside on what appeared to be a faint trail. It *was* a trail that Carlos had painstakingly created to not look like a trail. It was narrow and steep but it afforded better footing than the talus slope or some of the washes Abe had negotiated this day.

When they reached the ledge, Abe was just about done in, and Carlos felt sympathy for him. He helped his grandson remove his pack and sat him down on a log to rest while he brought him his canteen. Abe took a drink, then another and looked out over the view the ledge commanded. The forest below extended wider than it was long and more trees grew down over the edges until they could no longer stay rooted in the rocky soil. In the hazy blue distance Abe could see rocky spires that could only be Monument Valley. At least now he was oriented north and south!

The light breeze caressed Abe's sweaty face and made him feel chilled. He debated putting on a shirt over his t-shirt but decided he would warm up soon enough as the sweat on his body evaporated. He was more than content to sit there for a time while Carlos moved around on the ledge and inside the cave beyond the rock wall.

"Are you hungry?" asked Carlos.

"I could eat," said Abe, wondering how many calories he had burned on the hike to Carlos's dwelling.

Carlos retrieved two freeze-dried meal pouches from Abe's pack inside the shelter and began boiling water on a small stove. While the water heated, he tore the tops off the pouches and removed small tabs from inside. "These are oxygen absorbers that keep the contents fresh but they don't taste too good," Carlos explained.

Soon the water began to boil and Carlos measured out a quantity and poured it into each pouch. He stirred the mixture then sealed both pouches. After about five minutes, he opened the pouches and stirred the contents. He re-sealed the pouches and let them sit for another five minutes. After that he opened them up and they were ready to eat though much too hot for most people's taste until they cooled down some.

"Have you ever had one?" he asked.

"I didn't even know they existed. Actually I'm surprised," said Abe, "I expected we'd have to shoot a couple of grouse for dinner."

"I prefer not to shoot around here, it disturbs the wildlife and the spirits. I do take game now and then from farther away but it's such a mess to dress out the carcasses and these freeze-dried meals aren't bad."

"You surprise me, Grandfather. I expected you to adhere to the old ways. I've always been told that Singers are loners who commune with nature and follow the ways of their predecessors. You're kind of an anomaly, you speak impeccable English, talk about modern things but live here."

"That is not all, young Abe. I try to stay current with the goings on around me." He went into the shelter for a moment and came out with a stack of newspapers from his pack. "These aren't just for making fires and wrapping waste," he said with a grin.

When the meals were ready and cooled off some, Carlos handed one to Abe along with a spoon. He sat down next to his grandson on the log and they dug in. "Hey!" Abe said in surprise around his first mouthful. "Spaghetti and meat sauce? And it's pretty good too!" He smiled with pleasure and dipped into the pouch for another spoonful.

"These are double helping pouches but if that isn't enough, I can fix another," Carlos offered.

"No," said Abe around a mouthful of spaghetti, "this will do fine, thank you."

"No, thank *you!*" said Carlos with a smile, "you carried them up here!"

After they ate, they both settled back on the log and watched the sun disappear in the west. It was truly God's country and neither tried to attach any words. As it started to get dark, it occurred to Abe that he had no place to sleep and no bedding. He voiced his concerns and felt mortified that he had forgotten that detail.

"I have sleeping bags and just happened to have cut extra boughs for a mattress softer than the hard floor. You'll have to find your own comfortable spot on them but it can be done."

As they went inside the shelter, Abe noticed that it was nearly 9:00 PM. He was something of a night owl, but this night, he was more than ready to crash. Tired as he was, he didn't get right to sleep; it was too quiet and to start with the branches were lumpy.

Once Abe found his comfortable spot, he was out like the proverbial light and slept peacefully and dreamlessly until Carlos's stirring the next morning woke him. "Good morning, grandfather," he said.

Carlos stopped his rummaging in the packs and turned to his grandson. "Good morning, Abe, how are you doing?"

Abe did a roll call of his body and, other than a little tightness in his quadriceps, felt better than he expected to feel. "I'm doing well … so far."

He unzipped his sleeping bag and sat up. He stretched as much as he could from his sitting position then yawned hugely.

"In the back of the cave, among the large boulders you will find a small pool of water," Carlos told him. "It is a spring I dug out. It does not run very far before it returns underground but it is sufficient for our purposes. Dip what you need from it then wash up outside, we must not contaminate the spring. The next closest water that I know of is about four miles away and we would have to pack it back here."

Abe stood up then went about getting dressed. He went to the rear of the cave and found the small pool. There was a bucket nearby and he filled the bucket about half full then carried it out to the terrace. A short while later he returned to the shelter, ablutions completed, and saw that his grandfather had fixed them both a breakfast of jerky, trail mix and coffee. Abe didn't hesitate and dug right in.

After they finished eating and were finishing up their coffee, Abe asked, "Grandfather, I have a question – well, I have many questions, but right now this one is first in line. The night before we left to come up here, you came to me in a dream. It was definitely you and that's why I looked so surprised when I first saw you yesterday."

"It is true I visited you that night in your dream. I sensed that you were anxious about meeting me and more so about staying with me, and I thought seeing me might make you a little less apprehensive."

"How did you do that?"

"I can't tell you, for I do not know exactly. I am always conscious of my dreams but it takes many years of concentration to project – for lack of a better word – my consciousness onto someone else. And not everyone can "receive" me which makes it much more difficult if you are trying to help them heal. I am known as a Singer, a Healer. I heal by songs and chants directed at the Spirit World. Sometimes I use herbs and nearly always use a sweat bath which purifies the mind and body. I cure people with specific chants and songs according to what they need. I am fluent in two songs/ceremonies that have been passed on to me by Singers after a long apprenticeship. It takes years to learn and even now I am still learning. Someday I hope to hand the responsibility on to a younger, deserving member of the tribe. It takes many years, much study and endless dedication to become an *Hatáálii*.

"You would be old to begin the training but it has been accomplished before. I know you have other plans, but you are a prime candidate, you are more aware than most, you are related to an *Hatáli* , and you are Diné.

"I'm not trying to recruit you, Abe, but you're so full of questions you would be a good candidate."

105

"I'll give that some hard thought, Grandfather. It never occurred to me before now."

"One request," said Grey Hawk. "Please call me Carlos, everyone does. Every time you call me grandfather, I think you're talking to someone else."

Abe chuckled and nodded, then changed the subject, "What are your plans for today?"

"I have no plans other than to answer as many of your questions as I can," said Carlos.

# CHAPTER 9

Abe nodded, suddenly unsure of where to start. Finally, he said, "Tell me about my dad. I know I'm not supposed to talk about the dead, but I hardly know anything about him. I was only five when he died and I don't remember him at all."

"Your father's clan was from Window Rock. We - my wife and I - agreed to their proposal of a wedding between him and our daughter, Patricia Sweetgrass. They were married in a traditional Navajo ceremony and he came to live with us as is tradition. He was an easy-going young man with a quick smile and a real talent for working on cars. He could make anything run. He had gone to the BIA [Bureau of Indian Affairs] school in Window Rock and was more indoctrinated into the *Bilagaana*'s ways than Patty was, but they seemed to get along well and you were born in 2001.

"Your father was every inch the proud papa and would have taken you to work with him but his wife put her foot down. As I said, he was a whiz mechanic and well-liked by the clients at the Chevron station in Window Rock where he worked. He got that job right after he came here after being married into our clan. He always wanted to join the Army for the training he could get in mechanics and he finally persuaded his wife to let him join in 2004. After boot camp, he was sent to specialist schools for Abrams tanks, of all things, then shipped to Afghanistan where he joined a tank platoon

107

as a driver and general maintenance mechanic. He had wanted a company-level position where he could work on machines all the time but what he wanted and what he got were two different things. He was killed in an ambush by a Taliban anti-tank team. The tank blew up and his body was never recovered. Your mother tried several times to get the citation that accompanied the Bronze Star medal but was always told the citation was classified and could not be released."

"Why? He got blown up! What's classified about that?" Abe asked indignantly.

"They led us to believe that the medal came for something he did before he died but they couldn't or wouldn't say what."

"That was almost twenty years ago; I wonder if it has been declassified."

"What the American military does and why is unfathomable to me," said Carlos.

"I know about the headstone with his name on it back in Shiprock. That's all that's left of his legacy besides me, I guess. That is really sad. Mom got his life insurance money from the government but it didn't last very long. She heard that there might be other benefits but she never looked into it."

"Your father was a good man, a good husband and father. Those who knew him won't forget," said Carlos. "It was a good match we made for your mother and the only regret I think she had was losing him."

"What about your side of the family, Grand ... uh ... Carlos?"

"I am of the Near the Mountain Clan and my parents arranged our marriage just as we did for your father and mother. I came to live with your grandmother in Window Rock after I began my training as a Singer.

I sing the Enemyway Ceremony which uses prayer, talking circles, drumming, sweatlodges, and other traditional healing practices to help relieve veterans of pre- and post-combat stress and sustain connections with family, community, and our culture.

"I sing the Blessingway. As opposed to the other Diné Chant Ways, which are used to effect a cure of a problem, the Blessingway (*Hózhójí)* is used to bless the one sung over, to ensure good luck, good health, and blessings for everything that pertains to them. It is also thought of as being good for hope. I sing Blessingway ceremonies for expectant mothers shortly before birth is due, or young men leaving for the armed forces. I perform the Blessingway ceremony frequently since it is sort of the source for all the chants."

"How long did it take to learn them?"

"I am still learning them. Even veteran Singers can forget words or phrases that affect the ceremony."

"Mom said you were very good, and much in demand," Abe offered.

"I was very busy until my wife died. Suddenly all I wanted was solitude and time to contemplate life. Your mother understood this and urged me to go. It took me years to restore *Hozo* or to once

109

again regain my equilibrium. I now walk in beauty and that is why I avoid people like Robert Begay. He is an evil man and to become involved with him would destroy my *Hozo* probably for all time."

"He'd come after me if he knew or even suspected I had your knowledge, right?" asked Abe.

"Yes. If he learns you have spent time with me he will assume I have shared the knowledge, he will pursue you until he either gets what he wants or kills you," Carlos replied soberly. "He might use you to coerce me and if he does capture you I shall try mightily to free you, but you must understand that in the end, one or two lives is not worth giving up the secret to a man like that."

Carlos stood up and looked all around at the view from his terrace. He said, "This land has healed me, and is sacred to all Navajos. I have decided that *not* to share the secret with you is wrong. Tomorrow morning we will walk and I will show you. It is not enough merely to tell you; to understand, you must see. Do not forget to bring the flashlight from your pack."

Carlos spent the afternoon exploring Abe's knowledge of his heritage. Abe knew very little about the Navajo Creation Myth, the Hero Twins or the other lore of his people. Learning about his Navajo heritage would have fallen to his father or a maternal uncle but Abe had neither. The closest thing he had to a maternal uncle was Raymond Tsinajine. Ray Tsinajine was *not* considered a suitable source of information on the topic. Abe sat in rapt attention as Carlos began to fill the wide gaps in his knowledge. When the sun started its downward arc into the western horizon, Abe realized that they had spent the entire day talking about Navajo myths and legends. He also realized he was hungry. As Carlos finished his tale about First Man and First Woman, Abe asked him if he was hungry. Completely surprised at the passing of time, Carlos felt bad for monopolizing Abe's time right through lunch then heard his own stomach growl.

Carlos asked, "What sounds good for dinner?"

"I don't know," said Abe, "what are the options?"

"Smoked wood rat or another freeze dried meal."

"Um, I think I'd opt for the freeze dried meal. What choices do I have?"

"I would have to go through the whole box of dinners to give you a list. Why don't I just grab two and you can have your choice. They're pretty good and designed not to offend anyone's taste," said Carlos. "Why don't you set the table while I boil the water?"

Abe laughed. Setting the table meant getting out two spoons, since the meals were eaten right out of the pouch they came in.

Carlos came up with two pouches and read the labels, "'Chili Mac and Beef,' or 'Mexican Chicken Adobo with Rice?'"

"They both sound good," said Abe, "just hand me one when the time comes."

As they ate, Abe said, "I never realized our Navajo mythology was so rich in gods and supernatural powers. Are there many more?"

"Oh yes," Carlos replied, "there are as many as sixty major ceremonial chants and, on average, a singer is well versed in one or two since they are very detailed and require much preparation including sweat lodges and sand paintings. Some are relatively short, lasting a day or two; others can last up to nine days. I have been sharing the stories or myths of our people that I know; no one person can know them all."

After dinner, they sat on the log on the terrace and watched the sun sink into the west and the night came alive with sounds. Even before the moon came up, their surroundings were illuminated by the light from so many stars. "Our people believe the stars are friendly beings and the laws by which they should live are written in the patterns of the stars," said Carlos as they both gazed upward.

"I didn't realize so many stars were up there," said Abe, reverence in his voice.

"There are a whole host of myths relating to the stars. We Navajos used star-watching skills to know when to hunt, when to plant and when to harvest. The stars even assist in healing rituals."

"There's just so much to learn!" Abe exclaimed. "It must be in my blood; I'm drawn to the history you speak of and want to know more."

"It is time to sleep. Tomorrow will be a big day for you," said Carlos as he rose from the log. "We will take packs with us but they will not be as heavy as the ones yesterday."

Carlos went in to bed but Abe remained on the log looking up. He marveled at how much he had learned today and was excited that it was just the tip of the iceberg. He watched a shooting star blaze across the heavens. He did not know that the Navajo believe that if one looks at a shooting star, it will bring bad luck. He was profoundly curious about what his grandfather intended to show him the next day but all that he had learned today distracted that curiosity. As he sat there gazing upward, his curiosity came back with a rush and he almost couldn't wait until tomorrow.

Abe finally went to bed after the moon rose and cast its ghostly shadow over the objects on the terrace and distorted their shape and size. Had he been superstitious, he would have been frightened but he had not been brought up that way and thus slept soundly until morning.

The next day was a carbon copy of the day before, bright blue sky and an unrelenting sun. It would be hot today and Abe would ask Carlos about carrying extra water if there were no water sources along the way. He emulated his grandfather by tying a strip of cloth around his forehead to keep sweat and his hair out of his face.

When he asked about carrying extra water, Carlos said, "One canteen must be enough. Water is one of the most precious of assets on the reservation and carefully husbanded. We have the luxury of a spring at our camp but that is rare and highly prized."

After breakfast, Carlos led them on a narrow cut of a trail up the side hill, comprised mostly of scree, behind the shelter. The footing was tenuous and Abe did not relish the idea of falling down the talus slope. They finally crossed the slope and were back on a rocky, dirt trail that probably had existed for centuries. It too was narrow and, for the most part, threaded its way through the boulders and occasional escarpments.  As they walked they gained elevation and eventually scrawny pinyón pines began to appear and increase in numbers as they hiked out of the rocky terrain into flatter territory of brush, wild grasses and trees.

Abe was pleased at the way he was able to keep up with his grandfather, and, like the other day, vowed not to fall behind.  Carlos stopped on a point that looked out over a canyon.  It was far too big and convoluted to be called a wash and had to be at least four hundred feet deep.

"Are we going to cross the canyon?" asked Abe.

"We will walk around it," Carlos answered after taking a swallow of water.

It took them an hour and a half to reach the head of the canyon after crossing dozens of dry tributaries that flowed into it.  They stayed high, near or at the tree line where they didn't have to cross all the washes and the going was easier.  Abe was glad Carlos stopped; it gave him a chance to gaze out over the vista of the massive canyon spread before him.  In four places that he could see, he could make out the ruins of cliff dwellers who had built above the depths below.

Abe took his cue to follow when Carlos set out away from the head of the canyon into a pinyón pine forest.  The trees were not particularly tall but grew close together and though there was a trail, Abe found his jacket brushing against trees on both sides in places, and the path was littered with needles and cones.  Wordlessly he followed his grandfather through the forest which alternated with clearings containing sharp red rock formations.

When Carlos made another abrupt turn off the trail onto an even fainter one, Abe said nothing; he had every confidence the older man knew where he was going. He found himself pushing through tree limbs and walking around rock outcrops. They walked for at least another hour and a half until they came to the edge of yet another massive canyon. This one wasn't as wide or deep, but it was also too big to call it a wash.

"We will hike down into this canyon," said Carlos. "The trail is steep but passable with plenty of hand holds and places to anchor your feet. There may be some loose areas where it is safer to go down on hands and knees, and if I do so, you do the same. Be careful, it is treacherous, and if you slip, it is a long, rough journey to the bottom."

*Well, at least he's not treating me like a child!*

Carlos slowly began the descent into the canyon. Abe could see him slide a little in the loose rock and grab for rocky handholds or even the tough plants that grew out of the canyon walls. But he kept his equilibrium and made steady progress downward. Abe decided to wait a little while so that he didn't dislodge rocks down on his grandfather's head but watched the man carefully, paying close attention to the route he took down.

When he deemed it safe, Abe began the descent, making sure of his hand and footholds and staying as close as he could to Carlos's path. Twice his rocky handhold broke free and tumbled

115

below but Abe was able to recover and kept moving downward. At least gravity helped but he dreaded ascending this same canyon wall.

Forty-five minutes later, Abe joined Carlos on a narrow ledge extending near the canyon edge about twenty feet above the bottom of the gorge. They shared it with two pine trees that, incredibly, grew almost right out of the rock. "Now we crawl," said Carlos as he sank to his hands and knees, and began working his way under the trees. Abe wished he had brought gloves. Not only would they have protected his hands from the sharp rocks above but from the stickery detritus under the trees. He kept a vigilant eye out for snakes and scorpions but, to his relief, encountered neither.

Just when Abe was starting to wonder how big the trees were, Carlos stopped. Through the tree branches, Abe could just see a narrow cave mouth nearly eclipsed by the branches. Carlos reared up on his knees and removed his pack. "You will need your flashlight and to push your pack ahead of you."

Grateful that he wasn't claustrophobic, Abe shucked his pack and retrieved his flashlight, then followed Carlos into the cave mouth no larger than a manhole cover. Once again he was grateful – that he was tall and lean like his grandfather.

The walls were remarkably smooth and there was sand on the floor. It was still a tight fit and Abe struggled to keep up with Carlos. When the tunnel narrowed noticeably, Abe expected his grandfather to start to back up but he kept going, struggling to drag himself through the tight quarters. Soon Abe was enveloped in dust and could feel sand everywhere from his shorts to his hair.

Abe estimated they had crawled another two hundred feet in the narrower tunnel when Carlos stopped for a moment, appeared to set his flashlight to the side along with his pack and stood up! Overjoyed, Abe followed his grandfather into a small chamber about the size of a conventional hogan. Abe stood up and started to brush the sand from his mouth and hair as he looked around him.

# CHAPTER 10

It looked like someone had sculpted the walls into graceful curves and bends in layered, varied hues of red, yellow, almost white and purple. The parallel lines of the layers swooped and swirled in horizontal bands then vertically in elegant stripes that inexplicably made Abe feel relaxed. The curves and colors were soothing and Abe wondered about the sculptor(s).

"This is incredible! It's beyond description. Who could have done this?" he asked Carlos.

Carlos smiled. "It is beautiful. Nature created one of Her wondrous sculptures for us by scouring the walls and roof with wind, sand and water. It is how these formations came to be and the cause of how they will change in the future. But this is not the reason I brought you here. Follow me farther into the cave."

Their flashlights illuminated the kaleidoscope of colors and swirling patterns as they made their way deeper into the cave. After about a hundred feet, the cave grew into a large grotto filled with mostly horizontal bands of color. More remarkable were the petroglyphs etched into the sandstone bands on both sides of the cave.

"Behold, the history of the Diné and further back in time to the Ancestral Puebloans," said Carlos. "It is almost possible to create a story as you read the glyphs from left to right in each band.

I have no skill in reading the ancient carvings but even I can see a hunt, or a battle, or even a planting festival in the stone. They appear to be in a sequence as if the carvers were telling a story not unlike the verbal histories the Diné hand down. I have seen other sites where symbols are carved over other symbols confusing what message may have been left. These carvings have been undisturbed for centuries. No passersby have left their mark over an ancestor who carved a message or story earlier.

"The images seem to get more modern, the farther we go into the cave. At one point there are clearly horses and men with swords killing people and later, natives are astride horses fighting and hunting.

"Can you imagine what would happen to this place if men like Robert Begay were to learn of it? That is why I have kept it a secret since I found it," said Carlos.

"It is magnificent," said Abe, at a loss for another descriptor. "How did you find it?"

"It came to me in many dreams. I did not understand them at first but they persisted. Finally, the spirits led me to this place, driving me as a hungry coyote is led to a kill. It took me many trips to find the cave but eventually, the way came to me, again in a dream, and we are here."

"I was under the impression Robert Begay expected treasure, gold and riches," said Abe.

"It is what you would expect of him. He has no heart for his people and would sell the whole Navajo Nation if it was within his power."

"How did he find out?" asked Abe.

"He does not know exactly, but is convinced I have discovered something very valuable and he wants a share or, preferably, the whole thing," Carlos replied. "One of his men must have heard a rumor in Mexican Hat. I told a couple of people I had found something very valuable up on Cedar Mesa. Naturally, Begay would think in terms of dollars.

"We can't let that happen!" Abe exclaimed. "This site is priceless to the Diné and to those who study their ancestors. It must never be contaminated."

"The only way to keep it pure is to not tell anyone," said Carlos. "If Begay captures one of us, he is most likely willing to lay hands on us to induce us to tell what we know. Under the right kind of torture, telling all is inevitable. But Begay knows that if he has my grandson – who refuses to say anything no matter what – or if he gets me and you're still free, the reverse is true. We must ask the question, are we willing to jeopardize each other's lives to preserve this secret?"

Abe was silent as he winced almost in pain at his grandfather. "We have to get him off our trail! The only way I can think of is to fight fire with fire, but that's not the Navajo way. He thinks like a *biligaana* and must be convinced to give up his search by using *biligaana* ways." He paused, then said, "Perhaps my friend Bob can help. I trust him and I owe him my life."

"I do not think he needs to know about this," said Carlos as he waved both arms around the grotto.

"I can tell him that it is something of great historical value to the Navajo."

"Would that satisfy him?" asked Carlos. "Is that enough incentive for him to go up against Robert Begay's thugs?"

"I believe Bob would protect me, no matter what the reason. The more he knew the more motivated he would be. But it almost sounds like we would be using him, and that's not right."

"No. Like we would be hiring a gunfighter out of the old west. Let us think on this more. Come, there is still much to show you."

As they walked further into the site, Abe saw row upon row in bands of color, unsullied petroglyphs etched into both undulating walls. In the third grotto, natural ledges had been created above the bands by the erosive powers of nature. They were high, now safe from any water current from the monsoons, and on them were perched countless items of pottery, figurines, everyday utensils, even flutes and drums. In pristine condition, these pieces included a variety of styles with different decorations. Among them were figurines representing all facets of native life including deities dating back to the beginning.

Abe knew he was out of his league just being here. He recognized the things as priceless and the knowledge that could be gleaned from the progressive petroglyph panels even more so to history. A vision of Robert Begay's thugs sundering this unspoiled collection of ancient art left Abe outraged.

"Robert Begay must never learn of this!" he exclaimed, repeating himself.

Carlos said nothing but continued walking into the next grotto. Here the bands of color grew slightly wider which made for more detail in the carvings possible. Abe marveled at the fine workmanship and found that even he could sometimes understand what the artist was trying to impart.

"Jeez, Carlos, how far do these friezes go?"

"There are at least six more chambers. We have not even arrived at the presence of the horse or guns yet."

"It's almost too much to take in at once," said Abe. "My eyes start to blur when I try to look at too much at once and my brain zings around in all different directions."

Carlos chuckled. "Then it is good that we are not outside traversing a ledge." He stopped suddenly as they were about to walk out of a gallery and Abe nearly ran into him.

"What?" asked Abe.

"Do not be concerned … but I must stop for a while, I am not ill or in pain I just need to stop. I must sleep, for dreams are calling to me."

"But … grandfather, what should I do?"

"Don't worry. I will be fine, and then I will awaken. In the meantime explore the other chambers so that when I return, we can go. We may have to spend the night but I know from experience it does not get as cold in here as it does outside." Carlos removed his pack and sat down on the sandy floor. With the pack as his pillow, he settled down and in moments was asleep.

Abe was almost in a panic. He was deep inside a subterranean gallery with no idea how to get home and his grandfather was no longer conscious. He feared for the older man's welfare.

*Take deep breaths and calm yourself. You are not in a crisis, and things will be back they way they were soon.*

The words came unbidden into Abe's head. He took that deep breath, then another. Then he stopped. He had heard of hyperventilating and didn't want that to happen. But he was surprised, he was no longer quite so anxious. He tentatively took another deep breath and felt himself relax a little. He walked over and checked on Carlos. His grandfather was breathing deeply and regularly and Abe could feel his strong pulse at his neck. He felt helpless not being able to do something for Carlos but another part of him told him he didn't *need* to do anything.

Abe stood there in indecision for several thumping heartbeats. Then he remembered what Carlos had told him to do, *"In the meantime explore the other chambers so that when I return, we can go."* He turned his back on the chamber and his grandfather and started walking through a narrow passageway to the next chamber. As he entered, he paused. *Should I go back and turn off Carlos's flashlight?* He finally opted against it, deciding that Carlos had left it on and what was good enough for Carlos awake was good enough for him asleep.

Only two more chambers contained petroglyphs and pottery. He found it interesting that horses and rifles did not appear until late in the second-to-last chamber. Abe remembered that the Spanish Conquistadores with their horses and firearms didn't land in Mexico until the early 1500s. That suggested to him that if these friezes were chronological, much history had played out before the white men arrived.

What should be done with this trove of native history and artifacts? To photograph it and submit it for analysis would beg more questions than answers and he certainly couldn't see an archeological expedition or anthropological team entering these sacred spaces without making a horrible mess of them. And the pottery? Would it remain, go to the highest bidder or languish gathering dust in a museum, gallery or private collection? What was the right thing to do, or was there more than one right thing to do? There were certainly many ways to do the wrong thing.

Abe came out of his reverie and headed back toward Carlos. He had briefly stuck his head in the two unmarked chambers, the last bearing a huge channel eroded from the sandstone that was clearly the underground river's outlet.

Carlos Grey Hawk was awake and sitting up when Abe returned. He looked up a little dazedly at his grandson, smiled then yawned.

"Abe! Your timing is very good, but we must spend the night here. It is too late in the day to try to hike out of the canyon. Besides, we have much to discuss." Abe involuntarily glanced at his watch and saw that it was nearly 4:30 PM, much too late to try to scale the steep wall out of the canyon.

"No hot meal tonight," said Carlos, "we'll have to settle for jerky and trail mix."

"That will do," said Abe, "what did you learn from your dreams?"

"I have become the guardian of this place," Carlos began. "It has been a Shrine to native peoples for centuries, always guarded by one *Hatááłii* who passed it on to a successor through the years until the last Singer was killed in battle before he could pass on the secret. The petroglyphs and decoration on the pottery is as close to a written history as the Navajo, the Ancestral Puebloan and, perhaps, even older ancestors ever had. I will call it the Shrine of the Ancients."

"Since only the best carvings and pottery were left here – for posterity – there was a great fear that the Shrine's location would be discovered and looted as so many native sites had. There might be other sites like this, but I see this one as a glowing example of the farsightedness of early leaders. Not only was the knowledge preserved but steps were taken to ensure it was not destroyed later by others, not unlike the Egyptians.

"Judging by the images in the later petroglyphs, updating of the Shrine appeared to have ceased after the Spanish invasion but probably before the American Civil War or the Long Walk of the

Navajo. I have no background in anthropology or archeology, I am guessing that the date of last refreshing of the site, but it is late enough that I wonder at the validity of further updates."

"But Gran – Carlos – Egyptian pharaohs meant for their possessions to never be found, since they were for the pharaoh's use in the afterlife, not to hold for some future generation. It sounds like these petroglyphs and the objects that went with them were meant to eventually be shared or studied. I guess that's the bottom line question, what is this shrine *for?*"

"Having become the caretaker of all that resides here, perhaps its purpose rests with me, since I have no further instructions," said Carlos. "In a way it seems an awful waste to leave such priceless relics moldering in a cave – though a beautiful one – until they are dust once again. The alternative is to announce their existence to the world and invite expert examination and interpretation as well as probable defacement, theft and profit-taking."

"I wish we could know whose idea this was to begin with," said Abe. "At least then we'd know what level of leadership initiated it. Maybe it's a question for the president of the Navajo Nation since it affects the entire Nation and others who are no longer here to represent themselves. As a matter of fact, that sounds right to me."

"That is a perfect solution assuming there is no corruption in the government. I am not saying there is, only that it is human nature and whoever initiated this to begin with made sure human nature did not enter into it except with one solitary *Hatááłii* at a time. It is a responsibility I would rather not have, but I can see that I have little choice in the matter.

"There is another issue," said Carlos. "It is a question of succession should I decide not to disclose the existence of the shrine. The decision would pass to my successor, another *Hatááłii*. It is long past time for me to begin to train an apprentice. You, Abe, are the logical candidate. We are related by blood, you clearly have the mental abilities and aptitude and you already know about this Shrine."

"I am honored that you'd even consider me," said Abe. "But aren't I too old to begin the apprenticeship? I have heard that from several sources. Besides, I want to go to college and have the means to do so. How would I make time for both? Then there's Meredith to consider. Having a girlfriend or even a wife would complicate the apprenticeship even more."

"These obstructions are not insurmountable," said Carlos. "I had a wife, and I went to Diné College for two years while I was an apprentice. Make no mistake, it was an arduous task but I managed. I graduated with an Associate Degree in Native American Studies which, surprisingly, dove-tailed nicely with my apprenticeship."

Abe looked pensive. "I had originally thought that I'd like to major in Administration of Justice but in the short time since I left home, I'm not so sure. Thanks to Bob, I've been exposed to more Diné culture in the past few days than I have in my whole life up until now. I find I'm fascinated by the petroglyphs and what they mean not to mention the history of the area around Monument Valley and Mexican Hat.

"Do you think we ought to explore the outlet from the Shrine just to see if there is another way out of here? All the water that cut this had to have gone somewhere."

"Yes. I tried that and the water apparently just went back into the ground. I was hoping to find an underground lake but no luck, all the water went deeper."

"What are we going to do about Robert Begay and his thugs? He seems to have several friends around Mexican Hat but those who, like Adrian and Adam, don't like or trust him, won't give him the time of day. It's a good thing too or they'd have snatched me up early on."

"Let us put the matter on the shelf for the time being and have something to eat. Will it bother you to remain in the Shrine tonight?"

"Not at all, as long as a rattlesnake doesn't choose to cuddle up with me."

# CHAPTER 11

Abe was suddenly awake. Something was rummaging in one of the packs in the pitch black of the Shrine. Trying to calm his thumping heart, he slowly and quietly reached out from beneath his space blanket for his flashlight. Grabbing it like a club, he aimed it at the noise and clicked it on. Carlos was on his knees, hunched over, both arms elbow deep in his pack.

Carlos paused in his search and straightened up. "Good morning, Abe, did you sleep well?"

"Good morning. What are you doing?"

"Packing up, it's time to head back."

Sure that it was the middle of the night, Abe looked at his watch and was astonished to see that it was a little after 6:30 AM.

"Get up, Abe, and get packed. There is a storm coming, and I would like to be back before it arrives. You can eat on the way if you are hungry."

Abe didn't hesitate. He started to put everything he had taken out of his pack back in, and was ready to go in minutes. They started back through the Shrine. Abe found that he was looking at the walls from a different perspective. He did not want anyone to desecrate this place; then and there he decided he would do whatever he could to preserve it.

When they emerged from the cave, Abe had to close his eyes against the brightness, though it was overcast. He saw that Carlos had also paused to let his eyes adjust then set off up the side of the canyon.

When they reached the rim, Abe was grateful when Carlos stopped to rest. Five minutes later they were on the trail and Carlos was setting a fast pace. When it seemed like they were getting close, Carlos suddenly took a side trail off to the right.

He said, over his shoulder, "There is a point where you can see the ledge and the mouth of my cave. I always like to check for activity instead of blundering into trouble. From behind two pinyón pines, they watched the front of the cave for at least fifteen minutes, until Carlos deemed it safe enough to proceed. Thirty minutes later, they were removing their packs and thirty minutes after that the lightning and thunder commenced and it stormed until dark.

As they watched it rain, Abe told Carlos of his decision to become an apprentice. Though he didn't show it, Abe could tell the older man was pleased and immediately set about teaching his new student by relating some of the creation stories. Abe found the legends fascinating but wasn't nearly so thrilled about the singing and told Carlos so.

"I have never been able to carry a tune and have nothing in the way of a singing voice."

"Your voice is not nearly as important as the chant you are repeating. It is important that you get the words right and it takes a great effort to remember them and get them right. No Singer is perfect, but some are very very good and it shows."

"You mean the quality of your Sing might determine whether the patient gets better?" asked Abe.

"Only the patient can answer that," Carlos replied. "Not all Sings are successful and, in my humble opinion, modern medicine is a wonderful adjunct to a traditional Sing. There are those who feel my 'modern' ideas' on the subject run contrary to tradition but the old traditionalists are not, quite frankly, as successful as we 'modern' Singers in treating maladies of the body human."

The lessons went on continually until the day Carlos announced it was time to go down to Harley Uskilith's place. Abe was surprised, two weeks already? The time had flown by. The trip down did not seem nearly as arduous as the trip up had been. Perhaps it was the fact that more of it was downhill or their packs were substantially lighter, but Abe decided it was because he was in better condition.

Bob and Adrian were already there when Carlos and Abe arrived. Abe was very glad to see Bob, but saddened to know that his time with his grandfather had come to an end, at least for now. He had brightened considerably when Carlos told him that it was nearing time for him to come down off the mountain permanently. He had resolved his conflicts and now walked in beauty as every Navajo should. His value as a Singer was wasted when he was not available; he was, after all, a Singer for his people.

Carlos asked Bob and Adrian about Robert Begay and his thugs. Adrian had seen the two hoods in the green and white Ford pickup cruising through Mexican Hat but had had no contact with them. Predictably, Abe asked about Meredith, and Bob was tempted to tease him a little but opted just to say she had been at work, and they had had dinner together. Bob also mentioned the fact that mail for Abe had arrived at Bob's home in Santa Fe and Abe remembered he had sent in a change of address. He asked what the mail was, and Bob protested, "I don't open other peoples' mail, not even yours. But I did notice the return address, and it was from Tucson," he added with a devilish grin.

"Did you at least bring it with you?" asked an indignant Abe.

"Sort of," said Bob grudgingly, "it's back in my room."

"Bob!" Abe said in exasperation.

"Okay, okay, it's on the front seat of the pickup. Here are the keys," he said and tossed his keys to the young man who somehow didn't seem so young anymore. As Abe went to get the mail, Bob asked Carlos, "How is he doing?"

"He is a fine young man despite Raymond **Tsinajine** being his male role model. I think his heritage really sank in when we were in the mountains. He has decided to become my apprentice as a Singer and follow the traditions."

Shocked, Bob asked, "He's not going to go to college?"

Carlos chuckled. "Yes, he plans to go to college and maybe marry Meredith while he becomes an apprentice."

"That's a lot on his plate," Bob observed.

132

"Yes, he will have to do some juggling of his time to manage it but it can be done. I know, I did it," said Carlos matter-of-factly.

"Me too!" said Bob. "I made it through three years of college before deciding that was enough for a wife and a career in law enforcement. I don't think not having a degree held me back but, then again, I never aspired to higher rank."

"Do not sell yourself short, Bob," said Carlos. "Abe looks up to you not only for what you were, but what kind of a man you are. That is something to be proud of."

"Coming from a kid like that," said Bob with a grin, "that means a lot."

"Now, what about Robert Begay and his henchmen?"

"You wouldn't believe how much thought I've given that. The best that I've been able to come up with is to take Abe back to Santa Fe until it's time to start school. It's only few weeks away. He won't like being six or seven hours away from you, nor will he like being nearly that far from his girlfriend but I'd say his life and well-being trumps both."

"He knows he and I will be separated, at least for a while. I'm going back up on the mountain for a while but not forever. I plan to finish what I started up there then head down closer to civilization and to Abe."

"Carlos, you are always welcome to live at my house in Santa Fe," said Bob. "There's plenty of room and, of course, unless you object, Abe will be there until school starts."

"That is very generous of you, but I need to go back to Shiprock and re-connect with my people, including Abe's Aunt Beaulah. She is a good woman married to a bad husband and I must take some responsibility for that, since I arranged her marriage to Raymond Tsinajine. I cannot interfere with her marriage to him, but if she wanted to divorce him, I would support her. Normally, I would suggest that Abe accompany me to Shiprock but considering the threat over his head and his relationship with you, he's better off with you away from Shiprock."

"You are his blood relative and I'll accede to whatever your decision is. If Begay finds out Abe is in Santa Fe, I still have many friends wearing the Santa Fe Police Department badge who would like nothing better than to mete out justice to those two deserving souls."

"Yes, perhaps the ways of the Old West should not be forgotten."

"When do you think you'll come down from the Mesa for good?" asked Bob.

"I would guess no more than two weeks."

"How will you get from Mexican Hat to Shiprock?"

"My pickup is parked at Adrian's. He uses it to go to Kayenta for me so it is run pretty regularly."

"Okay, otherwise I would have offered to come get you."

"That is very kind of you but we have imposed on your good nature far too much. Your tour of the red rock country has been delayed yet again, and for that I am sorry."

"Nothing to be sorry for. I'm here doing what I'm doing because I want to be here and Abe has needed someone to be there for him. I'm glad I am able to help in some small way. By the way, I got him a cell phone. Would you like the number?"

Carlos laughed. "I may be the only Navajo Singer with his own cell phone but yes, all three of us should exchange numbers." They accomplished the exchange in short order and Bob repeated that Carlos had only to call to get an immediate response.

"Very well. Let me go say goodbye to Abe and you can be on your way. Safe travels," said Carlos as he offered his hand to Bob. Bob took it and a look of understanding passed between them. Between them they would do whatever it took to keep Abe safe and afloat.

Carlos walked over to where Abe was talking to Adrian. Carlos nodded at Adrian and said to Abe, "Let us walk. It is time for you to leave, and there are a few things that must not be left unsaid." He took Abe's arm and walked him out of earshot of everyone else.

"We have arranged for you to stay with Bob in Santa Fe until your classes begin. You will probably be living in a dorm to begin with in Tucson, yes?"

Abe nodded but did not respond.

"We are in perfect agreement to remain silent about the Shrine?"

Again Abe nodded, his eyes locked on his grandfather.

"You are troubled," said Carlos.

"I'm worried that you're going to be up there by yourself. What if something happened?"

Carlos smiled. "Thank you for worrying. I have lived here on the Mesa for over ten years and thus far I have survived. That you are concerned will make me more careful. I shall return in about two weeks but must first go to Shiprock to make contact with our family, including your Aunt Beaulah. If you are still in Santa Fe after that, I may come see you. Bob has offered me space in his home. If you have already started college, Bob and I will probably visit you in Tucson, just because we will miss you and want to know how your life and studies are going."

There were tears in Abe's eyes. "Is it proper for his grandson to hug a *Hatáli?*"

Carlos opened his arms wide and Abe stepped into the embrace. It was hard for them both not to sob outright but managed to maintain their decorum until Carlos nudged the young man toward Bob's pickup. As Abe walked away Carlos said, "Oh, I forgot. Bob bought you a cell phone. It is already programmed with both our numbers and ours with yours. When I get down off the Mesa, and into cell phone range, I will call you just to let you know."

Abe stopped, turned around and gave Carlos a smile that tugged at the older man's heartstrings. It was the saddest smile Carlos ever remembered seeing.

Bob was already in the pickup with the engine running. Abe put his pack in the back seat and climbed in next to his friend. "I sure hope he's okay," Abe murmured as he waved until Carlos disappeared.

"For what it's worth, Abe, I don't think I've met a man more able to take care of himself."

"I know. But he's older, and Begay's men are around. I can't help but worry."

"Well," said Bob, "at least it's something new to worry about. I seem to recall riding up here that you were worried about meeting him. Look how that turned out."

Abe sighed and watched Adrian's pickup ahead of them. Then he remembered his mail and looked down at the large packet on the seat addressed to him from the University of Arizona, Registrar's Office. He opened it and leafed through the contents.

"It says I have to be there the first week in August to register and get settled in the dorm. That's only a month away! I hope Carlos makes it to Santa Fe before then."

As he drove, Bob retrieved a small box from beneath his jacket lying on the seat. He handed it to Abe and said, "Carlos was supposed to tell you about this. I thought having your own phone would be mandatory at school, especially for the first few weeks. Carlos's phone number and mine are already in there and your number is in our phones." He chuckled. "Carlos thinks he might be the only *Hatáli* with a cell phone!"

Abe laughed. "He might be. But it's a sign of the times. As the older, traditional Singers die off, we'll probably start to see more of the new ways. Are we going all the way to Santa Fe today?" Abe asked, a little anxiously.

Bob grinned. "I hadn't planned on it but we can if you want."

"No," the young man said a little too hastily, "we can go tomorrow. Where are we going to stay tonight?"

"Makes no difference to me; do you have a preference?"

"The place we stayed at last time, La Posada Pintada, was okay, wasn't it?" Abe said with a grin, knowing Bob was messing with him. "Why fix what ain't broke?"

"I suppose you want to eat at the Twin Rocks Trading Post too," Bob said, trying to sound exasperated.

"*YES* I do, so step on it!.

Abe was surprised that Bob had already taken a room for him at the same motel. Abe was in and out of his room in no time. Bob didn't even bother to get out of the pickup. They made it to the parking lot of the trading post before Meredith was due to get off work and have her dinner. Abe ran in and when he saw her behind the counter, he broke into a wide smile and said, *"Yá'át'ééh."*

When she scurried around and enveloped him in a big hug, he was surprised but pleasantly so. "Hi!" she whispered before she pulled away and looked him up and down. "You look good. The time outside agreed with you. Did you find your grandfather? How did it go?"

Abe looked around then put his finger to his lips. She caught on right away and said, "It's so good to see you."

"Can you have dinner with us?" Abe asked, flushed by the physical contact.

Meredith looked at her watch and nodded. "Shall I call Aunt Rita to join us or to come a little late?"

"By all means invite her to join us," said Bob as he walked up to the pair. "How are you, Meredith?" She didn't have to answer, her face was flushed and her smile was spread ear to ear.

"Okay," said Meredith, "I'll call her right now."

"We'll go get a table," Bob mouthed while Meredith was on the phone. She nodded and Bob led Abe into the dining room where they found their usual table available.

As they sat down, Abe said, "I must say, it's nice to be in civilization again. I appreciated how Carlos was living, but I don't think I'm cut out to do it as long as he has."

"Won't you have to do it as part of your training?" asked Bob.

"Probably, and I can do it, but at this point it's not my preference. Carlos didn't have to live up on the Mesa, but he had lost his wife and needed to come to grips with the grief and being alone. I, for one, am glad to see he's ready to join us again."

"Your presence probably had nothing to do with his decision, right?"

Abe smiled. "I hope it had a *lot* to do with it. I don't want him to be so inaccessible. He's a good man and he'll be a great mentor. I can't tell you how glad I am to have found him."

"Well good on you.  There is something to be said for family ties.  In talking to Carlos, I could tell that your presence has changed his world – for the better.  You two are like matched book ends which bodes well for both of you."

# CHAPTER 12

"Not to change the subject, but changing the subject, did you happen to see Robert Begay?" asked Bob.

"No, is he here?"

"I'd be surprised if he wasn't and I'd bet he knows we're both here and has called his men. I don't think he knows for sure where you've been, but it's a good guess he's assuming you have seen Carlos in spite of his efforts.

"I have to ask, though I won't hold it against you if you can't or won't answer, do you now know what Carlos's secret is?"

Abe looked around him carefully then nodded his head. "I can't talk about it, I made a promise."

Bob caught Abe's eye then asked, "Is it worth someone getting hurt or even killed over?"

Abe dropped his eyes. "Carlos and I think so."

Bob saw Meredith heading their way and said, "I won't ask again, I respect your decision and will honor it." He stood up to welcome the young woman to the table and Abe followed his lead. Abe even pulled out her chair and helped her get settled. She immediately reached over and claimed Abe's hand.

"You guys look pretty serious, what have you been talking about?" she asked.

"Robert Begay and his intentions," said Bob, giving Abe a wink. "We figure he knows we're back – how could he not since we're sitting in his restaurant? Did you reach your aunt?"

Meredith nodded. "She was already on her way so she should be here any time."

"Good, then we'll wait for her before we have Abe regale us with his adventures in the wild."

Abe asked, "Did you get your packet from U of A?"

"Yes, I'm so excited! Aunt Rita is taking me to Many Farms to see my family the last week in July, then heading right to the U of A campus so I can register, get my classes, get established in the dorm and find my way around the campus so I can see where my classes are."

Abe looked at Bob. "If Grandfather doesn't show up in time, can we do pretty much the same thing?"

"I don't see why not. Maybe we can team up with Meredith and her aunt and make a day of it," said Bob. "As undergraduates, you're bound to have some of the same classes though maybe not at the same time."

"That would be too much to hope for but you never know," said Meredith.

Just then, Rita Makespeace entered the trading post and, with a grim look on her face, approached the table. Bob and Abe again stood up but Rita looked angry and didn't notice when Bob pulled out her chair for her. "Those damned guys in the green and white pickup followed me all the way from Montezuma Creek! They kept driving up real close to my rear bumper then backing off and laughing." She finally sat down after thanking Bob and nodding her head at Abe.

"I didn't even notice them watching the house until I walked out to get in my car. They turned around right behind me and followed me all the way to Bluff!"

"Where did they go when you pulled into the lot?" asked Bob.

"I don't know but it's a good thing they didn't get close enough for me to tell them what I think of them."

"That probably wouldn't be a good idea, Rita," said Bob. "These guys …."

Abe interrupted, "They just walked in the door and seem to be waiting to be seated. Nope, they decided to seat themselves. Here they come."

Two rough-looking Navajos in jeans, cowboy boots and plaid flannel shirts swaggered by the foursome's table, both smirking as they went by. One was taller than the other, maybe a little over six feet tall and husky with a belly that just about hid his western belt buckle. His face was pock-marked and his nose had clearly been broken at some time in the past since it favored the right side of his face. His partner was slimmer, a couple of inches shorter and very bow-legged. His eyes were set close together and his failing attempt to grow a beard made him look more scraggly than he would have been otherwise. They didn't say anything but took a table three booths away.

The two women and Abe looked to Bob for direction. They could hear the rumble of conversation but nothing specific from the pair since there were other diners in the room. "Just keep your voices down and be careful what you say. I doubt they know about your going to the U of A, so let's not give them a freebie. I guess they must have followed you home one day after you picked up Meredith and, failing everything else, decided to watch your place to see if Abe showed up."

"Well, they certainly would not have found Carlos Grey Hawk there!"

Rita ordered an iced tea and they placed their orders for dinner. "So, Abe, where have you been and what have you been doing?" asked Meredith.

"I know I have been on Cedar Mesa for the last several days but I still have no idea where or how to go back. I met Carlos – he wanted me to call him that instead of grandfather because he would think I was talking to someone else – and we talked for a while. Then we donned *heavy* packs and he led me way up into the high country to where he was living in a cave. The hike took five or six hours and we walked down in and out of so many washes I lost count. To be honest, mostly what I saw was Carlos's heels since I didn't have the energy or wind to look around me much. I know we were higher than Harley's place but I don't know what the elevation was.

"We finally came to a fairly level forest – at least more level than the washes had been – and his cave was on the other side of the trees. We had to climb a rocky hill up to his cave but it was nice once we got there. There was a big flat area outside the cave with an amazing view all the way to Monument Valley, and he had dug out a small spring inside the cave that gave him water. We had to be really careful not to contaminate the spring since the closest water from there was about four miles away through more washes and rocks. It sure felt good to put that pack down!

"We talked a lot. He told me about my dad, who I didn't even remember, and other members of my family which my uncle never told me about. We talked a lot about his being a Singer and I found that I was fascinated with the lore and legends I had never heard before. We hiked around some but mostly got to know each other. He's really a good, honorable man and I'm proud to be related to him. The more he told me about Diné history, the more interested I got. He told me it is traditional for a Singer to have an apprentice so he can hand down his knowledge and train a successor. I asked to be his apprentice and he agreed even though I planned to go to college … and other things. I am pretty old to begin the training but he was convinced I could do it because he did. He went to Diné College and got a degree in Native American Studies. The things he told me, combined with what Bob has shown me convinced me that my path is as a Singer in addition to following a degree path other than law enforcement.

"It was a wonderful visit and I can't wait to see him again. He plans to move down off the Mesa in a couple of weeks and go to Shiprock where he will reconnect with the family he has had no contact with since my grandmother died. He might even stay with Bob and me in Bob's house in Santa Fe for a while but I'm pretty sure he will live in Shiprock on a more permanent basis."

"A Singer!" Rita exclaimed. "You're reaching high, Abe, good for you."

"Do you now know why Robert Begay and those guys are after him?" asked Meredith.

"Yes, and Carlos swore me to secrecy so I can't talk about it. Suffice it to say it's worth keeping secret."

"Those guys …." said Rita. "What are we going to do about them?"

"As long as they don't do anything overtly, there's not much we can do," said Bob. "I'm very worried that Begay will decide that Abe knows where Carlos is and he will try to pry it out of him by whatever means it takes or, *vice versa*. If they find Carlos, they may threaten Abe with harm to force Carlos to divulge the secret."

"Is it worth all this, Abe?" asked Rita.

"Yes," Abe said firmly, looking her in the eye, "it is that important."

That pretty much ended the conversation about Carlos's secret. No one wanted to trick or force Abe into talking about something confidential and so they just let the topic die. Meredith started talking about her classes and what to expect. Abe chimed in and said that many of his first term classes were basic English, History and the like; Meredith agreed and they hoped some of those classes would coincide in time and place.

They finished dinner with casual conversation before it was time to go. Begay's men got up to leave and the larger man made a point of saying to his companion as they passed the foursome's table, "Robert will be glad to know; now maybe we can see some action." The comment was obviously for the foursome's benefit and Bob took it as a threat.

"We're going to have trouble with those guys, no doubt about it, and probably sooner than later. Rita, I can't see you or Meredith being in any danger but Carlos and Abe are directly in the sights of those guys. They don't know where Carlos is or what his plans are so Abe, you're the target. We'll leave for Santa Fe tomorrow morning and make the rendezvous with the ladies the first week of August.

"Meredith, Abe now has a cell phone and I'm sure he'll give you the number. Don't share it with anyone; if no one knows the number, it is more difficult to track. I'm hoping our time in Santa Fe will be peaceful, but if we get any indication Begay's men are around, Abe, you and I will take stricter precautions."

"Rita, I had hoped this would just be a friendly dinner, not a strategy session and for that I'm sorry. I don't need to tell you it's unavoidable, nor need I suggest you two keep your eyes and ears open, just in case."

Rita's lips were set in a firm line and Meredith looked scared, and like she was about ready to cry. As Rita reached over and took Meredith's hand, her lips softened into a smile, and she said, "We'll get through this, honey."

Meredith let out with a huge outrush of air. "I just don't want to see anyone get hurt," she said, looking at Abe. She had captured his hand and was holding on like it was a lifeline. "Don't get hurt, Abe. Whatever the secret is, it's not worth your life."

Abe squeezed her hand then let go. "Some things are worth dying for if it comes to that; Carlos and I already talked this through."

"Well, I think we should head home, sweetheart," said Rita. "There's no use fretting about it now, it will be what it will be and we will play our part as well as we can."

"Shall we follow you home?" asked Bob.

"Let's see what those men outside do," Rita replied. "If they stay here – which they likely will – there's no need. If they follow, then yes, please."

"If they follow you out of here," said Bob grimly, "they won't get as far as Montezuma Creek. We'll be right there with you."

They all rose and headed for the exit. Bob separated himself, and went to pay the bill. Abe caught up with Meredith and pulled her into an embrace. She clung to him, her breath coming in sobs. "It will work out," whispered Abe, "you'll see. If they don't follow you, call me when you get home so I know you two are safe."

Meredith suddenly took both her hands and placed them on Abe's cheeks. She kissed him hard then fled out the door. Rita was right behind her just as Bob returned to the exit. "Everything okay?" he asked.

"Not exactly," said Abe as he rushed out the door to look for the green and white Ford pickup. He spotted it in the back row then located Rita's SUV as it pulled out of the row closest to the trading post. The Ford pickup did not follow. Abe watched the SUV drive out of sight, then kept his eyes on the pickup. He could see both men inside but all they appeared to be doing was smoking and drinking beer.

Bob came out on the veranda in front of the trading post and directed his gaze toward where Abe was staring at the pickup. "Looks like they stayed put, no surprise there," he observed.

"Yeah, I just thought I ought to wait a while to be sure." Abe glanced over at Bob who had walked up beside him. "What did you mean when you said they would never get to Montezuma Creek?"

Bob looked Abe straight in the eye. "What do you think I meant?"

"Some bad thing would befall them before they got there?"

"Something like that."

"Good," said Abe with a nod, "We're on the same page."

They found they could sit at one of the tables on the veranda and still keep an eye on the pickup and its occupants. "We're going to have to tangle with them eventually," Bob predicted. "I don't want you getting involved if you can avoid it, these guys don't care about me, but they want you mostly intact. That means that if you start raising hell and get them distracted, it will be easier for me to deal with them one at a time. Hopefully we can lose them on the way to Santa Fe but if we can't, I can arrange a nice welcoming committee for them."

They waited until it started to get dark then drove over to La Posada Pintada. The Ford pickup waited for them to drive out of the parking lot before the driver even put it in gear. Bob didn't try to evade them, just drove sedately to the nearby motel and parked in front of their rooms. The Ford pickup parked across the street, its occupants not trying at all to stay covert.

Abe grabbed his backpack from the back seat and started to get out. Bob reached out a hand and put it on Abe's arm. 'They would be very foolish to try to grab you out of your room tonight," he said, "but no one said they were smart. If they try to bust into your room, start yelling and make as much noise as you can. I'll probably hear them before they get to your door but just in case, make sure I hear *you*, okay?"

Abe nodded, a worried look on his face.

"Try to get some sleep, I mean, after all this is the first bed you've slept in for a while. Might as well enjoy it. If it'll make you feel better, wedge a chair under the door knob. Good night."

"Good night," said Abe as he slid out of the cab and headed for his door. He let himself in and closed the door behind him. Bob could hear him engage the locks.

Bob got out of the pickup and unlocked the door into his room. If it were him, he definitely would make a try at abducting Abe sometime during the night. Something about having a bird in the hand and not knowing where the boy had been these past several

150

days had to have been very unsettling for Begay's men. They wouldn't want to risk losing him again.

Bob snapped off the lamp between the two beds then took off his jacket and draped it over the chair. He drew his Glock model 22 .40 caliber from his belt holster as he sat down on the bed. He pulled the slide back just enough to ensure there was a round in the chamber. He hoped he wouldn't need it, but if he did, he would *really* need it.

Begay's men looked like brawlers. Bob could brawl with the best of them, but had learned that he got hit less often when he used finesse instead of brute strength. He had come to prefer an unanticipated kick to the knee or crotch over a headlong roundhouse lunge. He wasn't averse to striking the first blow, especially when the odds were against him. He learned a long time ago that one fought to win, not by the Marques of Queensberry Rules, especially when outnumbered.

He bunched up the pillows on one of the beds and lay back on them in the dark. Barely any light leaked into the room from outside which is what he wanted – no light to dim his night vision. He didn't expect to get much sleep tonight, but Abe could handle driving to Santa Fe tomorrow. He tried to anticipate how Begay's men would attack and common sense suggested they would just try to bash in the door, grab Abe and leave before Bob had a chance to react. For a while he toyed with the idea of sitting up through the night in Abe's room but didn't want to upset the boy any more than necessary. Besides, this way, if they did succeed in making entrance into Abe's room, Bob would be at their backs and he knew full well how to exploit that.

Bob pondered what could be so precious as to make a senior Navajo man and a youth swear an oath to die before divulging the secret. It couldn't be a stash of gold or treasure, the Navajo was not known for being avaricious or preoccupied with money – except for the likes of Robert Begay. If it was a matter that affected the entire Navajo Nation, wouldn't they take it to the president or at least some higher authority? So far as Bob knew, neither man had mentioned anything about getting the Nation's leadership involved, so either it wasn't a Nation-wide issue or they didn't trust those in power. He wondered if there was as much corruption in the Navajo administration as there was in the various levels of the *Bilagaana* government.

To Bob, time seemed to drag when he thought about minutes going by but when he thought of other things, he was surprised to see half an hour then even two hours slip by. Sooner than he realized, it was nearing one in the morning when he heard the scuff of boots on the concrete sidewalk outside the rooms. When he heard whispers, he rose from the bed and positioned himself next to his unlocked door. Bob put his ear to the door trying to hear what was being whispered but it was too soft. He looked out the peep hole but saw nothing.

When he heard the first boot land on the door next to him, Bob quietly opened his door a crack. The first blow of the boot had awakened Abe and he started yelling and making as loud a fuss as he could.

The second kick splintered the door at the locks and the whole door slammed open. Abe was yelling his head off, as Bob slipped out of his room to the threshold of Abe's. Both invaders were standing just inside the door trying unsuccessfully to see in the dark. The larger of the two men was behind, closest to the door and Bob threw a roundhouse kick into the back of the big man's left knee. The man screeched and the knee collapsed, leaving the man writhing on the floor, on his side holding the injured limb.

The smaller man had made it to the foot of Abe's bed when he heard his partner cry out. He glanced around and saw Bob standing over the injured man. He made a snap decision and went for Abe as he drew a ten-inch hunting knife from a scabbard on his belt. He lunged at Abe, gathering up his legs, still under the covers. Before the man could even bring the knife up or threaten Abe, the young man pulled one leg free and kicked the man in the face. Tangled up in the blankets, there wasn't much force to the blow and only succeeded in making the man angry. He descended on Abe, working his way up the boy's torso, until suddenly he froze.

Bob had reached the light switch and found the uninjured man on his hands and knees on the bed frozen in place with Abe's knife at his throat. The man had already dropped his own knife and Bob grabbed him by the hair and dragged him down to lay beside his partner.

Bob had heard a familiar jingle of heavy metal, reached into the man's jacket pocket and came out with a set of handcuffs. To the uninjured man, he said, "Lay on your stomach and reach your arm around the leg of the bed, do it now!" The man hesitated and Bob kicked him in the arm pit which made the man cry out. "Do it or I'll work you over good!" ordered Bob.

The man stuck his arm under the bed, which was screwed to the floor with only had about six inches of crawl space. Bob grabbed the man's arm from the other side of the bed and ratcheted a handcuff onto his wrist, then pulled the arm out the other side of the bed leg where he snapped the other handcuff onto the injured man's wrist. He didn't bother to lock the cuffs, hoping they would cinch down on both mens' wrists if they tried to struggle.

Abe, meantime, was hurriedly getting dressed. Once he had his shirt buttoned and his boots on, he looked at Bob who was looking in distaste at the two bodies on the floor. "You okay?" Bob asked, glancing at the young man.

"Yeah … thanks to you. Now what?"

"We leave. Leave these assholes for the San Juan County Sheriff's Office to deal with." To the two men, Bob said, "I'm only going to say this once - back off. We were gentle with you this time but next time the gloves are off. Do you understand?"

The big man was in too much pain to respond. "What about you?" Bob asked the smaller man as he nudged him with his boot.

"Okay! Okay, I understand, just don't kick me again!" he whined.

"Search 'em both Abe and put everything up on the bed. One of 'em is bound to have a handcuff key."

Abe was none too gentle with the two men as he rolled them one way then the other as he searched them. Both had large caliber revolvers in belt holsters and the smaller man had a .380 automatic tucked into his boot. Abe relieved the two thugs of guns, wallets, pocket knives, keys, coins and, most importantly, phones. Abe had to search into the small man's watch pocket of his jeans to find a handcuff key that he placed with the phones. He laid the trove on the bed and looked questioningly at Bob.

"Take a look in the wallets for drivers' licenses, I'd like to know who these two are. If we're lucky, there are warrants for their arrest." Abe fished around the first wallet and found an Arizona identification card in the name of Walter Bitsillie with the big man's photo on it. The second wallet, belonging to the shorter man bore an Arizona driver's license in the name of Henry Begay.

"Henry, are you related to Robert at the trading post?" asked Bob. Henry was silent. "Henry? Do I need to kick you again?" asked Bob as he moved over close to the man.

"Yes," said Henry's muffled voice since he was face down in the carpet. "We are cousins."

"Well, that makes sense to have a relative in on Robert's shenanigans," said Bob. "How much is Robert paying you to grab the kid?" Again Henry was silent.

Bob nudged Henry's side with his boot. "Henry?"

"Five hundred dollars each," gritted the man.

155

"It looks to me like you two are going to lose money on this venture. Not only are you not getting the kid, I'm taking your guns and phones; they're going to be expensive to replace; I'm really sorry about that."

"Take some pictures of everything with your phone, Abe, including the guns and phones, so we can send them to the Sheriff's Office investigator who draws this case. Include some pix of how we're leaving them, to compare with how they are found by the police. Also take a few of the door - what's left of it - and the door jamb."

Bob whirled around when he heard a sudden intake of breath behind him. It was the desk clerk standing at the door looking in. "What's going on here? Who are these men?" the man asked in a shaky voice.

"These two men kicked in the door and tried to kidnap Abe here. I'll leave it up to you to call 911 and get the Sheriff's Office over here. We can't stay, but I'll give you my card to pass on to them. We're not running away, we just don't want to be here if more of these men show up, okay?"

"O ... okay. What should I do with them?"

"Nothing. Leave everything as you see it so the Sheriff's Office can have a good crime scene. The men are secure and not going anywhere, but I suggest you ignore their pleas and threats to help let them go. The Sheriff's Office will know what to do, all you need to do is call them. As far as the damage to the door and door jamb, I'd make sure you let the prosecutor know what it cost to fix so he can get restitution for you.

"Tell the Sheriff's Office everything including the license plate number off my pickup and our descriptions if they want them and that we took their guns and phones. We'll wait while you go to the office and call. Then you can come back here and guard the crime scene until the authorities get here. Any questions?"

The clerk shook his head as he accepted a card from Bob, then rushed back to the office to call the cops. While he was gone, Bob and Abe loaded their gear in Bob's pickup and waited for the clerk to return.

It took the clerk ten minutes to run back to the crime scene. Bob and Abe were already in the pickup. The clerk walked up to the door and said, "The Sheriff's Office wants you to wait for them."

"I told you why we don't dare. If more men show up this could turn into a gunfight and neither we nor you want that," said Bob. The clerk shook his head and backed away from the pickup as Bob nodded, put it in reverse and backed out of the parking spot.

"I'm not in the mood to take a bunch of 'short cuts' to get to Santa Fe. I'm going to get us down Highway 191 to I-40 and then *you* can drive us east to Santa Fe, okay? asked Bob as he drove west through Bluff.

Abe nodded but said nothing, just stared out into the darkness. After a while, he asked, "They really would have handcuffed me and taken me, wouldn't they?"

"They weren't there for a tea party, bud. Right now we have a little time to get ahead of them, and you completely out of the picture, first by getting you out of Utah and into Santa Fe, then finally to Tucson. Are you okay, you didn't get hurt or cut?"

"No, I'm fine."

"You're pretty quick with that knife," Bob said with a wry grin.

"I assumed you knew I would have it with me. I wasn't about to let that guy cut me."

"It never even occurred to me, but you sure simplified taking the second guy down. Otherwise I would have had to draw down on him while he held a knife to your throat. At that point his options would have been to give up or get shot."

"You'd have shot him?" asked Abe, a little surprised.

"The first chance I got. Basically the guy's a coward, but frightened men are unpredictable under stress, and I wasn't about to let him cut you."

"What are you going to do with the stuff we took?"

"The guns I'll turn over to Santa Fe County when we get there. I want to go through the phones and see what connections to Robert Begay I can find. I know it's considered tampering with evidence but damn it, lives are at stake and we have to take advantage of any lull in time we can to get you out of here."

"In view of what we've seen, how can we keep Carlos safe from those men?"

"I doubt Carlos would sit still for a body guard," said Bob, "he's just too independent. Besides he has many friends around Mexican Hat like the ones who flattened the bad guys' tires. If he can get to Shiprock undetected, maybe he'll be okay."

"I wonder if he'll even try to sneak out of Mexican Hat when he comes down from Cedar Mesa," said Abe. "He has a lot of pride and believes that his dreams will warn him of any danger. When we were up on the Mesa together we talked a lot about Robert Begay and what he was trying to do. The best word I can use to describe Carlos's attitude was disdain."

When they got to I-40, Bob surrendered the driving duties to Abe. He gave him a credit card and said, "If you need fuel, or are hungry, use this, but try not to wake me up, it was a long night and I really am getting too old for this."

# CHAPTER 13

Carlos Grey Hawk was feeling something he hadn't felt in years. He was lonesome! In less than two weeks, Abe managed to inadvertently and totally disrupt Carlos's routine at his shelter. He found himself restless and not content to do the regular things required to exist in his mountain retreat. He missed having Abe to talk to and to

teach; more than that, he missed the *presence* of a kindred spirit.

Living alone all these years had allowed Carlos to gather plants and herbs for his *jish* (medicine bundle) that would normally be collected by his apprentice. He used them frequently in his ceremonies. All had been carefully packed away anticipating their need at the next Sing. Now he packed them up in anticipation of his move down off the Mesa. He dug, and carefully lined with rocks, three varmint-proof vaults where he would store what he didn't need down below including canned and freeze-dried foods, most of his bedding and many of the day-to-day utensils he would not need, at least until he was settled in his own hogan. As a result, he had reduced his pack load down the mountain by about sixty percent. He still had a formidable pile of possessions to move, and debated making more than one trip.

Carlos finally decided on two trips. It was safer, and when he arrived at Harley Uskilith's place with the first load, he could send word for Adrian to come get him, then fetch the remainder of his cargo from his shelter. He also decided that he need not wait two weeks to come down off the Mesa. He had been back "home" for two days and could only anticipate four more days to have everything at Harley's, waiting for Adrian with Carlos's pickup. He was surprised that he found himself so eager to make the transition.

The first trip to Harley's was uneventful even though Carlos kept a weather eye out for Robert Begay's men. Harley was home, and bade Carlos store his belongings in his shelter to keep them safe from predators, both two-legged and four-legged. Harley grudgingly had to go to Mexican Hat tomorrow anyway so he would pass Carlos's message on to Adrian Tso when he saw him in town. That usually meant that Adrian would respond generally in two days, giving Carlos time to retrieve his other load.

Harley invited Carlos to stay the night and go back up in the morning but Carlos had the bit in his teeth now, and wanted to get the move over with. His mind was far beyond today, and on the contact he would have with his wife's only sister who had inherited Carlos's and his late wife's home in Shiprock. He hoped she would allow him to stay for a while so he could reconnect with his and his wife's clans. He hoped the sister was still alive after all these years because they had always got along well, but if she was not, he would find a sympathetic relative somewhere in Shiprock, or among his own clan in Farmington.

It was nearly dark when Carlos returned to his cave. It had been a long hike down and back and he was tired and footsore. He made himself a quick meal of a freeze-dried entrée then settled down for the night. As he lay there waiting for sleep, he was puzzled that he had not had any dreams about Robert Begay or his men … or Abe for that matter. He worried Begay's thugs might have made an attempt to abduct Abe, and was glad Bob was with him. Bob had plenty of experience dealing with criminals. It took a while for Carlos to fall into a deep sleep. If he dreamed, he didn't know it, and slept hard through the night.

Carlos awoke a little hung over from sleeping so deeply. He had hardly moved all night and his back was tight. He forced himself to get up before the sun and lit a candle just so he could see what he was doing inside the cave. He ate another freeze-dried meal (milk and granola) for breakfast then prepared his final pack for the trek down the mountain. By the time he was ready to set out, his head had cleared and he welcomed the bright blue sky and the birds chirping all around. He wondered if he would ever live in such serene surroundings again.

This pack was not as heavy as the first one and Carlos made good time down to Harley's place, arriving just before noon. Adrian Tso was already there with Carlos's pickup and fully charged cell phone. They were still far out of cell range but Carlos tried to call Abe anyway but, as he expected, got nothing.

"You probably haven't heard the latest on Abe and the *Bilagaana,* have you?" asked Adrian.

"No, I have had no news since they left," Carlos replied, his body language urging Adrian to continue.

"I heard Robert Begay's two men from the green and white Ford pickup broke into Abe's motel room in Bluff last night to kidnap him."

Carlos's heart leaped into his throat and he suddenly had trouble breathing. He didn't have to urge Tso to continue, "The *Bilagaana* crippled the bigger man, and Abe had the smaller man at knife-point. The *Bilagaana* used the two mens' handcuffs to secure them so they couldn't get away, took their guns and phones and left before the police arrived. He told the motel clerk to give all his information to the cops and he would catch up with them later once he got Abe out of danger. He was worried there might be more men waiting to try again.

"Abe was not injured and got away with the *Bilagaana* before anything else happened. The Sheriff's Office finally showed up and arrested both of Begay's men but only took one to jail. The other one wound up in the hospital in Blanding. I hear his knee is broken."

"Where did Bob and Abe go afterward?" asked Carlos.

"No one knows, but the *Bilagaana* left his phone number so the police could contact him."

Henry Begay finally got his phone call from the jail at 4:30 AM, "Robert? It's Henry. I'm in trouble and need your help."

163

"Do you know what time it is?" Robert growled.

"I can't help it. It's the first chance I got to call. I'm in jail and Walter is in the hospital. Robert, we lost them!"

"Watch what you say," said Robert.

"Can you come bail me out?" Henry asked plaintively

"Where are you?"

"The San Juan County Jail in Monticello."

"Yeah, I'm on my way. Keep your mouth shut, don't talk to anyone."

"I'm not saying nothing."

"Keep it that way."

An hour and a half later, Robert Begay marched his cousin out of the jail.

Once they were in Robert's Cadillac Escalade, Robert said, "Okay. Tell me what happened."

"We didn't have no choice," said Henry. "That damned cop lost us a couple of times and we were afraid he'd do it again. Right then we knew where the kid was and figured we'd better grab him while we could."

"So what happened?"

"We waited until after we figured everyone was asleep – way after midnight – and just decided to bust in the door, grab the kid and get out before the cop could react. The bastard must have been waiting for us. Walter busted in the door just like we planned and the next thing I knew he was yelling and rolling around on the floor. I saw the cop behind him and decided to go for the kid and maybe

164

bargain my way out. Next thing I knew the kid had a big knife at my throat; there was no doubt in my mind he would've cut me if I'd a tried something.

"The cop drug me off the bed and took the handcuffs out of my pocket. He made me stick my arm under the bed behind the bed leg then drug it out the other side and put a handcuff on my wrist. Then he grabbed Walter's wrist and put the other handcuff on it. The bed was screwed to the floor and only about six inches high so we couldn't crawl underneath and around the bed leg.

"Walter was moanin' and carryin' on and was no help at all. He kept saying 'He broke my knee, he broke my knee.'"

The cop had the kid take everything off us and put it on the bed. Then he took our cell phones and guns and he and the kid took off. He was worried that we might have help in the area. I wish we had.

The Sheriff's Office arrived and looked things over, took pictures and some evidence, then they unhooked us and put me in the back of a patrol car. They called an ambulance for Walter and took him to the hospital in Blanding. Walter was sure his knee was broke but I never heard what they found out. Can we stop by and see him on the way back to Bluff?"

"What did you tell the Sheriff's Deputy?" asked Robert.

"Nuthin'. He read me my rights but I didn't say nothin'."

"Okay, let's go to Blanding."

Forty minutes later they pulled into the hospital parking lot. Since it was still early, Robert easily found a space near the entrance, and he and Henry walked in together.

They found Walter still on a gurney in the ER. "What's going on Walter?" asked Robert.

"Just waitin'," said Walter. "They gave me a shot that made the pain go away then they x-rayed my knee. The doctor said nothin' was broke but I had what he called a hyper-extended knee. That's when it's bent the wrong way. You should see it, it's all black and blue already."

"What did the doctor say about admitting you or releasing you?"

"He said he didn't see no reason he couldn't put me in a brace and let me go. That's what I'm waiting for. I got a score to settle with that cop."

"Do *either* of you have any notion where they went?" asked Robert. Both men shook their head.

"So do I need to hire someone else?"

"No," said Henry. "Now we got our own reason for finding the kid, and we'll still keep workin' on findin' them."

"I hope you're successful," said Robert. "It's a good thing I haven't paid you anything so far, I might consider it a bad investment."

"You can rely on us, Mr. Begay," said Walter.

"Okay, let's get back to Bluff. Where's your pickup?"

"It should be parked in the parking lot at the motel. We parked it close to the kid's room since we figured we would have to drag or carry him out. Unless the desk clerk had it towed …."

Henry's pickup was still parked in the lot. With the help of his brace and a pair of crutches, Walter managed to get himself in the passenger seat. Since no pharmacy was open at that hour, the ER nurse gave Walter a small quantity of pain pills to tide him over until he could fill the prescription the doctor ordered for him. Walter and Henry decided to head for Mexican Hat; they had had enough excitement for one day. They still had a six-pack of Coors between them from their surveillance – enough to get them home.

*****

At once concerned and relieved, Carlos dropped Adrian off at his house in Mexican Hat then began the two-hour drive to Shiprock. He noted his pickup had a full tank of gas so he headed toward Bluff without stopping. He was well outside of Mexican Hat when he called Abe.

"Grandfather! I'm so glad to hear from you, I've been worried," said Abe. "Where are you, are you alright?"

"I'm fine, Abe. I just left Mexican Hat headed for Shiprock; where are you?"

Both had slowed their speed since neither was using a hands free phone.

167

"We left Farmington about an hour ago."

"Adrian told me you two had a little excitement this morning," said Carlos.

"Yes, but thanks to Bob, we're on our way to Santa Fe. One of the bad guys is in the hospital and the other is in jail so hopefully we won't have to worry about them for a while."

"What happened?" asked Carlos.

"Those same two guys from that green and white pickup kicked in the door of my motel room and tried to kidnap me. Bob was right there waiting for them. He disabled the big guy and yanked the other one off the bed where he was trying to grab me and hold me at knife point. He took too long and I had my knife at his throat before he could do anything but untangle himself from the blankets.

"Bob handcuffed them both. It was the funniest thing. One bad guy was on the floor with his arm stretched under the bed and the other one handcuffed to him from the foot of the bed. They could barely move and that's the way the Sheriff's Office found them. One got sent to the hospital and the other went to jail.

"Are you already moved out?"

"Yes," said Carlos, "it was very quiet after you left and I missed you, so I came down a few days early. I will still go to Shiprock first then try to make it to Santa Fe. How long will you be there?"

"Until the first week of August," said Abe. "Then I have to go to Tucson to get registered and ready for my classes including getting settled in my dorm. Maybe you could come with us and help me get settled?"

Just then Bob's cell phone began to ring over the pickup's blue tooth sound system. He wasn't really asleep so just sat up and answered it, "Hello?"

"Mr. Connelly?"

"Yes, who is this?"

"I'm Detective Gene Whittaker from the San Juan County Sheriff's Office. Is this a good time to talk?"

"Let me take you off blue tooth; my friend is on another phone with his grandfather." Bob disconnected the phone from the sound system. "Okay, now we can talk and not over the top of their conversation." Bob motioned Abe to pull over in the next wide spot.

"Well, it seems we have some unfinished business. Is there any chance you're anywhere near Monticello, Utah?"

"I'm afraid not. We're about an hour east of Farmington headed for Santa Fe where I live."

"I see. And there's no possibility of your turning around?"

"No. Please believe I'm not trying to be difficult but my friend, all seventeen years of him, is in danger from people around Bluff and Mexican Hat. As you probably know, they tried to kidnap him early this morning."

"Yes," said Whittaker. "Was anyone other than the one suspect injured?"

"No. Uh, how is he?"

"Not too bad. A hyper-extended knee. No permanent damage as long as he takes it easy for a while and doesn't try to overdo it."

"Good. Believe it or not, I tried to be as gentle as I could. Had I had a choice, he wouldn't have been injured at all but with two of them and one of me and Abe tangled up in bed …."

"Abe?"

"Abe Red Wolf. He's the one they tried to abduct."

"I see. This seems rather complicated; I wish we could sit down together and sort it out. All we know is what the desk man at the motel told us, your card and what little evidence we seized from the room. I'm afraid a judge will "No Complaint" them and dismiss the case without a victim."

"I'm not surprised but at the time, I was far more worried about reinforcements coming over the hill and the melee turning into a shooting. Both these guys were armed with handguns and one with a knife you should have found in the room."

"Yes, and only Henry Begay's fingerprints were on it."

"I'm not surprised," said Bob, "he was the only one who handled it."

"Can you tell me what happened?"

"The whole thing or just what happened this morning?"

"I'd settle for an account of what happened this morning until I can get you and, uh, Abe sat down for statements," said the detective.

170

Bob walked Detective Whittaker through what happened at La Posada Pintada from the time they pulled in until the time they left.

"So you have their guns and phones?"

"Yes, I wasn't about to leave the guns anywhere near them. I planned to turn them into the Santa Fe County Sheriff's Office where I used to work and asked that they be shipped back to you. In retrospect, I should have left the phones with the desk clerk but he didn't look all that reliable. I was pretty sure they would show a strong tie to the man who was responsible for hiring these two yahoos, Robert Begay, who manages the Twin Rocks Trading Post."

"Yes," Whittaker said, "why did he do that?"

"It's kind of a convoluted story but it boils down to a Navajo Singer coming across something on Cedar Mesa and Begay wanting the information for his own purposes."

"What did the Singer find?"

"He won't tell anyone but insists it's priceless," Bob replied.

"That doesn't help our case much."

"He says the secret is worth dying for and I believe he means it." Bob glanced over at Abe who was chattering away with Carlos. "I also suspect he has told Abe but he too is keeping it close."

"Well, whatever the reason, it's against the law to abduct someone forcibly and be armed during the commission of the felony. Unfortunately we still need a body to testify."

"Look, we're going to Tucson in early August, maybe we can detour up to Monticello then? By then, if we're lucky, things will have blown over."

"I have a feeling that's the best offer I'm going to get," said Whittaker. "When you send those guns back, send the phones with them. We'd like to take a look at them too."

While Bob and Detective Whittaker made arrangements to send back the evidence, Carlos continued his conversation with Abe. "I can't promise I'll be available then Abe, but I surely will tr - Uh oh. The green and white pickup just passed me heading toward Mexican Hat. Wait. I can see his brake lights, he's going to turn around."

Abe interrupted Bob's conversation, "Carlos says the green and white pickup just passed him and is turning around."

# CHAPTER 14

"I'm *sure* it was Carlos Grey Hawk driving that white pickup we just passed," said an excited Walter Bitsillie. "Turn around, he's the one we really want. Mr. Begay would forgive everything if we could bring him the old bastard."

A little doubtfully, Henry Begay turned his pickup around and mashed the accelerator to the floor. They could see brake lights come on intermittently on the white pickup as they sped to catch up.

"Yes," said Carlos, "they are definitely coming back toward me."

"Don't hang up, whatever you do, Carlos," said Abe as he signaled Bob to listen to his conversation. "Where exactly are you?"

"I am about a mile, maybe two, west of the Highway 191 intersection. They are coming up rapidly."

"I don't know if you can copy what else is going on," said Bob to Detective Whittaker, "but Carlos Grey Eagle, the actual target of Robert Begay, says that the bad guys' pickup just passed him, turned around and now are coming up behind him at a high rate of speed."

"Where are they?" asked Whittaker.

"Near the 191 junction."

"Tell him to head toward Bluff. I'll see if I can round up a deputy or two to help."

Bob relayed Whittaker's directions to Abe who relayed them to Carlos.

"I will stay on 191 going toward Bluff but I believe they will catch up to me before I reach the town," said Carlos in a calm but tense voice.

Abe relayed to Bob, "He doesn't think he can make it to Bluff."

Bob to Detective Whittaker, "He doesn't think he'll make it."

"Tell him not to stop unless they give him no choice and to keep his phone on with you so we know where he is," said Detective Whittaker. "Meanwhile let me get on the radio and see what I can scare up."

"He is close enough now that I can see two people in the pickup. Now the driver is flashing his high beams as if he wants me to stop," said Carlos.

"Don't stop," said Abe, after overhearing Whittaker's instructions to Bob. "Keep going as long as you can. We have their guns so you don't have to worry about that, just try to stay on the road and get into Bluff."

Bob nodded his agreement.

Carlos reported, "Now they have come up alongside me and are motioning me to pull over."

"Whatever you do, don't do that," said Abe. "Keep going as long as you can."

Bob relayed the activity to Whittaker who said, "Damn it, I'm on hold!"

"Get turned around, Abe, we have to go back," said Bob curtly.

Abe motioned frantically at the phone in his ear. Bob nodded and took the phone from him and put it to his other ear. Abe didn't hesitate but did a tire-screeching u-turn and headed back the way they had come.

"Detective, now I have both phones; hopefully when Carlos says something you'll be able to hear it directly from him."

"They are trying to force me into the ditch by swerving at me from my side of the pickup."

"Carlos, this is Bob; Abe is busy driving like hell back to you. Try to get ahead of them again."

"Their pickup is faster than mine, and if I try to go any faster, I will probably crash."

"Okay, stay calm and try to keep your pickup on the road, The Sheriff's Office is coming from Monticello and we're just west of Farmington." He didn't want to say none of them would likely get there in time to help the old Singer. He only gave calm reassurance while making sure Detective Whittaker heard everything Carlos said.

"Damn it," said Detective Whittaker. "We only have two units on, and they're together, covering Grand County up in Spanish Valley on a big disturbance. I'll grab the other detective and we'll head out from here in Monticello"

"They are swerving, trying to force me off the road. I almost went into the ditch," said Carlos, as calm as if he was watching the sunset from his shelter.

"They almost ran into me this last time, and forced me into the park at Sand Island."

"Carlos! If they reach you, don't fight them. Don't give them a reason to hurt you, okay?"

"Yes. They are right on my bumper in the park and the parking lot here at the boat ramp is a dead end," Bob could hear the phone rustling against fabric and assumed Carlos had put it in his shirt pocket."

Bob could hear Carlos's door open and a voice yell, "Get out of the truck old man … right now!" There were some scuffling noises and the sound of what sounded to Bob like handcuffs ratcheting. Carlos was trying to ask what they wanted but the male voice told him to shut up and get into the driver's side of a truck. The engine roared to life and Bob could hear rattling bumping as it was driven from the park back out onto the highway. The engine accelerated its roar to where it was difficult to make out any conversation inside the vehicle.

Again Carlos's voice asked what they wanted, and again he was told to shut up or get hit again.

Abe's mouth was set in a grim line as he drove. He said nothing but Bob could see his jaws clenching and clenching again over and over.

"We'll get him back, Abe," said Bob.

"If they hurt him …." said Abe, tears filling his eyes to the point he had to dash them away.

"Detective? Have you been recording all this?"

"Yes," said Detective Whittaker, "from the beginning, but the signal is breaking up between my phone and the one the victim has; I can't understand everything."

"Where are we goin'?" asked a voice over the phone.

"We gotta take him somewhere. Robert won't want him seen around the trading post or at his house, and it ain't smart to take him to our place. Where can we take him that's isolated and quiet where we can do a little persuadin' if we need to?"

"Somewhere on the Res, that way those *Bilagaana* cops won't bother us."

"Robert's going to want to see him; it shouldn't be too far away from Bluff."

"Kayenta would be good, that's not so far."

"Do you have friends or family there?"

"My *Shimasani* [maternal grandmother] lives a little ways out of town. She is old and lives by herself since no one in the family will put up with her drinking or her temper. She doesn't like no one, but if I brought her a couple of jugs of red wine, she probably wouldn't say anything if we used her barn."

"Can we trust her?"

"No but she never goes out to the barn. It isn't like this is going to take forever."

"What's her name?"

177

"Millie Nez."

"And she won't poke her nose into our business?"

"She can't hardly walk, and nobody listens to her anyway."

"I guess all she can say is no."

"I didn't plan on asking her. While I distract her with the wine, you take the old man into the barn. The big doors should be partly open and it's never locked. Find something sturdy to handcuff him to. I don't think he'll be like *Ma'ii* [Coyote] and gnaw his hand off to get free," he laughed. "We'll give him a couple of blankets and some water. He'll be okay."

"Don't forget I can't walk except on crutches."

"Then I'll give her the wine and I'll go to the barn."

"What if he dies?"

"Just as long as it's after he tells Robert what Robert wants to know, who cares?"

"Are we going to rough him up some?"

"Depends on what he's willing to say and what Robert wants us to do."

"I hope so, it'll be payback for what that *Bilagaana* cop did to me."

✶✶✶✶✶

By the time Bob and Abe arrived at the Sand Island State Park, Detective Whittaker was there along with another detective and a marked patrol unit from Blanding. Detective Whittaker was taking pictures of the area around Carlos's pickup which was sitting parked close to the San Juan River with the driver's door standing open. The other detective and the uniformed officer were scouring the area near the river bank for Carlos or evidence.

Abe hit the brakes and was immediately out of Bob's pickup and running toward the white one. "Whoa, whoa, whoa," yelled Detective Whittaker as he took hold of Abe's arm and stopped him. "There's no one in the pickup," said the detective who towered over Abe at six foot three.

"But that's my grandfather's pickup!" Abe protested.

"I know and right now I'm taking pictures of an undisturbed crime scene so unless you want to screw up some evidence, stand back. Like I said, there is no one in the vehicle but there is a little blood. Let me take my pictures and collect my evidence, then you can have a look. Maybe you could help those other officers look for your grandfather?"

Abe felt that was a waste of time. He knew Henry Begay and Walter Bitsillie had kidnapped Carlos.

"There are footprints in the sand suggesting that only one person approached the pickup but two left it. What kind of shoes does your grandfather wear?"

Abe hesitated. "He wears hiking boots when he's out by himself but prefers cowboy boots when he's in town."

"That fits. A pair of tennis shoes approached the pickup but a pair of tennis shoes and a pair of cowboy boots walked away.

179

Now can you see why it's important not to contaminate the crime scene?"

Bob walked up to them in the meantime. "Detective Whittaker? I'm Bob Connelly. It's good to finally meet you," Bob said as he offered the detective his hand. "Well, it looks like you got your wish, here we are in person."

Whittaker shook Bob's hand, then Abe's. "It's Gene. Thank you for coming though I know wild horses couldn't have kept you away. So far all I've done is shoot pics and taken a quick glance inside the pickup. The Blanding PD officer, who was the first one here, was sharp enough to check the inside of the pickup from the passenger side therefore we have undisturbed footprints on this side. There's some blood inside but not enough to suggest a major injury. That's all I know. My partner is out canvassing with the Blanding officer whom we probably should kick loose so he can go back to his jurisdiction."

Bob nodded and Detective Whittaker called his partner on his portable radio. "Les? Why don't you turn the Blanding PD officer loose so he can get back to town?." There were two clicks on the radio and soon the Blanding officer came walking back to his patrol car.

"Hey Gary? Thanks for the cover; we were really caught out on this one. Both our units are in Spanish Valley covering Grand County on a near-riot."

The officer waved then got in his car and left.

Whittaker turned back to Bob. "As you know, the cell phone signal petered out about twenty minutes ago. The last few minutes of the recording are mostly garbled, but some words can still be made out. Something about Kayenta was the last thing I could understand for sure."

Abe waited impatiently for Detective Whittaker to finish taking his pictures, taking blood samples and dusting for latent fingerprints. When the detective motioned Abe over to the vehicle, he said, "Have a look. Be sure to tell me if anything looks out of place."

Abe found nothing amiss except for some drops of blood on the steering wheel and on the floor mat in front of the driver's seat. He turned to Detective Whittaker and asked, "Shouldn't we be heading to Kayenta?"

"And do what?"

"Look for Carlos, look for the green and the white Ford pickup!" Abe exclaimed in frustration.

"Abe, Detective Whittaker can't go there without a court order and *that* would be iffy," said Bob. "He'd be out of his jurisdiction and wouldn't even have the rights of a citizen since it's on the Reservation. It's the same situation we had with your uncle in Shiprock except we might not find such an understanding Navajo Nation Police Officer. We need to know more before we try to barge in and raise hell."

"That's right, and our best lead is that recording," said Detective Whittaker. "I think all three of us should listen to it again, in a quieter place where we can rewind it if we need to. Maybe we'll catch some more words."

"Maybe I should go see Robert Begay and twist his neck until he talks," said Abe with rage in his voice.

"That would wind you up in jail, Abe, with Begay free to operate at will," said Bob, trying to reason with the incensed young man.

"We have to do something! We can't just stand around talking," Abe cried.

"I agree," said Detective Whittaker. "Let's go to our Blanding satellite office and see if we can pick up any more off the recording. After that, I'll have it computer enhanced but that will take some time."

Grudgingly, Abe consented to drive his grandfather's pickup to Blanding PD in lieu of having it towed. He didn't like the idea of driving *away* from the direction his grandfather had probably been taken, but he didn't see any alternative.

Henry Begay remembered to politely wait outside his *Shimasaní's* house until he was invited in as it was done in the old days. "*Hatsói ashkiígíí* [grandson]. Why are you here?" Millie Nez demanded, "you never come around unless you want something."

"*Shimasaní*, it is good see you again, it has been too long," said Henry in what he hoped was a hearty voice. "Look, I have brought you a gift just because I missed you."

The old lady's eyes brightened and lost their suspicion at the sight of the two gallon jugs of Carlo Rossi Sweet Red Henry placed on her kitchen table. "Thank you, *Hatsói ashkiigíí* [grandson], no one ever brings me gifts anymore," she muttered again.

"How is your health, *Shimasaní?*" asked Henry, not caring what the answer was but knowing he should ask the question.

"I am well enough, except for my arthritis and bad heart. I need a Blessing Way Sing, then I would be much better."

"I am sorry you are not well. Have you inquired about a Singer?"

"Who listens to me? My *ach'é'é; hatsi'* [daughter] never comes to see me because she thinks I drink too much and have a bad temper. Why shouldn't I? No one cares anymore."

"It is not right, *Shimasaní*, I shall speak to my *shimá* [mother] about this, perhaps I can help. But now I must go but I won't forget. *Dóó ni'áásh* [until we meet again]."

Henry walked back out to the pickup and drove it down near the front of the barn. As he expected, the large barn doors were ajar – their hinges almost past useful service – and he parked right next to them so his driver's door was hidden from the house by the pickup. He hustled Carlos into the barn which was empty except for some rusty implements, a few old bales of dusty hay and some birds.

183

As he expected, there were eyebolts screwed into the posts next to the stalls for tethering horses and Henry knew one of these would work well for "tethering" Carlos.

He unlocked one of the handcuffs from Carlos's wrist and fed it through the eyebolt and ratcheted it closed. There was a hay bale next to the stall where Carlos could sit down fairly comfortably as long as he didn't try to wander.

"There. Now we will know where you are at all times until Robert is ready to speak to you. Maybe later I'll come by with some blankets, water and maybe even some food. Until then, stay put and keep quiet. I don't want you upsetting my grandmother, understand?"

Carlos nodded but said nothing.

Henry shook the handcuff attached to the eyebolt one more time and nodded in satisfaction. He walked out and climbed into the pickup. "It's done, he won't be going anywhere. Let's get out of here. It's too early to call Robert but it's not too early to have a drink to celebrate!"

# CHAPTER 15

They had listened to the recording over and over again, slow, fast, and on headphones to everyone's exhaustion. "Kayenta" was clear as a bell but the scratchy white noise that came after it was simply impossible to decipher except in brief pockets of communication when the words were discernable but out of context. "Old but lives by herself ..." was clear enough but who lived by herself and where?

"Jugs of wine ... ," and "Gnaw his hand off ...," caused a great deal of consternation until they put it in perspective with the two suspects' predilection for drinking and using handcuffs.

"Abe?" asked Bob. "Could you tell if maybe they switched to the Navajo language and that's why we're having so much trouble?"

"No," Abe replied, "they are talking just English, I would have caught any Navajo words."

"We're going to need to get someone from the Navajo National Police in on this," said Detective Whittaker. "I think Kayenta is a good place to start our search, and finding an older woman who is related to one our suspects seems a logical place to begin our inquiries but we need someone familiar with the records system to do the searches. From years of working with the Rez, I have some pretty good contacts but they won't be in for a couple of hours yet. Meanwhile, I suggest we go find some coffee and something to eat and bounce this around some more."

There was no opposition to Detective Whittaker's suggestion and they found a local café just opening that had fresh coffee and bacon and eggs on order. Predictably, Abe was anxious to *do something* and it took a firm hand by Bob to calm him down.

"It would make sense to stash Carlos at a place where an older woman lived by herself," said Detective Whittaker. "All we need is one good lead."

"Perhaps calling Adrian Tso might be a better way to open up the family trees than starting with police records," mused Bob. "He's a long time resident of Mexican Hat and probably knows everyone around there and he'd do whatever he could to get Carlos out of this jam. Same with Adam Benally and that clerk at the San Juan Inn. Maybe any or all of them know people in Kayenta with the same knowledge.

"I know you can't be a part of it," said Bob, "but I don't intend to wait for the Navajo National Police to bat this around. As soon as I am convinced we know where he is, I'm going in after him. Cops have to follow protocols; I don't."

Gene Whittaker winced. "That's risky. The Navajo National Police is very sensitive about anyone infringing on their jurisdiction even though they're usually slow to act. You may find Carlos Grey Hawk but you might run afoul of their courts."

"I don't care. As long as we get him back, I'm willing to face the music."

The look of gratitude Abe gave Bob only strengthened Bob's will to see the matter through.

After they ate, Detective Whittaker and his partner left to hunt up some of his Navajo contacts at the Kayenta police station. Leaving Carlos's pickup at Blanding PD, Abe and Bob headed for Mexican Hat to find Adrian Tso and the others.

Their first stop was the Exxon station. As luck would have it, they caught him between jobs and he stopped to talk with them.

"Mr. Tso, do you remember us? I'm Bob Connelly and this is Carlos Grey Hawk's grandson. Robert Begay's two thugs abducted Carlos this morning at the Sand Island State Park and are holding him somewhere, probably in or near Kayenta. Carlos was able to leave his phone on when they grabbed him and we were able to hear part of the conversation between the thugs. What we could make out included Kayenta and something about leaving Carlos at a place where an older woman lived by herself. We're assuming she's a relative of one of the thugs who are Henry Begay and Walter Bitsillie. They were the two in the green and white Ford pickup who were up here asking about Carlos a while back."

Adrian Tso shook their hands then shook his head when he heard the news. "Carlos was so sure he'd be safe, he took no precautions and look where it got him. He is stubborn as any mule I know of. I recognize the two names but don't think I can put a face with either name. But I'll start asking around town; there are a lot of people in Kayenta related to folks here so maybe we'll get lucky."

187

"Do you know anyone in Kayenta as knowledgeable about the people there as you are about residents of Mexican Hat?"

"There is a *Bilagaana* doctor in Kayenta – an old timer – who treats a lot of the Navajos willing to come to him. His name is Doc Emory and his clinic is on the right just before you get to the big ninety-degree curve coming into town. You would probably have better luck going to see him than trying to call him on the phone. He's sort of cantankerous but he cares about his patients."

Adrian Tso agreed to ask around Mexican Hat while Abe and Bob headed for Kayenta. It was only about a forty-five minute drive and they found Doc Emory's clinic without any problem. They had to wait about half an hour before the doctor could see them.

They had been escorted into an exam room that obviously doubled as the doctor's office. After a short wait, a tiny, wizened white man with thinning white hair walked in.

"What's this?" he asked, "you two don't look sick or injured."

"No Sir, we're not," said Bob as he handed Doctor Emory a "retired police officer" business card. "We're trying to locate Abe here's grandfather who was abducted early this morning near Bluff by two Navajos. We're afraid for his welfare as he has information they are willing to force out of him even if it means his life."

"What does that have to do with me?" Doctor Emory asked querulously.

"We were able to overhear part of the suspects' conversation and they mentioned Kayenta and leaving the victim with an old woman who lived alone probably out of town."

"What's her name?"

"We don't know; that part of the recording was garbled. We're trying to contact folks around Kayenta with older relatives who live alone. The suspects are Henry Begay and Walter Bitsillie and the woman might be related to one of them."

Doc Emory squinted at Bob's card at length before he asked, "How do I know you're not just trying to find helpless people to pull a scam on?"

Abe spoke up emotionally, "Carlos Grey Horse is my grandfather and I'm scared they're going to hurt him. We're not trying to sell *anything*."

"Carlos Grey Horse?" asked Doc Emory. "The Singer?"

"Yes."

"I know him by reputation. He's supposed do Blessing Way and Enemy Way Sings and is very highly thought of around here." He paused for a moment and looked up as if thinking. "Let me think about this. It might take a while, I have a full waiting room, but if I think of anyone, I'll call you. I don't think this falls under any HIPPA regulations."

"Thank you, Doctor," said a grateful Abe.

"Now get out of here, I have patients waiting."

As they drove away from the clinic, Abe asked, "What do you think about checking at the local pharmacy? They usually know who is old and maybe if they live alone."

Bob shook his head. "You're right about them knowing, but considering the HIPPA regulations, they'd be prohibited from divulging that kind of information. And I can see why. Even though we have the best intentions, there's a privacy issue."

"What is HIPPA anyway? I heard Doc Emory mention it."

"It's the Health Insurance Portability and Accountability Act which is designed to prevent discrimination and preserve the privacy of individuals. The government had this old lady in mind when they enacted the law. The more I think about it, the more sure I am that we got lucky finding an old country doctor willing to listen to us. Now if he can only come through."

They hadn't reached the outskirts of town when Bob's phone rang with a number he didn't recognize. "Hello?"

"This is Doctor Emory. The only patient like the one you're looking for I know of is Millie Nez. I know for a fact she lives alone because her family won't put up with her temper and drinking. She lives off Highway 163 past the solar farm in an old mobile home. There are some outbuildings there too but I don't think they're in use. I ought to warn you, she's a firebrand if you cross her whether she's drunk or sober. Send the young man to talk to her, at least he's Diné. I wish him luck, he'll need it." Doc Emory didn't wait for a thank you, just dropped the phone back into its cradle.

The one-sided conversation had come out on the pickup's stereo system via Blue Tooth so Bob and Abe heard the same thing. "Thanks, *I think,* Doc," muttered Abe.

"Well, we're headed in the right direction," said Bob cheerfully.

"Easy for you to say," Abe replied gloomily. Then he brightened, "Maybe we've found the needle in the haystack."

When they spotted the acres of solar panels on the left, Bob slowed way down and they began looking. There wasn't much to see; the ground was mostly creosote bushes and mesquite but it was fairly flat. Millie Nez's place was easy to spot, it was off by itself on the northwest side of the highway. A farmer's gate slumped in the dirt. Bob drove up close to the mobile home. A ramshackle barn with the big doors ajar stood about a hundred feet from the house.

Abe said, "The polite Navajo way to visit someone unannounced is to wait until they invite you in but I don't know if the old lady will even realize we're here. Let's give her a few minutes then I'll go up to the front door."

Five minutes seemed like an hour to Abe and he jumped out of the truck and cautiously walked up to the porch and waited a little while. When there was no response he stepped onto the porch and knocked at the door.

"Who's there?" bellowed a raspy voice. "Go away, this is no trespassing property."

"Grandmother," said Abe soothingly, "My name is Abe Red Wolf." He then formally introduced himself by citing his lineage. I am not selling anything or trying to get money from you. I am looking for my grandfather, Carlos Grey Hawk, who was abducted earlier today near Bluff. We have reason to believe he might be hidden here."

"Grey Hawk? The Singer?" asked the voice.

"Yes, Grandmother."

"Well, he is not here."

"May I look in your barn?"

"No! You can get off my property and be quick about it or I'll call the cops or get out my shotgun. There's no one here but me!"

Abe turned to step down off the porch when the voice yelled, "And don't come back!" He went back toward the pickup shaking his head. He glanced at the barn, noticed that the doors were partly ajar and was sorely tempted to stick his head in to look around. Instead, he honored the old crone's demand that he leave and got back in the pickup.

"*That* was a waste of time. Doc Emory wasn't kidding, she's a mean one."

*****

Millie Nez listened as the vehicle in her yard turned around and left. *Carlos Grey Hawk had been abducted?* She wondered why; a nicer, gentler man she had never met. He had conducted a Blessingway ceremony for her a few years before and it had done wonders for her arthritis. It had to be the same man. The more she thought about him, the more she wondered what her grandson had been doing at her place. When he left, she knew he didn't drive away immediately, and wondered why.

Her curiosity got the better of her and she grabbed her walker and set out for the barn. Millie wasn't nearly as infirm as her family thought, though she did like to use her walker for balance. She was plenty strong to walk on her own. She took her time, careful to avoid the rocks and uneven places in the path from the house to the outbuilding. *The doors are open wider than they were.* That made her suspicious … and more cautious. She stood at the door for several minutes and just listened. She could hear only the scuffling and chirping of the barn swallows that lived here during the breeding season. Other than that she heard nothing.

Finally she peeked around the edge of the door and stared into the barn's interior. At first she could see nothing until her eyes – used to full sunlight – adjusted to the gloom. There sat Carlos Grey Hawk slumped against the gatepost into one of the barn's stalls. He looked up at her though he couldn't make out who it was due to the sun's glare behind her.

"Carlos Grey Hawk, the Singer?" said Millie Nez.

"It is I, Grandmother, you remembered?"

"How could I forget, you did me a great service. Why are you here?"

"Your nephew, Robert Begay, hired your grandson and another man to kidnap me and hold me until I gave them certain information which I am not willing to do. I am sure the kidnappers are talking to Robert Begay right now. I must escape. Will you help me?"

"What keeps you from leaving?"

"I am chained to this gatepost with handcuffs. Do you have bolt cutters or, perhaps, a hack saw?"

"Let me think. It has been a long time since I was here. Yes, I think there is a hacksaw … somewhere" said Milllie, looking around the interior now that her eyes had at least partly adjusted to the dimness."

"We must hurry, your grandson and his friend might be back anytime."

"Of course. Let me think." She made her way slowly to a makeshift work bench and pulled out a drawer. "Yes!" she said triumphantly as she pulled a dusty hacksaw out and showed it to him. She walked back over to Carlos and handed him the saw. "I do not know how sharp the blade is. While you cut, I will look for another blade."

Carlos pulled the chain taut and began sawing on one of the links. The steel was hard and he wasn't doing much more than scratching the surface.

"I am afraid this blade has been used many times," he said loud enough for Millie to hear.

"I am looking for a better one."

She vigorously rummaged in the drawer, moving objects around so she could dig deeper. At last she pulled out two loose hacksaw blades. "Here!" she said, "I think these are better."

She handed one to Carlos who awkwardly switched blades. The new blade immediately bit into the steel of the chain. "Yes," he said, "this is much better." As she stood there watching him work, he said, "Perhaps you can keep watch in case they return?"

She nodded and made her was to the open door. "Nothing yet," she said.

Carlos barely heard her as he channeled his energy into setting himself free. The blade was cutting the tempered steel more slowly now but was over halfway through the link. Finally, he gave up and switched to the other blade and within just a couple of minutes cut through the link. He rose immediately and stretched out the kinks from sitting in one place so long.

"Grandmother, I must leave immediately. I offer you my humble thanks and vow to return when this matter is settled. Your generosity will not be forgotten."

"Perhaps another Blessingway ceremony can be arranged?"

"Yes. If I survive, yes."

"Stop at the house and at least take one of the gallon jugs of water and some of the jerky," she said as Carlos headed for the barn door.

Carlos trotted to the house and found the water on the kitchen counter and the jerky in the refrigerator. He also found a small day pack hanging from a hook near the back door and took that too.

When he emerged from the house, Millie was standing outside the barn door watching. He raised the pack and she nodded. He set off at a trot north, almost parallel to Highway 163 but out of sight of the road. He kept to the washes as much as he could and stayed low among the brush when he couldn't.

Milllie went back into the house and returned to her wine and her TV show. She was very angry and was looking forward to telling off her grandson.

Two hours later, Henry and Walter wandered back to Millie's place with some water and blankets for Carlos. Neither approached the house but went right to the barn. Moments later Henry came running out of the barn toward the house. "He's loose!" he yelled at the top of his lungs, "Where is he?"

He ran up on the porch and burst into Millie's house. "Where is he?" Henry demanded, "How did he get loose?"

Millie was primed. "You don't burst into my house without being invited and I most certainly did not invite you but since you're here I have a few things to say to you. You may think I'm an outcast since I live alone but I'm nothing compared to what you have done. Kidnapped and injured a Singer? What on earth have you become? Wait until the clan finds out. You will be ostracized if I have anything to say about it and I am pretty sure they will listen to me instead of you. You have disgraced the whole clan and I am ashamed to be associated with you. Now go and *never* come back!"

Henry looked like his grandmother had just whipped him. He turned on his heel and left, closing the door sedately behind him.

When he got back to his pickup, Walter was on the phone to Robert Begay.

"What do you mean he escaped?" Robert Begay yelled into his phone. He was standing in the entry of the trading post and half a dozen people paused in response to his outburst. He turned his back and headed for the door marked "Private." "How on *earth* could he escape from a handcuff without a key?"

"He cut the chain. Henry just found out his grandmother gave the old man the hacksaw and helped him get away. It wasn't our fault, Mr. Begay."

"Like hell it wasn't your fault!" roared Begay once he had disappeared into his inner sanctum. "*You* left him there and didn't even check to see if there was any tool he could use to get free. This is on both of you and if you don't find him, you're going to pay – in blood!"

*****

Meredith was on the phone to Abe in an instant. "Abe? I think your grandfather has escaped! He got away from those two thugs somehow. I don't know any details, but Mr. Begay was just out here in the entry yelling 'what do you mean he escaped.' Then he went back into his office and I couldn't hear anymore. I hope that's what this means and I don't lead you on a wild goose chase."

"I don't know what else it could be," said Abe matter-of-factly. "I just wish we knew from where he escaped so we could find him and help. Thank you for calling, that it was you who called means a lot to me."

"I know it does," Meredith said softly, "I'm glad I was the one who heard it and was able to call you. I'll let you go; I know you have things to do. Call me if you can?"

"Count on it and … thank you."

As Abe disconnected the call, he whooped, "He got free! Carlos escaped!"

Bob tried to pin him down for details but Abe didn't have them to give. "I wonder if that old lady helped him escape from her barn. Let's go back and find out even if she yells at us.

"Carlos is an experienced desert rat; if anyone can survive out there, he can. What we need to do is intercept him and get him to safety."

"And keep those goons off his trail. Robert Begay has to be some kind of irate!"

Bob was driving and turned them around and headed back to Kayenta. Though they were closer to Mexican Hat and had to notify Adrian and the others, they needed a starting place.

# CHAPTER 16

Bob was on the phone to Detective Whittaker right after he heard the good news. "He has a lot of Indian country to cover before we can get involved," said Gene Whittaker.

"My guess is he'll head for Mexican Hat or directly up to Cedar Mesa where he'll feel safe. Those two mutts aren't going get off their lazy asses and go looking for him; they'll just 'road hunt' like they did last time. Which brings us right back to where we were, as I see it" Bob said.

"Except when we find the two thugs, they'll stay in jail no matter what kind of injury the one has," said Detective Whittaker. "And I think we have enough to go after Robert Begay for conspiracy considering the evidence we have, and may get, if one or both of his goons wants to roll. That would wrap everyone up that's involved *but* it doesn't preclude Begay trying again when he's out on bail or, more likely, on his own recognizance."

"Like I said," said Bob, "we're right back where we started."

"I disagree, especially if Carlos can find a home in Shiprock or temporarily with you in Santa Fe. If he's a normal grandpa, he's going to want to spend time with Abe and if Abe is in Tucson ... well, who knows what Carlos might do."

"My money is on him settling in Shiprock; that's where most of his family is and it's a fair distance from Bluff or Mexican Hat.

Unfortunately it's also a fair distance from Tucson, where Abe will stay as long as school gives him what he wants, and Meredith is around."

"What about you, Bob? What's your angle in all this?"

"Good question. I kind of fell into this mess after damn near hitting Abe in a rain storm while I was on my way to Bluff. I guess you could say I've kind of become a Dutch Uncle. I've grown attached to Abe and don't want to lose that connection with him and I'm pretty sure he feels the same way. He doesn't really have a helluva lot of family besides Carlos and a nice aunt in Shiprock who is married to an asshole. Abe was lucky he got out of there when he did. He's on the cusp of some life-changing experiences and I see myself as just being around to help him when he needs it, give advice and enjoy his company."

"Sounds like a Dutch Uncle to me," chuckled Gene. "I wonder if this is something you could have done if you were still working."

"Highly unlikely, but now that I'm retired, I'm allowed to get personally involved and I like it."

"Not me! Connie and I have enough family drama with the kids and grandkids!"

After hanging up with Detective Whittaker, Bob looked over at Abe. "You look like you perked up a bit. Are you ready to tangle with Millie Nez again?"

"I'm ready to kiss her feet if she's the one!"

"I doubt that would be necessary. I thought I'd walk up to her house with you and maybe a *Bilagaana* telling her through you in Navajo would make it official that she done good for her own people."

Abe chuckled. "You're learning the language!"

"I'm too old and don't hear well enough to learn much, but I thought it appropriate in this case. Hopefully she'll thaw enough to tell us it was she, and what kind of shape he was in when he left and in what direction."

"We both know he'll head for the Mesa and probably to his old hideout. I just hope I can find it again," Abe said. "I'm so relieved he escaped; it just goes to show you can't let your guard down with the old guys." He laughed and punched Bob playfully in the arm.

Bob nodded with a wry grin. "At least not *that* old guy."

When they got to Millie Nez's home, they waited to see if she would notice their arrival. After several minutes, Abe got antsy and wanted to hurry up the process. They got out and approached the porch waiting a while longer before going up on the porch and knocking.

"If that is you Henry, go away! You are no longer welcome here!"

Bob and Abe looked at each other and grinned. "It's me, Grandmother, Abe Red Wolf, from yesterday. May we come in to talk for a minute?"

"I suppose you won't leave me alone until you do, so come in," growled Millie Nez. As they entered the front door, Millie chose not to get up to greet them but scowled from her rocking chair.

"This is Bob Connelly," said Abe. "He is a retired *Bilagaana* policeman." Abe almost said "from Santa Fe" but at the last minute decided that was too much information. "He wants to thank you for helping my grandfather yesterday, and wonders if you could answer a few questions. We are trying to locate my grandfather to take him to safety from those men who kidnapped him."

"Ask your questions," said Millie Nez gruffly.

"Thank you for saving his life," said Bob, waiting for Abe to translate into Navajo.

Millie only nodded impatiently.

"Was he injured?"

"Only a small cut over his eyebrow," said Millie. "He was stiff from being in one position handcuffed but he looked okay to me once he got up."

"Did he have anything with him when he left?"

"Only a gallon jug of water, a bag of jerky and a small backpack."

"Did he say where he was going or how he was going to get there?"

"No."

"Abe's grandfather is a friend of mine as well," said Bob. "We want to find him and make sure he is well, and protect him if necessary."

Bob walked over to the old woman and knelt down in front of her. He took her hand, looked her in the eye and said, "Ahéhee' [thank you]."

It flustered the old lady and all she could do was smile. "Now when you find him," she admonished, "don't forget to remind him about a Blessingway ceremony."

"We won't forget, Grandmother," said Abe.

They got back in the pickup and headed back toward Mexican Hat. "I checked," said Abe, "it's forty-two miles from Kayenta to Mexican Hat, maybe a little shorter if he goes overland but he still has to cross the river and Mexican Hat is the most logical place."

"If Begay is still in the hunt, he'll be camped there too. In July the water depth fluctuates making crossing somewhere not at a bridge iffy but knowing Carlos, probably doable. Sitting waiting for him at the Mexican Hat bridge doesn't seem to be a good use of our limited resources. How many ways are there up to the Mesa without using the Moki Dugway? Carlos probably knows all of them. Seems to me he'd probably show up at Harley Uskilith's at some point and that's probably where we ought to start thinking about looking for or waiting for him. I hope Begay hasn't found out about Harley yet.

"I would prefer to intercept him much much sooner, out in the desert away from the Mesa, for his sake, but I suspect he's too wily to ever be spotted. What do you think, Abe?"

"After having spent time with him, I know Carlos to be a consummate woodsman and desert dweller, and unless he's stranded on a rocky ledge high above a canyon, he can evade anyone. I too would love to pick him up sooner rather than later, but he's going to be very cautious around anyone and will probably fade back into the background before making his presence known even if he identifies someone."

"That's a pretty good assessment. Something else that crossed my mind," said Bob, "is who can we still trust? Begay will up the ante now and his money might tempt someone who so far has been loyal to Carlos."

"You mean like Adrian or Adam or even Harley?" Abe asked, shocked. "I can't imagine any of them giving Carlos up for money."

"But what if he dug up some dirt on one of them and held it over his head? That's a classic *Bilagaana* tactic and Robert Begay is obviously playing by white man's rules," Bob said.

"What do you suggest?"

"Not much we can do other than keep our plans and ideas close to our chests. I don't like distrusting people either but for Carlos's sake, we ought not forget human nature."

"I just find it amazing that a guy like Robert Begay would go to all this trouble when he doesn't even know what the payoff is for sure," said Abe. "He must have some idea; otherwise, he's chasing a wild goose and he's too savvy for that."

As they neared Mexican Hat, Bob asked, "What are we going to tell Adrian and the others?"

"I say let them draw their own conclusions and they'll probably be pretty similar to ours. Tell 'em Carlos escaped with the help of the woman and is at large and we don't have any more of an idea where he is than anyone else. As far as waiting for him at somewhere like Harley's, if Carlos sees a strange vehicle or a face he doesn't recognize, like I said, he'll probably just fade away and we'll never even know he was there. Our ace in the hole is knowing where his shelter is; hopefully, I can find it again."

They arrived at the Exxon station and Adrian Tso was still there working on an ancient pickup. They told him what they had learned and that Carlos had escaped.

"Boy, that makes my day," said Adrian with a big grin. "I hated the idea of those two jerks holding him. Now we just have to wait for him to make contact. Waiting for him somewhere is a waste of time."

"Can you think of anything at all that we can do besides wait?"

"Nope," said Adrian, "maybe bring his pickup over to my place so he has wheels when he surfaces. I don't think Carlos wants to stay on the Mesa anymore, and I think young Abe has much to do with that."

With promises to stay in touch, Bob and Abe got back in Bob's pickup and headed for Blanding to recover Carlos's pickup. "Adrian seemed steady as a rock," didn't he?" asked Abe.

"Yes, and that's because he is, until he might be faced with a crisis he knows nothing about right now," said Bob, feeling very cynical.

"I *hate* the very idea," muttered Abe.

They retrieved Carlos's pickup and Abe drove it back to Mexican Hat where they parked it at Adrian's house. The mechanic's two little girls stared out the window at them with wide, curious eyes. Bob was for calling it a day and they returned to the La Posada Pintada, not sure they were going to be allowed to stay there anymore. It was the same clerk and he didn't bat an eye as he helped them fill out their registration forms.

"I should thank you for how you handled things the other night," he said. "You could have been a lot rougher on the room and it wasn't your fault they kicked in the door. How about I put you in rooms closer to the office in case there's trouble again?" Both nodded their acquiescence then left to transfer their gear to their rooms. They then headed to Twin Rocks Trading Post for something to eat.

Abe was especially eager to get to the restaurant ostensibly to see Meredith and thank her in person for her very welcome phone call about Carlos. When he walked in she was busy with a customer so he just watched her, marveling at what an attractive young woman she was. When she saw Abe, Meredith's face lit up like a morning sun. She finished with the customer, then came around the counter and embraced him and pecked him on the lips.

"I'm *so* glad to see you and know you're okay!" she exclaimed. "Did you find Carlos?"

Abe's smile faded. "No, as far as we know, he's still out in the desert by himself."

"And you can't help him if you can't find him?"

Abe nodded glumly.

Meredith looked around her to make sure no one was close enough to hear what she said next, "Robert Begay was walking through the entry just a little while ago, and he was on his phone again, angry, and telling someone to round up about ten riders tomorrow and begin a track of the 'old man' from 'Millie's' place. He started to say something else but all I heard was guns before he spotted me and ducked into the back room."

Abe glanced at Bob to make sure he heard this, then turned back to Meredith. "That's good to know, but I'm afraid our coming in here puts you in jeopardy."

Bob stepped up to the young people and said, "He's right. This guy will stop at nothing to get what he wants and if that means a few casualties along the way, so be it."

"Surely he wouldn't bother me? I'm just a clerk!"

"But you're a clerk connected to me," said Abe. "If he thought you were passing information on to us, the least he would do is fire you. Who knows? I wouldn't put it past him to exact a little retribution too. I think you need to be very careful and don't let him catch you on the phone, especially after you've heard something. You're in a position to learn and pass on some timely information but the timeliness can wait if it means your welfare, okay? Maybe you can call us on your break from somewhere private."

Meredith grimaced but nodded in agreement. "The last thing I want to do is become a problem for you."

"And the last thing we want is to deprive ourselves of your information, but like Abe says, your welfare comes first," Bob added. "I also agree with Abe that this probably should be our last meal here at the trading post. It's mighty ironic that the man who we most want to bring down is the manager."

Meredith showed her disappointment, but put a good face on it and escorted them to a table. "When will I see you again?" she asked somewhat plaintively.

"Maybe we can drive over to Montezuma Creek on one of your days off?" Bob suggested.

"Yeah!" said Abe enthusiastically. "Besides, I'll call you tonight."

"You'd better," she said, shaking finger at him. "I know! Why don't you come for lunch the day after tomorrow? I'll clear it with Aunt Rita whom I'm sure won't have a problem with the idea."

"The only thing that would prevent that is if we get a line on Carlos," said Abe.

"Have dinner while I call Aunt Rita."

After Meredith returned to the register, Bob brought up a topic he had been toying with for a while. "I wonder if it's legal to fly drones over BLM and Navajo Nation lands? That may be an efficient way to cover more ground than those horsemen if it's legal."

"I know on Nation property it's okay if you're not flying over one of the tribal parks or harassing wildlife or something like that but I don't know about BLM land."

"Well," said Bob, "we have phones, let's find out!"

Bob spoke first after perusing his phone, "It sounds like the rules are similar to Navajo rules, no flying over parks, wildlife or anywhere it disturbs living creatures. That shouldn't be too hard to do in country that's considered part of the Mojave Desert."

Abe had already moved on to drones. "It says here there's a place in Blanding where you can rent or buy one."

"Really? I never would have guessed Blanding had a drone shop."

"It's part of a trading post, not a drone-dedicated business."

"Let's go see 'em tomorrow," said Bob with enthusiasm.

When they paid the bill, Meredith said, "Aunt Rita said lunch at noon the day after tomorrow and don't be late!"

"I've never been late for a meal in my life!" said Abe, laughing as he hugged his girlfriend.

When they walked into the Cedar Breaks Trading Post in Blanding the next morning, there was no doubt they had entered an eclectic collection of merchandise ranging from Native crafts to … drones! They were met at the counter by a younger man wearing an Indian patterned long-sleeved shirt and jeans. He was in his early twenties and appeared eager to please.

"How can I help you gentlemen?" he asked.

Bob spoke up, "We're interested in renting a drone for a few days."

"Well, you came to the right place," said the man, waving to a corner of the showroom where three drones were hanging from the ceiling. "Are you familiar with flying one? Have you flown one before?"

"Well, n n n no," stuttered Bob, "I thought they were supposed to be easy to fly."

"Oh, they are. But they're even easier for someone who has used a joystick in, say, video games before," the man explained.

"I have," Abe offered. He looked at Bob and explained, "I had a friend at school who had a flight simulator game we used to play all the time."

"Perfect," said the salesman, "the controls on a drone are almost identical to most flight simulators except there are more software safeguards such as Auto Return, Follow Me, Hover and Collision Avoidance." From that point forward the salesman was talking to Abe, not to Bob, and Bob didn't much like it. He didn't say anything, he just wanted them to get their hands on one and get gone so they could put it to work.

"What kind of features are you looking for?"

Abe and Bob looked at each other and shrugged. "What's available?" asked Bob.

"How long of a flight time?" asked the sales clerk.

"As long as possible and about a mile range. Does that kind of range require line-of-sight control?" asked Bob, arching his eyebrows at Abe who nodded.

"You can get it both ways but it's much cheaper with LOS control."

"We will need high altitude and excellent zoom capability," said Abe.

The salesman was punching data into a laptop as fast as they could feed it to him.

"What else *should* we have?" asked Bob.

"Auto Return is almost an automatic anymore," mused the clerk. "You might consider Follow Me, Hover and Collision Avoidance. Generally speaking, for the type of aircraft you describe, it will already have that and possibly more."

"Is there such a critter as we've described?" asked Abe.

"There is, and we have them on the shelf; those are fairly common requirements. Now, the UAV comes with two batteries and an AC charger. Do you have a small inverter or DC charger capable of recharging your batteries in the field?"

Bob shook his head. "Doesn't one come with the kit?"

"Some do, some don't but, quite frankly, the factory chargers are slow and can only do one battery at a time. If you're looking for extended flight time, you'll need more batteries and a faster charger that can charge multiple batteries at once."

"This is getting complicated and we only want to rent one, not buy the company!" Bob exclaimed.

The sales clerk nodded sympathetically. "That's why when we rent a kit; we make sure everything you need is there."

"At what kind of cost?" asked Bob.

The clerk pecked away on his keyboard for several minutes. Finally, he said, "I can rent you a UAV as you described, with four batteries, extra props, a multi-battery charger and even a camera feature that locks on a selected target for $350 for a week."

"What about damage insurance?"

"Coverage up to the value of the kit is automatically included."

Bob looked at Abe and shook his head. "Pretty steep."

Abe nodded, then said, "But it's still the most efficient game in town."

Bob sighed. "You're right." He asked the clerk, "How soon would you have a kit available?"

"Whenever you call for one; as I said, we have a few in stock."

"What about training?"

"We include one of our own training videos and strongly recommend you test fly the UAV in a large uncluttered space until you have the hang of it. Like I said, they're not hard to fly but it sounds like you have specific needs for it and that might take a little longer to get the hang of all the options. I'm sure your son will pick it up much faster, the younger ones usually do if they have video game experience and a flight simulator is the best."

"Okay," said Bob with another sigh as he pulled out his wallet. "Better bring one out, I guess we'll take it."

# CHAPTER 17

Bob and Abe were up early the next morning, as the sun came up, eager to try out their new toy and to get an edge on the riders who were probably gathering to begin their track. Bob stopped in open country near the unoccupied airport and they broke out the drone. They had watched the video three times the previous evening after dinner and felt reasonably confident they wouldn't crash and burn.

While Abe assembled, Bob skimmed the owner's manual which didn't say anything new. They were surprised that this one came with a console bearing a small video screen that they both could watch no matter who was flying. Abe went first and slowly took off and brought the craft up to a low hover. He executed some maneuvers to test the vehicle's flight controls then ascended a few hundred feet. The console told them how far the drone was from them and how much life was left in the Lithium-Ion battery. They were relieved; both had worried that the craft would just fly away and not respond to commands to return because it was out of range. Abe activated the camera and found its image remarkably stable, even at a higher altitude.

Next, Bob gave it a try and was predictably less accomplished than his younger charge. He emulated Abe's maneuvers but didn't fly it as far away as Abe had, deciding Abe was clearly more competent than he. He was concentrating more on the camera's capability and hoping they could use the subject lock on feature if they spotted Carlos.

"One thing we haven't thought about is what to do if we spot him. If he sees the damn drone he'll try to evade it, unless we can get a message to him that it's us. His phone is bound to be dead by now. The book says this model doesn't have much payload capacity – a few grams – but if we could attach a note to it to warn him of the trackers, and set it down where he could see it, we might have a chance. We would also need to include a paper and pencil in case he wanted to respond."

"A little zip lock bag with a piece of paper and a small pencil would do the trick, don't you think?" asked Abe.

"I guess we'll have to test fly the unit with the baggie tied on and hope it doesn't weigh too much or create too much drag."

"Carlos has about a thirty-six-hour head start and, as fast as he travels, might well be nearing the San Juan River by now," said Abe. "We should concentrate on shallow areas of the river where he could conceivably cross. I guess Muley Point is as good a vantage place to start looking unless you have a better idea.

"If it wasn't so obvious, Carlos would probably think of the shallows near Mexican Hat where some of the rafters take out. Maybe he'd try in the middle of the night. Then again, that would place him not far from the bridge at Mexican Hat and people."

Bob added, "The sales clerk said something about an infrared capability on the camera so maybe we shouldn't just plan on watching during the day?"

"Wouldn't it be great if we spotted him a little ways upstream from Mexican Hat? We could pick him up and be away from the trackers before they even knew what happened. That reminds me, we'd better have a good supply of water and something to eat when we find him."

"Okay," said Bob, "let's head for Muley Point and put this bird to work."

The river below Muley Point wasn't necessarily the best place to ford the San Juan River but from its vantage point, to see a lot of the river was excellent. They found a wide open rocky surface near Muley Point East and launched the drone. Abe guided it over the precipice and flew away from the cliff for a distance to ensure line-of-sight before descending closer to the river. They agreed that keeping the drone fairly high would minimize the chance of anyone hearing it and the camera resolution was so good, they ascended another two hundred feet. Abe started over the river and traced its course almost to maximum range of the bird before turning and making a swath on the other side of the San Juan. He learned quickly to slow down his flying so the camera could get good footage but they were still covering far more ground than they ever could on foot or horseback.

Twenty-five minutes went by in no time and Abe had to call the drone in to change batteries. It only took a couple of minutes to switch and they were airborne again picking up where they left off. It became an almost boring routine after a while, seeing nothing but desert brown and red, but they persevered, Carlos was worth the effort.

Once, Bob saw movement on the monitor. Abe hovered the drone and zoomed in with the camera. It was a Desert Bighorn ewe with her twin lambs working their way up from the river.

"It could just as easily been Carlos and he's just as sneaky," said Abe with a chuckle. After that, Abe flew even slower, not wanting to miss something that moved. Carlos would be expert at camouflage and if he stood still or, worse yet ducked under some brush or a tree, he would be invisible unless he moved.

It took them to mid-afternoon to decide that scanning the terrain during the day wasn't the best use of their time so they decided to go into Mexican Hat and see if anyone had heard anything.

They first stopped at the San Juan Inn and spoke with Adam Benally and the friendly Navajo desk clerk. Neither had heard or seen anything of Carlos, but they hadn't talked to Adrian Tso for a couple of days so they didn't know what he might know. Their trip to the Exxon station to see Adrian proved just as fruitless. They didn't tell any of the men about the drone and their plans, much less the existence of Begay's trackers.

At a loss as to what to do, they debated going into Bluff and checking out of their rooms so they could move down to the San Juan Inn which was closer to the action. They decided against it, people would wonder what they were doing. They wouldn't have much of an explanation.

Abe suggested they drive to Blanding and stock up on supplies for their overnight watch for Carlos. He thought they ought to buy Carlos some clothes since he would probably have just crossed the river. Bob agreed; they didn't want to be seen doing this in Mexican Hat or even Bluff. Blanding was big enough where they could remain more or less anonymous.

Mission accomplished, Bob suggested they stop at their motel and try to catch a nap considering they were about to pull an all-nighter. Neither slept well but it was enough to put them in the right frame of mind to endure what was coming. Bob also told Abe to remove everything from his room. If they rescued Carlos tonight, they certainly wouldn't be coming back here! He had paid through that night so if they didn't use the room no one would be upset.

On the way back to Mexican Hat, Bob pulled onto a dirt road that led to the Mexican Hat rock formation. They found that they could drive around the formation while less than a hundred yards from the river bank. The whole distance from the rocks to the town of Mexican Hat was flatter than anywhere else with mild banks down to the river – perfect for crossing. Carlos would know this, and that other crossing areas were miles away. Bob said that if he was Carlos, he'd wait until late at night while watching for Begay's men and slip across the river in an area they weren't watching. After all, they couldn't have people watching the whole distance from the Mexican Hat formation to the bridge at the San Juan Inn, could they?

They at last parked across Highway 163 on a rise overlooking the plain from Mexican Hat rock nearly to Mexican Hat town. The drone easily had the range to cover the area from their vantage point. They waited until dark then launched the drone. The range on the camera on infra-red was excellent and though images were small when zoomed out, anything warm that came within range would show up clearly.

For the first couple of hours, Abe flew over the opposite side of the river at almost maximum range hoping to spot Carlos before he crossed. He decided to continue to patrol that side of the river since they would need time to react to Carlos's presence when and if they spotted him. Reacting to him and making contact were two different things and they finally decided that if they could cross the highway and be close to the river while Carlos was still crossing, they would have the best chance to make contact before he tried to run. The idea of dangling a note no longer seemed feasible.

Occasionally Abe would make a run over the near side of the river looking for watchers but, surprisingly, they found no bodies or even any warm cars from the rocks to the outskirts of Mexican Hat town. If Begay failed to send watchers it would be a major error and one Bob and Abe hoped they could capitalize on.

At just after midnight, a small herd of sheep made their way out of the rocky terrain on the opposite side of the river and cautiously approached to drink. They stood out in great detail with the infra-red against the cooling rocks and Abe was at last convinced the camera would do what he had hoped it would do. Thus far, he had not recorded any footage on the micro SD card so he triggered the camera to test it on the sheep. He played it back and it functioned perfectly; he was high enough where even they didn't detect the drone.

Every half hour or so Abe had to bring the device in to change the battery. He was flying cautiously, not risking losing control of the bird. Abe was glad to have two extra, charged batteries at all times.

Just after one such battery replacement, Bob, acting as spotter, saw movement. "Over to the left," he said, "beyond that pointed boulder about two hundred yards above the river bank."

Abe banked the drone in that direction while zooming in the camera. It was clearly a person and he or she was being extremely cautious moving through the brush above the water line. The person would stop every two or three steps and look all around before taking a few more steps. The person didn't apparently hear the drone but Abe ascended another three hundred feet to be sure. When the person reached the river bank, Bob started his pickup but left it in park. When the person was a quarter of the way across the river, Bob shifted into gear and eased down from their vantage point to the highway. He drove to the access road to Mexican Hat rock and turned in. The person, now halfway across the river froze, then squatted down in the water.

Most of the infra-red image disappeared on the monitor but they could still make out the head, the arms and part of the torso. As Bob neared the person's location, more of the image faded as the person sank lower into the water until only the head was showing. When he stopped the pickup as close to the river bank and the head as he could, Bob could not see the person's head in the water.

While Abe monitored the drone, Bob got out of the pickup and walked down to the water's edge. He whispered loudly, "Carlos? It's Bob. Come on out of the water before you freeze."

"Carlos?" Bob said a little louder, hoping the Singer could hear his muted voice over the sound of the water. "Abe's in the pickup, we're here to get you out of here."

Suddenly Carlos was right beside him, dripping water and grinning from ear to ear. "How did you know I was here?" he asked.

"Well," Bob retorted, "it wasn't because you were making a racket. It doesn't look like any of Begay's men are around but let's get out of here anyway. We can be well on our way to Santa Fe by daybreak."

"Did you bring any dry clothes?" asked Carlos hopefully. "You made me duck down in the water and I'm cold."

"As a matter of fact, I think we do ... and something to eat and drink."

"The clothes first," he said as he started walking toward Bob's pickup. "Then water, lots of water. I ran out about noon yesterday and water has been on my mind since."

Abe, meanwhile, had packed up the drone. He got out to greet Carlos and stood watch while his grandfather changed clothes. Once done with that, Carlos said, "We should get going. Robert Begay has to have men watching the river."

"That's what we thought too but we haven't seen any sign of anyone. Maybe they're watching another section."

They all got in the front seat but before Bob started the truck and headed for the highway, he handed Carlos his key ring. "There's a handcuff key on there unless you've become attached to your bracelet. Carlos didn't waste any time shucking the single handcuff and nodded appreciatively when he handed the keys back to Bob.

When he started to turn the pickup to the right, back toward Bluff, Carlos stopped him. "No," he said, "we cannot leave yet. Turn left, toward Kayenta."

Bob did as Carlos directed but looked questioningly at the older man. "Aren't we tempting fate a little, here?" he asked, his voice laced with trepidation.

"Yes, we probably are, but there's something we must investigate before we can leave. We must get through Mexican Hat before dawn and then I'll explain. I'm going to lean over and put my head in Abe's lap, so no one will see me when we go through town." Less than ten minutes later, they were across the bridge over the San Juan River passing the Hat Rock Inn.

"Before you start, Carlos," said Abe, "you should know that Begay has ten men on horseback tracking you from Millie Nez's place. We figured they were about thirty-six hours behind you when they started but they had horses. We've been pretty darn worried even though I know from personal experience how sneaky you can be in the wild."

"If that was a compliment, I accept. I did not encounter men on horseback but I believe they are searching for more than just me and that it is the same reason Robert Begay has been pursuing me. I just do not know why ... for sure.

"You see, once I escaped from Millie Nez's barn, I traveled northwest assuming Begay's men would follow but would concentrate in a north or northeast direction unless they found my tracks. I figured to take a roundabout way back into Bears Ears and Cedar Mesa. I believe Abe would have known where to find me." Abe nodded.

"It was difficult finding concealment in the desert until I reached the San Juan River drainage and then deep canyons were plentiful. I skirted most of them looking for an easier place to ford the river but the river canyon was too steep and the water too deep and turbulent to think I could safely get to the other side. Before I turned around and headed for a sure crossing at Mexican Hat, I discovered a wrecked airplane in one of the tributary canyons.

"The wings had been torn off as the aircraft descended into the narrow, deep canyon but nothing caught fire which I thought unusual. The fuselage appeared beat up but intact and upright. It was at least an hour hike down into the canyon to the plane, but I did not think I could afford the time since I was sure Robert Begay would mount a search for me. I hated to leave without checking for survivors and there could be, since the wreck looked fresh. The plane was still shiny and not sun oxidized or dusty like things get around here.

"We must go back and check for survivors. I could not quit thinking about someone being injured in there and slowly dying because no one found him."

Bob asked, "Carlos, did you see any identifying numbers on the plane?"

"I did not look specifically for any numbers but don't recall seeing any. Are there not supposed to be numbers on the tail?"

"Yeah," said Bob, "almost all planes have to have a tail number." He looked at Abe who raised his eyebrows. "Are you thinking what I'm thinking?"

Abe nodded. "Carlos, that airplane might be the reason Robert Begay is looking for you. It could be an overdue shipment of drugs bound for the American market."

"That may be, but I would still feel better if we checked for survivors. There is a road that comes fairly close to the canyon," he offered.

"Define 'close,'" said Abe wryly.

"I'd much rather get within about two miles of the canyon and fly the drone over it," said Bob.

"Drone?" asked Carlos.

"It's what we used to find you," Abe explained. "It's a small airplane that is remotely controlled – by me – and has a very good video camera so we can look at things on the ground. It even has infra-red which helps spot things – like you – in the dark."

"Will people hear it above them?"

"It is very quiet and we fly high enough where no one can hear us. Did you hear us? We watched you arrive at the brush along the river, go through it and wade into the water. We even saw you duck down when Bob called to you."

"You did? I heard nothing until Bob called to me and for a minute I thought I was caught. I am glad it was you and not you-know-who."

"We can fly the drone over your canyon and check for anyone around and get some GPS coordinates," Abe suggested.

"If the coast is clear, I still would like to hike in and look for ourselves," said Carlos. Bob and Abe weren't as enthused about being exposed in the canyon for hours with a band of ten armed and hostile horsemen nearby.

"Okay, Carlos, Abe and I are outnumbered. We'll go check on that plane, but if we see riders within, say, a mile, we're out of there, okay?" Carlos nodded in agreement, and Bob turned the pickup back toward Kayenta. They traveled no more than four or five miles before Carlos directed Bob to turn right onto a dirt road. Luckily it was mostly dry because the deep ruts bespoke a trail of deep mud, partially buried boulders and many water cuts across the roadway.

They bounced and jostled over the track for what seemed like miles before Carlos indicated another right turn onto a trail that clearly was much less traveled since the ruts were not as deep but the cuts were just as plentiful. Soon they began encountering deeper washes that cut into the soil and required them to skirt the worst of

225

them as they approached the watershed. Now it was a matter of circling around all the washes until Carlos called a halt.

"We are less than a mile from the airplane. Do you want to launch your drone and take a look around?" he asked.

"Perfect," said Abe as he jumped out of the pickup and started unpacking the drone. When he launched it, he checked all the flight controls then set it on a north by northwest heading in search of the right canyon. Five minutes later he ascended and overflew *the* canyon but declared it and the surrounding area devoid of people. Abe recovered the drone and they drove closer to the canyon. They stopped, got out and looked over the canyon and saw the plane at the bottom. The walls of the canyon were rugged in the extreme - in other words rougher than hell. They had decided that Bob and Carlos would descend into the canyon while Abe kept watch overhead with the drone. He would drop into the canyon and waggle his wings if he saw anyone coming.

# CHAPTER 18

Bob and Carlos loaded day packs with water and a few snacks then found a lightly used game trail that dropped into the canyon. There was plenty of "four-point descending" involved but after about forty-five minutes they arrived at the bottom and made their way to the badly beaten-up aircraft.

Bob had thoughtfully brought along a tire iron in case they had to pry their way in. He yelled and pounded on the outside of the craft but got no response. He tried the passenger door that looked like the one least damaged and, remarkably, it opened. Bob snapped a couple of photos with his phone then quickly closed it again after catching a glimpse and a whiff of the bloody, bloated bodies in the two flight seats.

He told Carlos what he had seen and smelled and that was good enough for the Singer. Navajos typically shied away from dead bodies. Bob worked his way around the aircraft to the left-side cargo door. He had to do some prying but the tire iron proved its worth and soon the door was standing open. Two-kilo plastic-wrapped packages were stacked to the bottom of the windows in the fuselage. Bob could see no markings on the packages and didn't bother to open one for fear that it might be fentanyl powder. He was more than convinced that the load was illicit drugs and wanted nothing more to do with it.

"I said a prayer to help send the men to underworld and now we can go. We do not need their *chindi* [spirit] to return from the underworld to haunt us," said Carlos.

They both drank off a small bottle of water then headed back the way they had come. An hour later they emerged dusty and sweaty on the rim of the canyon.

"Well?" asked Abe as he called for the drone to return.

"Both men are dead," said Bob. "Exact cause of death unknown, but it was bloody and they had a rough ride. What say we get out of here?"

Both companions agreed and within moments they were back on the track going back the way they had come. "Were you able to get GPS coordinates for when I call this in to DEA (Drug Enforcement Administration)? I've been thinking about this situation and I'm wondering if we can use the drugs to set a trap for Begay and his men. We could somehow leak the location and he would jump on it with both feet if it wasn't too obvious. Then it would be up to DEA to arrest them when they came to recover the dope."

"How could we leak it to him without it looking suspicious?" asked Abe.

"Well, it couldn't be by providing him with the coordinates; Carlos would never have the equipment to do that. A map comes to mind but I don't think the Navajos are much on maps, are they Carlos?"

"Not maps on paper," Carlos replied. "Most of our map imaging is verbal and associated with known landmarks."

"Well, we're sure as hell not going to let you get captured again just so you can tell them where the plane is. They'd kill you afterward."

"That is probably true. I suppose, with Abe helping, me we could create a representation of the location of the airplane on paper for you, white man."

"That sounds much more plausible," said Bob, "but we can't wait long to do this, DEA is impatient and wants a payoff in the way of a quick operation. I know a guy with DEA to call and he'll go along with our idea as long as the chance of an arrest is high. I'll call him later today. Meanwhile, how about we get out of the hot zone and stay in Blanding tonight ... and get something to eat?"

It was well past full daylight when they passed through Bluff. They had debated going back for Carlos's pickup at Adrian's but decided that would tell Begay's men that Carlos had eluded them. Meredith wasn't yet on duty so there was no reason to stop in Bluff so they continued on to Blanding. He pulled in to the Patio Diner and told his companions, "Go ahead in while I make the call to DEA. Maybe my buddy there will have a good idea how to leak the location of the plane to Begay."

"Jim Campbell," said a terse voice over the phone.

"This doesn't sound like the DEA Special Agent *I* know," chided Bob with a grin on his face.

"Who is this?"

"Now you sound right, cynical! This is Bob Connelly come back to haunt you, you old bastard."

"Bob! I should have known. How's retired life?"

"It's not at all like I expected. I knocked around the house for a little while then decided to treat myself to a Utah/Arizona red rock trip. I got tangled up with a Navajo kid who I almost hit in a rain storm and now I have an offer for you I doubt you can refuse."

"Yeah? Try me."

"I know where there is what is left of a large Cessna aircraft – twin engine – chock full of dope and sought after by a Navajo crook who only needs the location to come running to recover it."

"Do tell. And how do you know all this?"

"The Navajo kid's grandfather is a medicine man and is off by himself a lot. He came across the wreck in a canyon north of Kayenta, Arizona. The bad guys have been after him for a while trying to get the location out of him. They tried kidnapping his grandson once and that didn't work so they finally managed to grab the grandfather who escaped from a place near Kayenta and that's when he found the wreck. We – his grandson and I – got to him before the bad guys did and got him the hell out of Dodge. He took us to the wreck because he wanted to be sure there wasn't an injured pilot inside. Both people up front were dead due to the crash. But the plane didn't burn and that's why I have pictures I'll send you of what's inside. I don't know what it is – I didn't look – but the plane is full up to the bottom of the windows with gray plastic bricks.

"Right now the kid, grandfather and I are in Blanding, Utah. We're going to stay here tonight and try to think of a way for the bad guy, Robert Begay, to find out where the plane is in a way that doesn't arouse his suspicions. He'll beat a path to the wreck and you will be waiting to take him and his crew of ne'er-do-wells off thereby saving countless lives and messing up a cartel payday."

"That's how I see it. I know you have to jump through numerous hoops to conduct an operation like this. We'll do whatever we can to assist but I know you'll need to move fast. Begay is actively trying to locate the grandfather to extract the information from him and we're sort of scrambling to stay ahead of him."

"I can see why you haven't called or written, you've been too busy! Sure, we can make something happen, but off the top of my head I'm much more inclined to bug the cargo, let the bad guys do the work of packing it out of the canyon, and grab them and the dope when they light somewhere. In your mind, is that doable?"

"I don't see why not as long as we don't wait too long. Begay had ten men, armed, on horseback tracking the grandfather before we rescued him, and there's nothing to stop them from running across the wreck except it's way the hell out away from everything."

"Robert Begay sounds familiar, I'll see what I can dig up on him. Meanwhile, I need to run this all past an AUSA (Assistant U.S. Attorney) and make sure he or she is onboard but it sounds pretty straightforward. Knowing you, it probably isn't but one can always hope," Campbell said with a chuckle. "Do you know where you'll be staying tonight?"

"Not yet. I'll text you the information when I get it, but I'm going to text you the pix right now."

"Okay. I'll arrange things at this end and, if I'm lucky, I'll see you sometime this evening in Blanding."

"Thanks, Jim. Doing this will take the heat off the old man and the kid, *and* puts some bad guys in jail hopefully owing a cartel."

After texting the photos of the scene, Bob walked into the diner just in time for the waitress to set plates down in front of three places. He hadn't known it, but he was having a chicken fried steak with hash browns, eggs over medium and, best of all, black coffee.

Bob sat down and Abe immediately asked, "Were you able to contact your friend? Oh, we ordered for you, we figured you'd be hungry."

"I did and I am. I sent him the pictures and he's going to run it by the prosecutors to make sure all the "t's" are crossed and the "i's" dotted. He hopes to drive over here from Albuquerque either this afternoon or evening. He's a good guy for a Fed." Concerned about listeners, they were careful not to discuss the case. That would come later after they got their rooms.

They opted for the Rodeway Inn on Highway 191 in the southern part of town. After transferring their gear to their rooms, Bob's room in the middle, the trio congregated in Bob's. "I don't know about you guys," said Bob as he collapsed on one of the beds, "but I'm bushed being up all night and Carlos you have to be more tired than me."

"I could do with a nap," said Carlos. "Do you think we're safe here? Begay must be looking for your pickup by now."

"That's why I parked between those two semis. Hopefully they're here until morning by which time we'll be ready to go again. I'll just text our location and room numbers to Jim Campbell so he won't have to bother the front desk. I also reserved a room for him next to ours.

"Now, does anyone have any concerns about how this operation is evolving? My idea is to hand this over to DEA and watch from the sidelines. The only thing we need to do – you two – is lead the Feds out to the crash site and make a map that I can read since I don't know the Navajo ways or landmarks."

"How would we get the map into Begay's hands without him being suspicious?" asked Abe.

"The floor is open to suggestions," said Bob.

"I think if I could 'accidentally' get close enough to Walter Bitsillie while he's still crippled, he could grab me, as he would undoubtedly try to do, I could struggle with him for a little while and drop the map out of my jacket pocket," said Abe. "I can't see that it would be all that tough to get away from him since he can't walk without help."

"And if he has a knife or a gun like he did last time?" asked Bob.

"You come to my rescue. Maybe kick him in the knee again?"

"Carlos?"

"It's risky. The idea of Walter – or even Henry - getting the map away from Abe is good, but catching Walter by himself without help might be difficult."

"Regardless," said Bob, "we need to get that map done before Jim Campbell gets here; otherwise he'll be sitting around waiting for it since that's the carrot for Begay."

Abe and Carlos went right to work using a topographical map, a pencil and Carlos's encyclopedic memory of the area. They traced the route from Mexican Hat on Highway 163 to the first turn off onto the rutted dirt track. Carlos had trouble gauging distances on paper but between him, Abe, and even Bob, they finally drew a facsimile of their route to the downed aircraft. They agreed that when they took DEA out to the site, they would write down mileages between landmarks just like Abe would do if he was directing Bob to the site for the first time.

"Now we need to write a note on it, from Abe to me, explaining what was out there and what I could expect to find. The map and the note would be more in character from Abe and, since he'll have the map in his possession, he should be the one explaining things to the *Bilagaana,*" said Bob.

Using several pages of motel stationery, they drafted a note to be written on the face of the map. Finally, they were satisfied and Abe set to work transferring the missive onto the map. When he finished, they all took one last look at it and pronounced it ready to go.

Then they all retired to their respective rooms and took a much needed nap. It had been a long night.

Bob was awakened about three hours later by an insistent knocking on his door. Groggy, he rolled off the bed, grabbed his Glock and eased over to the door. He looked through the peep hole and saw Jim Campbell standing there somewhat impatiently.

He opened the door, greeting Campbell with a big grin and a handshake. "It's about time you opened the door," groused Campbell good-naturedly as he walked past Bob into the room. "I didn't want to have to wake up your companions, but that was next on my list. How the hell are you?" Campbell was a classic fair-haired Scotch-Irishman with rosy cheeks and a perpetual smile. He had always been with DEA and had no aspirations of going any further up the ladder, he was happy doing what he was doing.

"Better, after the nap. We were up all night watching for Carlos and finally picked him up around 3:30 or 4:00 this morning. How are *you* doing and how is Diane? I know she fell and broke her hip, is she recovering okay?"

"That wife of mine is indestructible. She didn't even have to go to a rehab facility after they released her from the hospital. She's doing really well, walking every day and receiving in-home physical therapy. She sends her love, by the way."

"Glad to hear it. Let me go get the other two and we'll tell you what we know and what we've been thinking about doing."

Bob slipped out of the room but was back in less than ten minutes with two bleary-eyed Navajos in tow. He made the introductions and everyone took a seat either in a chair or on the bed.

"Before we get started, I should tell you we have an interesting file on Robert Begay. He has been named as a player in several loads of dope coming across the border mostly from Sonora. We've never been able to get anyone next to him so he's probably feeling pretty bullet proof and we'd like to change that. We think he's pretty high up the ladder with the *Sinaloa* Cartel and he could do some significant damage to them if we could turn him."

"You mean you want to offer him a deal for services he might render?" asked Abe increduously.

"Yes and no. If we get him clean on this load of dope, we would offer him a deal, but part of the deal would be several years behind bars."

Abe grinned. "I like the way you think."

"Okay, tell me the whole story. Mr. Grey Hawk, would you care to lead off since you found the plane?"

"Call me Carlos." Carlos presented a succinct account of what he had been doing on Cedar Mesa, his decision to return to civilization and his capture by Begay's thugs. He told of his escape with Millie Nez's help and his discovery of the wrecked aircraft.

Next Abe recounted his introduction to Bob, his efforts to contact his grandfather and his near abduction by Begay's men. When he began to describe the plan to get the map into Begay's hands, Campbell stopped him. "Let's get all the background out

236

first, then we'll discuss how we're going to make a go of this operation."

Finally, Bob told his story about nearly running into Abe, of deciding to give the young man a hand and his involvement in the case up to this point. "Our intent is to stay out of your way, only helping if you need us, and get Abe to Tucson in time to get settled before his classes begin."

"Well," said Campbell, "we've done operations like this before – successfully – and the circumstances of this one appear to be very positive, in our favor. Now, how were you thinking of getting the map into Begay's hands?"

"We discussed that most of this morning," said Bob, "in fact, we created directions to the plane on the topo map and we only have to put mileages between landmarks and it's ready to go. Our thinking was that this was a map for me so I could go out and look over the crash site. Navajos don't usually use maps like white people do so this was a way for a Navajo to explain to a *Bilagaana* how to find the site and it says so on the map. Show him the map, Abe.

"It's still up in the air is how to get the map into Begay's hands without rousing suspicion," said Bob. "He has some pretty dumb crooks working for him and we thought that if we could create a situation where the map fell out of Abe's pocket and was found by one of the thugs that would be the best way to legitimize the transfer of the location of the plane."

"Normally, we would use a go-between DEA informant to do this," Campbell advised, "but people like that here on the reservation are scarce. I think your plan is sound as long as no one gets hurt during the transfer. Do you have a scenario?"

"As far as we know, Begay and his men are still searching for Abe or Carlos and making Abe available seems the best method," Bob replied. "We just need to find out where the two bad guys hang out then wave the red flag. Carlos, do you have any ideas about this? For that matter, do you even know the two men who kidnapped you?"

"I know *of* them," Carlos replied. "Adam Benally knows more about them and mentioned that they spend a lot of time at Red Rock Auto Repair and Towing in Bluff. Adam used to be friends with the owner but once those two started hanging around, he went back to Mexican Hat. He said the green and white Ford pickup that followed you belongs to Henry Begay and he usually can be found working on it at Red Rock. He and Walter Bitsillie sometimes take calls for towing for the owner even though they are not licensed. That is one reason Adam left."

"So if the green and white Ford pickup is there, our boys aren't far away?" asked Bob.

"That would seem to be the case."

"Okay," said Bob, "here's what I suggest …."

# CHAPTER 19

The first DEA objective was to get the load in the wrecked plane wired so they would know if anyone was tampering with it and to track it. Jim Campbell had brought a three-man technical crew with their equipment van that doubled as a ground surveillance team. They were prepared to insert trackers in at least ten of the "bricks" in the plane – in case the load was broken up right from the beginning. The trackers would also act as alarms and would transmit a signal if one of the doctored bricks was disturbed. The receiver for the transmitters was already installed in an undercover DEA aircraft that should already be on the ground at the Blanding Municipal Airport about three miles south of town. Through Jim Campbell, the pilots/spotters and receiver operator each had coordinates for the downed aircraft and would be available on an Alert Fifteen status when given that signal by Campbell.

The technicians, along with Campbell, Carlos and Abe were on the way to the crash by one o'clock P.M. and anticipated a five-hour trip/installation. The techs would then return and become the surveillance team whose job was to surveil Begay and the two thugs until the DEA aircraft could take over. It would then become a waiting game until Begay made his move.

After leading the DEA crew into the site, Abe and Carlos would prepare for their encounter with Henry and Walter. The plan first called for Bob to drive by the tow company to ensure that the two suspects were there. He would then go to the Sand Island State Park where he would conceal his pickup but be prepared to ensure the encounter went the way they wanted it to go. Abe and Carlos would then go to the park where they would call in for a tow because they needed a jump start. When Henry and Walter responded, Abe would approach the tow truck to tell them they weren't needed, they had found the problem. He would be surprised it was Henry and Walter and try to make a run for it back to Carlos's pickup. With luck there would actually be no contact between Abe and, presumably Henry, since Walter was still crippled up. First choice was for Abe to fall down and drop the map, but he would be prepared to tussle with Henry before dropping the map. Both Carlos and Bob would ensure that the encounter went the way they wanted it to go. Bob would be in a position to confirm that Henry found the map and took it back to the tow company with him. They had to assume Henry and Walter would recognize the significance of the map and make it known to Robert Begay at which time a twenty-four-hour surveillance would be established on him.

Abe would make it back to Carlos's pickup and Carlos would take off out of the park. If the tow truck gave chase, they should be able to lose it and then return to Blanding. Jim Campbell would have overall command of the operation and, as soon as possible, would send Bob, Carlos and Abe to the sidelines while the DEA team took over but the local trio was to stay prepared to act if necessary.

Jim Campbell figured Robert Begay would wait until the following morning to go find the plane. Eager and greedy as he might be, he was smart enough not to try to find the canyon in the dark, much less try to make a descent to the bottom.

Assuming all went as planned, the next morning would find Bob, Carlos and Abe languishing in Bob's motel room listening to events unfold on a portable radio provided by Jim Campbell. Campbell would be in his undercover car loosely following Begay until the DEA aircraft could take over. Once the aircraft had Begay's white Cadillac Escalade targeted, the DEA ground team could back off a little and let Begay lead them out into the desert after the contents of the aircraft. Presumably, Begay would gather several men to help haul the dope to a hideout.

That would be the end of Bob, Carlos and Abe's involvement until it was time to go to court which would be months or even years. DEA would ultimately raid the hideout, seize the dope and arrest anyone at the site. The trio could then relax their guard since Begay and company would have bigger problems than trying to hunt down a Navajo medicine man and his grandson.

Robert Begay smiled as he paused to replay the message on his "informant line," "Robert, this is your cousin, Henry. I think me and Walter might have come across something you could use to solve the mystery with Old Man Grey Hawk. We were answering a call for Jake at Red Rock Towing. The call was for a dead battery so we took the tow truck to Sand Island to jump start whatever kind of car was dead. We were surprised when Grey Hawk's grandson jumped out of the pickup and came over to tell us they didn't need us. When he recognized us, he spun around and ran back toward the pickup as fast as he could go. But on the way back to the pickup, the kid tripped and fell. He scrambled to his feet, jumped in the cab and away they went.

'Course Walter couldn't chase because of his boogered up knee and the kid was back in the pickup and Grey Hawk was pulling out before I could catch up. But he dropped a map that must of fell out of his pocket. It was a topo map with a note on it to 'Bob' who I think is the kid's cop friend. It was a map showing the way to a airplane crash out in the desert south of the San Juan River. We was going to follow it out there but Walter thought we should probably check with you in case it had to do with why you wanted Grey Hawk.

"It looks like a map for someone who doesn't know the area, with mileages written down between landmarks and a note across the top from Abe to Bob and I don't imagine it's you! Call me back if you want it, and I'll bring it by."

"Bring it by the office …," said Robert, when Henry answered his phone. "… so I can at least take a look at it."

The Dynamic Duo walked into the Twin Rocks Trading Post twenty minutes later and asked for Robert Begay, Henry trying to impress the pretty girl at the counter by saying Robert Begay was expecting them. She picked up her phone, punched in Robert's number and told him he had two visitors he was expecting. Robert said he would be right out to get them.

The Duo did not recognize Meredith, but she pegged them as the same two from the green and white Ford pickup that had followed them the day she and Rita went out with Abe and Bob. As soon as the three men disappeared into the back, she was on the phone with Abe filling him in on what the Duo was doing with her boss.

After Abe finished the call with Meredith, he told Bob what she had said. Bob grinned. "Looks like they took the bait. Now Campbell and his team need to sit on them until they make a move."

Bob called Jim Campbell and relayed what Meredith had told them. Campbell jumped right on it, making calls and alerting people, starting with the DEA plane's crew.

When Robert Begay's Escalade left the trading post twenty minutes later, the DEA ground crew was on it and followed it out of town toward Mexican Hat. The DEA airplane took off a few minutes later and, after Campbell vectored it to the Escalade, Campbell's ground team backed off and let the plane run the show. Not surprisingly, Begay drove directly to Millie Nez's place where he met up with eight men in four pickups. With Begay in the lead, they left and headed north on Highway 163.

When Begay turned onto the rutted turn off, Campbell called Bob and caught him up on what progress they had made. When Bob offered his and his companions' services, Campbell declined but asked that they stay ready in case they needed more help. He had given them a portable DEA radio so they could keep up on the progress but asked that they stay out of the follow unless Campbell specifically requested their assistance.

Robert Begay had gathered together mostly shirt-tail relatives to help him move the dope. He was gratified that everything was coming together so smoothly and hoped his luck would hold. It grated on him to listen to Henry try to impress him with their actions, but vowed to keep his mouth shut and not drop them both alongside the damned road somewhere!

The talking stopped the farther they got out into the desert. Everyone was trying mightily to stay in their seats even with seat belts. Robert wasn't wasting any time, wanting to get out to the site, load the dope and be gone before anyone else stumbled across it. This would be his big score and, other than family, no one would be the wiser. He preferred dealing with family, they were less likely to turn against him if he treated them right and, in this case, he would be able to treat them very well in exchange for their silence.

He debated what to do with the two mutts in his Escalade. He should have left them in Bluff but he was afraid they'd start bragging around town. He doubted they could keep their mouths shut and it would take a very strongly worded admonishment to convince them he was serious. Perhaps he would have to break an arm or a finger or two to get their attention. It wouldn't bother Robert to issue such an order, and thought it might work as an example to the others.

After the third turn, Robert stopped the caravan to look at the map himself. He didn't trust his navigator and was not enthused about getting lost out in the desert. He read the notations for every change in direction and concluded that they were on track and getting very close to the site. He handed the map back to Henry and continued on until Henry announced, "We're here."

"Here" was on the side of a deep canyon and once Robert was out of the Escalade, he could see the fuselage of the airplane below. It looked like it would be a rough ingress and egress but a thousand dollars each would sweeten the deal with his men. He gathered them all together and made sure each man had a large backpack since it looked like they would need both hands to climb in and out of the canyon. Robert walked along the canyon's edge until he saw freshly scuffed dirt and rocks and assumed this was where Carlos had hiked down into the canyon. He started down, followed by his men except for the Dynamic Duo. Robert told them to stay on top and keep an eye out for interlopers. Walter wasn't much good for anything anyway, with his knee in a brace and it was a good excuse to keep Henry out of the canyon and seeing what Robert did not want him to see.

It seemed to take forever to reach flat ground again at the bottom of the canyon and even then they had to dodge big rocks and brush. They could smell the dead pilots long before they arrived and most of the men were unsettled being so close to dead bodies.

Robert could see where Carlos or his grandson had pried open the side cargo door and when Robert opened the door, he could see his fortune lying before him in gray plastic bricks. Without hesitation, he started the first man behind him loading up his pack. As more space became available due to the absence of the bricks, he had two men loading at once. He tried to keep a count of the bricks going out but with two loading at once, it was nearly impossible. He told each man to load as close to thirty bricks as they could carry, he didn't want anyone making two trips if he could avoid it – that would take too long.

As the loading process continued, Robert realized there were more bricks that he thought there would be. Four pickups were way more than enough to transport the haul but some or all of his men would have to make a second trip down to the plane. He passed the word on with the next man going up to send the first ones back down for a second load. He hoped they could finish in two trips. He didn't think his men would be amenable to a third trip in and out of the steep, dusty canyon and he didn't blame them.

As the last men made their second trip, Robert was relieved to see they would get the whole shipment out of the canyon. He debated checking to see how much money the pilots were carrying but thought better of it and headed back up out of the canyon behind the last man. When he finally made it to the top, gasping and wheezing, he found all the shipment loaded in one pickup and all four pickups loaded with men and ready to go. As soon as he caught his breath and drank down a bottle of water, he told everyone they were leaving and would be taking the cargo back to Millie Nez's place where they would store the load in her barn until he could get it sold. First, he had to figure out just what he had before he could peddle it.

The DEA plane alerted the ground team that the caravan of trucks was coming back out and the ground team gave them plenty of room. It would be a major victory to arrest all the transport crew now, but Jim Campbell wanted whoever would be buying the load. He didn't think Robert Begay had the contacts to mete out smaller quantities and would want to sell wholesale to one buyer. That the word would get back to the owners of the shipment was a given, but that was not Campbell's problem and he was thankful it wasn't; Mexican cartels had long memories and violent tempers.

Bob, Carlos and Abe hung around the motel in Blanding more-or-less marking time. They didn't want to not be available if they were needed, but they really didn't have much to do. When they were alone, Abe and Carlos brought up the topic of the Shrine and discussed letting Bob in on the secret. Bob knew they were talking about something but he didn't spend much time pondering what it might be; he was more oriented toward the DEA rolling up Robert Begay's group. He was curious, of course, but decided that if he needed to know, they would tell him in their own time and way. Meanwhile he stuck close to his phone in case Jim Campbell called.

And, finally, at about three in the afternoon Bob's phone rang. It was Jim. "Well, we have them back at that woman's place, what's her name, Millie Nez? There were four pickups and Begay's Escalade. From what we could tell, they backed the first vehicle into the barn there and, presumably, unloaded it since the vehicle was

247

sitting higher when they came out. We didn't have a very good eye on the place but drove by often enough to see. I've been in touch with my office in Albuquerque and the U.S. Attorney's Office; the affidavit for the warrant is about three-quarters done and should be signed a little after 5:00 PM. by a magistrate in the U.S. District Court for the District of Arizona. We're kind of crossing jurisdictional lines here from New Mexico to Arizona and have to be careful to make sure it satisfies their judge and prosecutor. I've done this before, and as long as you work with those in the right district, the end product is satisfactory and won't get dismissed or, worse yet, reversed."

"You know," said Bob, "I hate to tell you at this late hour, but we used a drone with infra-red-capable camera to spot, track and finally make contact with Carlos. We rented it for a week but have only used up three of the seven days. Would it be of any use to you?"

"Case law is all over the place when it comes to shooting video of suspects with a drone. My understanding *at this time* is that if you are controlling the drone from public property or private property with permission to be there and the drone is flying over the same kind of property, you're probably okay. It's too bad we couldn't have used it in the desert when they recovered the dope but that's water under the bridge and we probably couldn't have been in position anyway. Now, since they're active on private property, we probably can't use the drone while we're flying over them."

248

"Yeah, I was afraid of that. New case law comes in every day and it's hard to stay current. Okay, what can we do to help?"

"We'll be keeping an eye on the place around the clock until we hit it. It's going to be a crap shoot catching a buyer inspecting the merchandise and we may have to settle for Robert Begay as the main target so we want to be sure he's there when we execute the warrant. Do you or your people want to be there during the raid?"

"Probably not. They would enjoy seeing Robert Begay in handcuffs but if he saw them there, there would be no end to the repercussions. Carlos and Abe have to live here."

"Sounds about right to me. Reluctantly I should tell you that you can probably turn in that drone. I can think of all kinds of uses for it, but now that the bad guys are on private property, most of those ideas would probably be illegal. Oh well, I think our case is pretty solid without it but it would have been nice to have photos of each of the players while they were in action. You don't think they would have detected the drone?"

"Carlos never heard a thing. It was very quiet where he crossed the river, all there was was a little gurgling of the water along the banks. We were hovering at about three hundred feet and the video footage was impressive."

"I'll tuck that away in my pea brain for next time. Maybe we can make use of one and get good evidence from it. I can sure see some useful applications. Is it hard to fly?"

"Abe, being younger and very into video games was much more adept than I was but I flew it a bit and there's so many foolproof systems, it would be hard for a pilot like Abe to crash. It has collision avoidance software and automatic return to base programming which takes a lot of the challenge out of it."

"Gotta go. Looks like Begay's troops are getting ready to leave and I'd like to try to get some pix if possible."

"Okay. Call me if you need anything. We'll be around for another day or two if you have use of us."

"Okay. I'll call and keep you posted as things progress."

# CHAPTER 20

It was after dark when Bob next heard from Jim Campbell. "Well, we got them tucked in for the night," the DEA agent reported. "I have a team of two sitting on Begay all night, and another team of four watching Millie Nez's place. We're in pocket with the warrant and will follow Begay to Nez's place then execute the warrant right after he goes in the barn. This thing came together too fast to set up very good cell phone monitoring system. Our primary interest is when and if Begay finds a buyer. We'd like to snap up the buyer in the net too but we'd have to get very lucky to do so. I guess we'll take what we can get."

"Is there anything we can do to help?" asked Bob.

"Not really. It *should* be a straightforward operation. We'll come in a little behind Begay, secure everyone and search them then do the usual things one does at a search warrant. I'm hoping none of Begay's men get excited because if the shooting starts it will get messy. If a buyer shows up," said Campbell, "he'll bring enough firepower to ensure there's no rip off, which is always a possibility when unknown people are meeting unknown people. If there's a firefight between the buyer and Begay's men, the locals will get slaughtered since they don't have near the firepower the cartels have.

"I'm telling my people to hold in place until I give the word in case the deal goes sour – if there is a deal. That's the big problem

251

with having a buyer show up.  Mexican cartel soldiers are more about *machismo* than discipline and without a platoon of infantry behind me, I worry."

"If there's a gunfight, what will you do?" asked Bob.

"Hold my people back, in safety, if I can.  They will be well-armed and able to take care of themselves and they might wind up in the melee at some point, but I'll try like hell to keep them out of the line of fire – at least until it's necessary.  That's why I have so many troops down here."

"What time do you think the circus will start?"

"That's probably up to Robert Begay.  He'll kick it off when he gets to the Nez place.  Hopefully it'll be a low key operation, but as A.E. Houseman, the poet said, "Train for ill and not for good.""

"I'll be waiting by the phone, just in case; be careful and good luck."

"Thanks, I'll call you later."

Bob had a bad feeling about Campbell's operation, but he couldn't think of a thing Campbell had not already thought of and didn't want to encumber Campbell with a feeling.  Still, he worried, but there wasn't much he could do.

*****

Robert Begay was up at 05:00 AM the next morning and gathered his troops, less the ones guarding the shipment, at his house for a briefing. "The buyer will be arriving between 08:00 AM and 09:00 AM, and will have some men with him. Keep silent unless spoken to and keep your answers to a minimum. Keep your weapons at the ready but not aimed at anyone. If any of them raise a weapon, look to me for a signal before you shoot.

"The plan is for the buyer to examine the shipment and test its purity then spot weigh it. Each brick is very close to a kilogram in weight and I tested the product and it tested positive for crystal meth. All we have to do is accept their money and watch as they load it into their vehicle(s) and we'll all be a lot richer. Anyone have any questions?"

"If one of them suddenly brings up a weapon and aims it at me, I ain't waitin,' I'm going to put him down," said one of the men.

Begay sighed, "There's no way to know for sure what's going to happen but try to use restraint; we don't want a blood bath."

"I don't want to get shot, neither," said the same man.

"Neither do I," said Begay, "I want to be rich."

They broke up and headed for Millie Nez's place. Robert could see a rifle in every gun rack and figured that at least half of the men were carrying handguns as well. He fervently hoped they wouldn't need them.

When Begay's caravan arrived at the ranch, everyone parked helter skelter. The thought of combat erupting didn't even cross Robert Begay's mind. He took two bottles of sweet red wine into Millie and made sure she was well into one of the bottles before he came back outside.

The four men who had spent the night there were glad for the coffee and breakfast burritos their friends brought. They had alternated watches inside and outside the barn and reported nothing out of the ordinary. Campbell held his troops back until all of Begay's men were accounted for but before he could give the go signal, three jacked up four-door four wheel drive pickups blazed by his men and turned into the Nez ranch.

Counting himself, Robert Begay had twelve men, all armed and all alert but not combat trained. When the *Zetas Vieja Escuela* (Old School Zetas – a splinter group from the Zetas criminal drug cartel) arrived the attackers immediately started shooting with M16s on full automatic fire and the Navajos outside the barn didn't have a chance. They were all down, mortally wounded in a matter of seconds. The ones inside, including Robert Begay, panicked and scrambled for a way out or a place to hide.

The leader of the *Zetas,* Guillermo Aguilar, strutted up to the closed barn door, apparently not at all concerned about being shot, and yelled in heavily accented Spanish, "Roberto Begay, your only chance to live is to come out unarmed. Otherwise we will come in and everyone will die. You have five minutes."

Robert Begay was so terror-stricken, he was completely at a loss how to react. The four men with him grabbed him and hustled him to the barn door, opened it and pushed him out, slamming the door closed behind him. Begay stood there trembling as urine ran down his leg and puddled by his shoe.

"So you are Roberto Begay, the man who stole our shipment then tried to sell it back to us," Aguilar smirked. "How can anyone be that stupid? Can you give me a reason why I should not kill you right now?"

Begay just stood there trembling. Finally, he stuttered, "I … I … did … didn't know it was yours. Had … had I known that, I … I would have given it back."

Aguilar was standing at a forty-five-degree angle, four feet from Begay. He looked out at the desert then, in the blink of an eye, a machete gleamed in his hand and Begay's head was at his feet. Begay's decapitated body collapsed away from the blow, blood flowing around the neck as it pumped from the corpse after it hit the ground.

"Kill the rest of them, and make a statement that no one steals from the *Zetas Vieja Escuela!* Burn the house, then load up the shipment. *¡Vamanos!"*

The gunfire from the carnage inside the barn had just died down when more jacked up pickups roared up from the south and turned into the ranch's driveway and stopped, blocking entry or exit to the property. Four heavily armed men jumped out of each pickup and took up cover positions behind the *Zetas'* vehicles with their backs to the highway. They opened fire immediately and those *Zetas* outside the cover of the barn died before they could react. The armed group surrounded the small barn, awaiting orders, weapons at the ready.

Near the center of the newest phalanx a voice was heard, "You *Zeta* pigs in the barn, you are trespassing on *Sinaloa* territory. For this, you will die." His hand came down and a fusillade of gunfire riddled the old barn from all sides. "Burn it," said the same man and fires were quickly ignited against the old, extremely dry siding of the barn. In less that fifteen minutes, the old building was fully engulfed. Those *Zeta* soldiers who tried to escape the inferno through the door were quickly cut down until the barn door was blocked with bodies.

"Jesus," said Campbell as he viewed the slaughter through binoculars. He looked at his second-in-command and said, "Now, do you still disagree about bringing those Bearcats?" The Lenco Bearcat was a vehicle designed for military and law enforcement use. It was heavily armored and enabled law enforcement to close in tactically on an opposing force as well as support tactical rescue efforts.

"You're going to take on the *Sinaloa* Cartel?" asked his subordinate.

"I don't see as we have an option," said Campbell. "They have committed arson and murder on U.S. soil and we don't have time to call in a tactical military unit, if one would come. I can't see driving away and letting these bastards waltz back into Mexico unscathed. I don't think I'm going to mourn any of the victims but I'll be damned if we let these invaders go without a fight."

"You're the boss; issue the orders."

"Load all of our people in the Bearcats. They're supposed to hold a driver and a front passenger plus ten people so there should be enough room for everyone. No one, repeat, no one will accompany us unless they are tactically equipped with vests, helmets and fully automatic weapons. Damn, I wish I had that drone of Bob's now," Campbell muttered to himself.

"When they're loaded, bring them up and we'll position them behind the *Sinaloa* vehicles. Try to disable or block in as many of their vehicles as possible, we don't want high speed pursuits in addition to a standoff. Deploy personnel into reasonably safe positions including the gun ports in the Bearcats. These guys are using the same weapons we are and a .223 round isn't going to do much against the armor on these vehicles.

"I will try to negotiate with the leader, even though the cartels are not known to negotiate. When the first shot is fired from any *Sinaloa* shooter, it's weapons free. Obviously, if any bad guy tries to surrender, try not to shoot him and, if possible, take him into custody. Go ahead and relay this to the troops. We move out in two minutes."

Campbell's three Bearcats were hidden in a copse of trees about three eighths of a mile south of the Nez ranch. He had been parked closer, in an undercover pickup, and had been able to get a pretty good idea what had just gone on. He drove back to the Bearcats and took his place in the lead vehicle.

"Let's go," he said to his driver as he relayed the order over the tactical net which was received by every team member.

257

When they got to the Nez driveway, Campbell told his driver to drive between two of the *Sinaloa* pickups blocking the driveway. The Bobcat easily pushed them both back out of the way and opened a limited access into the yard. He started transmitting in English and Spanish, "This is the U.S. Drug Enforcement Agency, *la policia.* You are under arrest. Put down your weapons and put your hands on top of your heads and you will not be harmed." A .223 round glanced off the windshield. Then another and another. "Fire at will," Campbell ordered into his microphone.

He watched as three *Sinaloans* nearest the Bearcat dropped their weapons and turned toward the truck with their hands on their heads. All three were immediately cut down by gunfire from behind them. The confrontation quickly devolved into a stalemate. The *Sinaloans* had too much open ground behind them to flee so they had to stick close to the vehicles for cover since the barn was now a pile of smoking ash.

This went on for about five minutes then Campbell ordered his driver to bulldoze through two parked pickups ahead of him to gain access to some of the *Sinaloans* hiding behind them. The other two Bearcats followed suit and the volume of fire increased again as the tactical trucks forced their way forward.

Campbell could see *Sinaloans* standing and shooting at the trucks then retreating behind more vehicles. He could hear the rounds hitting the sides and windows of the Bearcats but nothing penetrated. Every now and then, he watched as another *Sinaloan* collapsed face down between the vehicles and he wondered how

258

many were left. The shooting tapered off again as Campbell ordered the driver to push aside some of the *Zetas'* vehicles to get to the Navajos' vehicles. Finally, one … then two *Sinaloans* threw down their weapons and put their hands on top of their head. No one shot at them and an arrest team from one of the Bearcats worked their way carefully toward them. From positions of cover, they ordered the two to turn all the way around to make sure there were no more weapons then to back up to where the agents were behind cover. The two were quickly secured in flex ties and placed in one of the trucks.

A team from each truck ventured out, conducting a vehicle by vehicle search looking for the wounded and the hiding. One team caught a *Sinaloan* hiding under one of the trucks and dragged him out kicking and screaming. It wasn't clear if the subject was scared or resisting but he was secured and placed with the others. Over the next four hours, DEA teams scoured the Nez ranch for suspects but only the three were found alive.

All told thirty-seven lives had been lost with three arrests. Campbell adroitly steered the media to DEA and local public information officers while he was deeply involved in the after action investigation.

He took time later that afternoon to call Bob, "Well, it really hit the fan," he said with a tired laugh. He told him an abbreviated version that covered the demise of Robert Begay and suddenly the trio's prospects took a lighter turn.

"I wonder if the word will sink into his thugs. Then again, the minute the police run across them, they'll cease to be a problem too," said Bob. The look that Abe and Carlos shared disturbed him, but he'd bring it up another time.

"This is bound to stir up hostilities between the cartels," Bob sighed. "From what I can piece together, the dope Carlos found in the plane belonged to the *Zetas Vieja Escuela* but this upstart Navajo crook named Robert Begay took it upon himself to appropriate it and then, ignorantly, try to sell it back to its owner. The *Zetas Vieja Escuela* decided to make an example out of him and his people and they all died – Begay by beheading, something that cartel is known for. The *Sinaloans* learned that the *Zetas Vieja Escuela* were infringing on their territory and took swift and decisive action though it cost them thirteen soldiers. I don't think the bosses are going to lose any sleep over that; what's a few more dead bodies?

"There may not be any overt war between the two organizations; after all, the *Sinaloa* cartel is far larger and well entrenched, but sometime in the future, *Zetas Vieja Escuela* will get even or worse. My understanding is that the dope in the plane was crystal meth, about half a ton which doesn't make it the largest seizure by any means but it put a hole in someone's pocket. There is any number of ways to value the stuff but figuring the value between one and two million is probably conservative depending on where it was going."

"Where are you, Jim?" asked Bob.

"I'm back in Albuquerque, they flew me back and I'll likely be headed for D.C. before long. This is going to be a political football and the media and the politicians are going to have a field day verbally masturbating themselves over it."

"I just hope none of the bullshit splashes on you," said Bob.

"I'm only a GS - government service employee - and I'm already eligible to retire so if they turn up the heat, I'll pull a Bob Connelly and bail. Seriously, I hope it doesn't come to that. I like what I'm doing and where I'm doing it and I'm not ready for it to end."

"Well, I'm glad you came through it okay; it sounds like it was a little dicey out there for a while."

"Yup. Remind me to send a nice thank you to Lenco for developing the Bearcat. That made all the difference and none of my people were injured which is wonderful."

"If we *ever* make it to Santa Fe before Abe's classes start, we'll be sure to look you up and at the very least buy you dinner. You done real good."

# CHAPTER 21

Bob, Carlos and Abe went out to pizza that evening, feeling lighter and less paranoid than they had in weeks. The pizza place was not busy and they pretty much had the place to themselves.

After they had acquired their drinks and were settling down at a table to wait for their pizza, Bob said, "The drugs on the plane aren't the end of the story, are they? I'm not trying to pry, but the looks you two have shared and your actions since Begay left the picture suggest to me that when you, Carlos, were talking about something of great value, it wasn't a planeload of meth. Abe said the secret was worth dying for and I admit, it piqued my curiosity but if it's Navajo business, it's none of mine, and I'll say no more about it. I'm available if you need help but that's because I think the world of you two, not because I want to know what's none of my business."

Abe looked at Carlos and raised his eyebrows in a question. Carlos nodded and took in a breath before beginning, "Abe and I have discussed this very point off and on since he learned of the secret and he believes it's safe to tell you. I don't hesitate because I don't trust you, but because I do not wish to burden you with something that, in your own words, is not your concern. I believe that we need a broader perspective than what we two can provide, and that is why I wish to tell you the secret, knowing you will not let it go further than we three without our approval.

There is a Shrine on Cedar Mesa. The Shrine of the Ancients. It is presently on Bears Ears National Monument land administered by the National Park Service. The shrine is as close to a written history of the indigenous peoples of the area dating back centuries. It is in the form of bands of petroglyphs in different grottos and, though no one actually can date petroglyphs, the stories that have been carved into the sandstone clearly go back to before the first white man arrived. I am well-versed in the lore of the Navajo people and can see the legends carved out on the walls in a linear, chronological pattern. The value of these legends is priceless and date to before the Conquistadores arrived since horses and swords are introduced into the carvings later in the chronology.

"Access to this Shrine has always been very secret and difficult to find, as it should be. Should the wrong people learn of its existence, they would destroy many of the carvings just to get a few panels out. That must not happen. It is a place of great beauty and value as a Native American heritage site."

Abe took over from his grandfather. "There are hundreds or thousands of intact pots in the grottos with the carvings. They are pristine and also chronological according to the styles, patterns and colors of different eras. The pots are obviously portable and a tempting source of millions of dollars to the wrong people. That's why we were so worried that Begay was trying to get the location so he could loot the site. Imagine our relief when we learned that he was only after a couple of million dollars worth of drugs."

Bob had to chuckle at Abe's irony. Then he grew serious. "Why are you telling *me* this? I know little or nothing of Native American history or art. I'm just a dumb retired police officer with time on his hands. Your secret is *safe* with me but why tell me?"

"We have been debating the idea of letting the Shrine's existence be known in certain circles. Historically, only one *Hatáli* was entrusted with the knowledge of the Shrine's existence at any given time. It was not handed down to me, I dreamed the location of the Shrine after it had lain unattended for, I am guessing, centuries, for whatever reason. It has enlightened no one, or been added to Native American collective knowledge and history. One might say that it might as well not exist for all the good it is doing the Diné. I have always been proud of how my people have orally handed down their history and philosophy from one generation to the next but this is an instance where the written word entered on everything from papyrus to marble endures better than the spoken word.

"Since access to the Shrine is so arduous, it makes sense to make a careful video record of all the contents, both for posterity and for study. Perhaps some bright young anthropologist can make sense of these carvings that has heretofore eluded us. Perhaps there is a primer or Rosetta Stone among the petroglyphs that would open up another language to us. That will never happen so long as the Shrine is kept secret.

"You, Bob, because we trust you and value your input, enlarge our perspective of the world. Yes, I know that you have not been a world traveler, an historian or a student of human dynamics but you are well-steeped in the ways of middle class Americans which is something where Abe and I are sorely lacking. We don't want this announcement to get out of control or come under the thumb of corrupt politicians which is what I fear the most.

"There is a fortune in ancient pottery in the Shrine that probably should be on display and under study in museums and in the Navajo capital, Window Rock. Some of those items can be found nowhere else and are, without exception, all museum quality. But being relatively small and portable, these pots are subject to theft and breakage which makes me fearful to make them available. I have visions of archeologists studying some of these pots and identifying their origin by the ancient maker with whom they are familiar having studied pot shards and the few intact pots available.

"In common vernacular, Bob, we need you to see through the *bullshit*, that would invariably come with offers to show these items. Their value to me is in their history and I fear that my over-protectiveness might be a weakness. I need someone to bring in that broader perspective now and then for both Abe and me. I want to hand these priceless items over to a trustworthy individual who will care for these pots as if they are his or her own. I am an *Hatáli,* a medicine man, that is what I have studied for years and what I do best. I am not a museum curator nor do I wish to become one. I have an apprentice to train and that will be difficult enough

265

considering the schedule he'll be keeping. I will turn over the location of the Shrine to another *Hatáli,* perhaps less encumbered than I, but *I* will make the decision about who that will be regardless what the President or anyone else says because I do not trust them."

"I can see that you feel very strongly about this and I respect that. I will do whatever I can to assist you but wouldn't it be wise to have more than one advisor?" asked Bob.

"I am sure there will be no shortage of people offering their opinions, but I can only listen to a few and they must be people I trust."

"How will you implement your plan?"

"I believe I should make an appointment with the President after a video is made of the Shrine and the pottery. It almost seems sacrilegious to introduce the new into the old but if it will preserve the old I must look forward, not to the side."

Their pizza came and the discussion was tabled while they ate. They discussed going to Mexican Hat tomorrow to get Carlos's pickup, and to touch base with those who had helped. They all agreed they were relieved that none of their sources of information switched sides as Bob had feared.

When they returned to their rooms, Bob called Jim Campbell but got a recording. He hoped Jim was not answering because he was catching up on his sleep but knowing how administrators worked, Jim was probably writing reports or answering questions and was probably in D.C. by now. Bob left a message for Campbell telling him that he, Abe and Carlos were probably going to head for Santa Fe tomorrow unless Jim needed them to remain in Blanding.

By Bob's reckoning, they had about three weeks before Abe needed to be in Tucson. They had a lot to do. Abe needed everything, from clothes to a laptop. They discussed modes of transportation around the UA campus; Abe thought he could get by just fine on foot. He would consider the merits of a bicycle or even a scooter after the first semester, but transportation was, for now, low on his list of priorities.

They retired early, not sure how well they were going to sleep, considering their pursuers were no longer around. Abe, of course, was on the phone to Meredith and told her briefly about her boss's demise and she was properly shocked. She had never had a conflict *per se* with Begay but admitted that she had not liked the man and certainly never trusted him. She speculated who might take over but decided it was above her pay grade; besides, she was headed to Tucson in just a few short weeks.

After breakfast the next morning, the trio headed to Mexican Hat to retrieve Carlos's pickup and belongings that were stored at Adrian Tso's place. After that, they split up with Bob returning to Blanding to return the drone while Carlos and Abe gathered components for Carlos's *jish* packets. It was the first time the two had had any time at all for *Hatáli* instruction of which there would be many many hours. They first drove to the Exxon station to see Adrian Tso and let him know that Carlos had moved out all his meager possessions and would ultimately be moving back to Shiprock.

They didn't notice the green and white Ford pickup parked behind the station until Walter Bitsillie and Henry Begay came around the corner into the mechanic area and stopped short. "Well, look what we have here!" said Walter with a smirk. He was walking without a crutch or a cane but limping heavily.

Henry just stood back and sneered, "Uncle Robert will be glad to see you."

Carlos and Abe stood near Adrian, unfazed by their comments. "Didn't you hear?" asked Abe. "Your Uncle Robert Begay was killed by members of a drug cartel yesterday near Kayenta."

"That's not true," said Walter, "you're lying just to get away. Robert still wants to see you and we'll take you both just to be sure." He took a couple of menacing steps toward Carlos and Abe, when Adrian stepped between them after picking up a large, heavy pipe wrench.

"Back off, Walter," growled Adrian. "If you don't, I'll lay this wrench alongside your thick skull. Don't you listen to the news? There was a big gun battle at Millie Nez's place yesterday morning. Robert Begay and all his men were shot down by the *Zetas Vieja Escuelas* who were then massacred by the *Sinaloa* cartel. Even the *Sinaloans* suffered casualties, I heard ten or twelve were killed.

"It's true, Henry," said Adrian, "sorry to be the one to tell you."

Henry Begay just stood there and stared at Adrian. He suddenly shook himself and reached for his phone. He called a number from memory and said into the phone, "Is it true about Uncle Robert? Was there a shootout at Aunt Millie's yesterday?" He listened for a while then looked at Walter and nodded. "Okay, I'm on the way."

He clicked off the phone and said to Walter, "It's true. Uncle Robert and ten uncles and cousins were shot to death by the Mexicans yesterday. They need me at home right away."

Walter started to turn but stopped and looked back at Carlos and Abe. "Lucky for you we have to go but you're not off the hook. Whatever Robert wanted out of you, *we want,* if we have to beat you to death to get it, that's what we'll do."

Abe started to say something, then shook his head and thought better of it. He and Carlos watched in silence as the Dynamic Duo disappeared around the corner of the shop.

"Lucky for the Begay clan there are others better qualified to take over than Henry," said Adrian with a shake of his head. He looked around at Carlos. "What was he talking about? Something Robert Begay wanted to learn from you?"

"I came across a wrecked airplane in the desert," Carlos explained. "It was full of drugs and Robert wanted it. Apparently he got more than he bargained for."

"I heard there were drugs involved," said Adrian.

269

"About half a ton of crystal meth worth upwards of two million dollars," offered Abe, glad to disabuse Adrian of the *other* reason Carlos and, later, Abe, had been sought.

Carlos and Abe headed up toward Cedar Mesa. Carlos assured Abe this was not an overnight trek and they would be back in plenty of time to have dinner with Meredith at the Twin Rocks Trading Post. Carlos had never met the girl but the more Abe talked about her, the better Carlos liked her. They spent the rest of the morning and much of the afternoon walking in the desert and woods, collecting mostly herbs, feathers and reeds. Carlos would have to make or trade for some of the other components including rattles, fetishes, small pottery bowls, whistles, shells, and, most critically, small, individual pouches of pollen.

On their way to Bluff, to the pre-arranged dinner with Bob, Meredith and Rita, Abe was full of enthusiasm and questions about the instruction Carlos had given him and asked if there were places around Santa Fe where some of these components might be found.

"You would be better off thinking about collecting components in the Sonora Desert around Tucson. It will be your responsibility to collect these components for the ceremonies and to assist me in other ways. Sweat baths are an integral part of a ceremony and you will be expected to build the fire to heat the rocks and take them into the sweat house. A fire is never kindled inside the sweat house but water must be on hand to create the steam that helps one sweat and to keep the participants hydrated."

The conversation continued unabated until they pulled into the trading post parking lot next to Bob's pickup. They went inside and found Bob and Rita at a table waiting for Meredith to get off work and for Abe and Carlos to arrive. Dinner was a relaxed affair since there was no specter of Robert Begay to haunt them and, in keeping with Navajo tradition, his name was not mentioned at all to keep his *chindi* from invading.

Bob and Carlos had had a chance for a short, private discussion before dinner and now Bob suggested that Abe take Meredith home while the elders had a discussion. Rita was surprised, but comfortable with the suggestion.

Once the kids were gone, Bob got right down to brass tacks, "Rita, Carlos and I have a problem that we're way out of our depth on. We're hoping, with your background with the Navajo Nation, you can help us out. Problem is, we need to know that you can keep what we have to say quiet until Carlos says otherwise."

"You're asking for my help but can't tell me about what until you've sworn me to secrecy. Is that about right?" she asked.

"Yes," said Carlos, "it is a serious matter that affects the whole Navajo Nation and if word got out prematurely, my life, Bob's and probably Abe's would be in jeopardy."

"That serious, huh? If it's illegal, I'm not your candidate; if it has to do with drugs, ditto. Otherwise, I'm very good at keeping secrets."

Carlos looked at Bob and Bob nodded. They were out on the front veranda and there was no one else around so Carlos decided it was safe to take Rita into his confidence – no one else would hear. He launched into the story, telling her what he had been doing on the Cedar Mesa for the past several years and that sometimes his dreams were very realistic and sometimes what he dreamed came to pass. He explained about dreaming about the Shrine and had no other explanation of how he came to find it. He described it in detail and Rita sat spellbound, taking in every word, not interrupting.

"Abe knows because even though he is a very green *Hatáli* apprentice, he is a living bridge between me and the rest of the Nation. If something happened to me, at least *someone* would know of the shrine's existence and, more or less, where it is. I brought Bob in, even though he is a *Bilagaana,* because he is trustworthy and knows far more about the outside world than Abe or I do. We look to him for perspective of the ever-encroaching white man's ways onto the reservation. He has proven his trustworthiness over and over, especially with Abe and me.

"But Bob knows nothing of Navajo Nation affairs and politics and I am hoping that is where you come in. How familiar are you with the present administration and president?"

"Up until three years ago, I was President Enid Yazzie's administrative assistant. What he knew, I knew, but it was far more than a nine-to-five job. He is a fine man, a hard worker and a caring man but he is easily distracted. He has so many things on his plate; it's hard for him to stay focused on the subject at hand sometimes. I could not have asked for a better boss but the pace and all the people coming in with their hand out got to be too much so, after twenty years, I took an early retirement and found a teaching job in Montezuma Creek. Enid appointed me to deal with the Nation's problems in the area and it has worked out well ever since."

"I honestly didn't know," said Carlos, "and please believe I didn't confide in you knowing you might have an in with the President. I frankly do not know what is best for the Nation and for the Shrine. I am just an old Singer who has run across an important situation that I do not know how to handle.

"At first glance, it seems logical to appoint a caretaker, another *Hatáli,* to oversee what becomes of this Shrine. Someone who can protect it from looters and vandals while sharing the Native heritage of many generations for future generations. The pottery should be removed and situated in places of security but available for people to see and appreciate. They deserve much study – as much as the wall panels – and perhaps a bright anthropology or archeology maven can detect a pattern that will enable us to read what the Old Ones have tried to share with us.

"You, yourself, would be a good candidate to be the overseer, except your knowledge of the history and lore of our people is lacking. That is not insurmountable but of the two assets, yours is the most important. For example, this Shrine is within the Bear's Ears National Monument and unless the Navajo Nation can trade parcels of land with the federals, it will remain there, vulnerable to depredation if its location is ever found out. Acquiring that land for the Navajo Nation will not happen quickly and the task

273

of making it happen must be handed down to another, qualified generation. That alone is a monumental responsibility."

"When will you go back in to shoot the video and still photographs?" asked Rita.

"The sooner the better," Carlos replied. "The President should see what we are talking about before he can make any decisions."

"Would it be possible to accompany you when you return to photograph the shrine?"

"It is a two-day trek to the site and an arduous climb in and out of a steep canyon. Then you must crawl through a very narrow tunnel. At least most of the tunnel is of sandstone so the floor is sandy and not so hard on hands and knees. The tunnel is the reason we cannot merely re-locate the shrine. To try to move the petroglyphs panels would be to destroy half of them and the expense would be astronomical."

"Okay!" said Rita brightly, breaking the almost oppressive mood of the conversation. "When do we leave?" Bob chuckled and even Carlos smiled.

# CHAPTER 22

"Something came up today that you should know about," said Carlos, looking at Bob. "After Abe and I got my pickup, we stopped by the Exxon station to see Adrian. We ran into Walter Bitsillie and Henry Begay, and they were their old disagreeable selves." He described the confrontation and Adrian's threatening Walter with a wrench.

"They did not know of the shootout or the planeload of drugs and were inclined to disbelieve us until Adrian confirmed what we were telling them and they backed off to go check the facts for themselves. Both promised that they were not done with us yet, that whatever valuable thing I found on the Mesa was still out there and they planned to make us tell them one way or another. Hopefully, they will learn the whole story from Henry's family but if they're not convinced, we'll have to deal with them."

"You forget, Carlos," said Bob, "we're headed for Santa Fe today, and you will eventually wind up in Shiprock, far away from those yahoos."

"What about Meredith and Rita?" asked Carlos. "They followed them to Montezuma Creek one day."

"I forgot about that," said Bob. "Okay, I'll hunt them down and make it *very* clear what happened with his uncle and what *will* happen if they so much as watch Rita or Meredith drive by."

"Oh, don't go to all that trouble, Bob," said Rita, "Meredith will be off to Tucson soon and I have a very persuasive Beretta .380 if necessary, and I know how to handle it. I keep it in the console of my Highlander so it's within easy reach."

"Are you sure, Rita? It wouldn't take much effort to convince those two," Bob said with a grin.

"I suspect you'd enjoy it too much," said Rita with a smile of her own. "Tell you what, if they come calling, I'll call you and we can 'persuade' them together."

"Deal, but call regardless of what the Dynamic Duo is up to. When the Sheriff's Office catches up with them, they're probably going to cool their heels in jail for at least a little while."

"Are we all on the same page?" asked Rita, "Does everyone have each other's phone number and all that?"

"Bob, when I'm ready to go back to the Shrine, I'd like you to accompany Rita and me. Your technical ability with photographic equipment has to be far greater than mine. Rita, do you know where we can rent the appropriate equipment?"

"Certainly not in Bluff. We *might* get lucky in Blanding," she replied.

"The guy who rented us the drone seemed to have a little bit of everything," Bob offered. "We can check with him."

"Yes," said Carlos. "It is a shame the Shrine is not outside, the drone would be invaluable."

"Yes. It's also a shame we can't do the photography before we leave for Santa Fe. That's over a thousand-mile round trip," Bob observed.

"Why can't we?" asked Rita. "If it's just a matter of getting the equipment together, and taking the time, why not now?"

"What about the kids?" asked Bob. "They probably don't want to have to go up there when they have so much to do to get ready for school. I could leave Abe a credit card and he could get all the things he needs such as clothes, a laptop and so on. Meredith, I'm sure would be glad to help."

"But where would they stay?" mused Rita. "We would probably be gone two or three days."

"They could rough it up at Harley Uskilith's," Carlos offered.

"That would tell them we didn't trust them," said Rita.

"I agree," said Bob. "If they want to be together, the only way we can prevent it is to send one to the other side of the country. Otherwise, they *will* find a way. The most logical place for them to stay would be at your place in Montezuma Creek; Rita, but if you're uncomfortable with that, I could set Abe up with a motel in Blanding. He'll have either my pickup or Carlos's and Meredith will have access to your SUV, I assume?"

Rita nodded. "Montezuma Creek makes the most sense but we should each have a 'birds and the bees' talk with them just to let them know we're thinking of them."

"Okay!" said Bob, rubbing his hands together. "Carlos, Abe told me you have a lot of stuff cached in your aerie up on the Mesa. What else should we gather together for, say, a four-day stay?"

Carlos thought for several minutes. Finally, he said, "If three of us are going in, we need to make sleeping accommodations for the third person. There are tree bough beds for two inside the cave that work well once you find a comfortable spot. An air mattress or foam pad would be the best for sleeping on rocky ground. There is water there, so whatever else you want to eat besides the freeze dried meals. I have sufficient utensils so other than food and sleeping arrangements for one I think we can manage. Abe and I spent a night in the Shrine using space blankets, and we just used flashlights for illumination. If you plan to shoot photographs, we should probably carry in some battery-powered floodlights. So, other than personal belongings, that is all we need. I have sufficient backpacks for all of us in my pickup."

"Okay," said Bob, "Tomorrow, Rita can go shopping for another sleeping bag, some kind of sleeping mat and eats, and I'll look into photo equipment in Blanding. Carlos, why don't you decide on whatever else we should take."

Rita said Abe could stay at her place tonight and Bob took rooms for Carlos and himself in the same motel in Blanding as before. They agreed to meet in the morning for breakfast, finish their planning, have a talk with the kids and gather their supplies for the trip into the Shrine.

At 8:00 AM the next morning, Rita, Abe and Meredith walked into the Village Inn Café in Blanding and sat down with Bob and Carlos. The two young people were sitting side by side and mooning at each other. Rita whispered to Bob, "I hope we're not too late for that talk."

Bob announced they had changed plans and Carlos, Rita and he were now heading back up to the Shrine to take pictures instead of going to Santa Fe. He handed Abe a credit card and said, "You need clothes, a computer and school supplies, that's what you and Meredith can do while we're on the Mesa. You can take my pickup since Carlos's already has his equipment in his."

"Why the change in plans," asked Abe.

"Not much sense in making an extra thousand-mile trip for nothing," said Bob. "By the way, you and I need to have a little chat after breakfast."

"Am I in trouble or something?" asked Abe, looking concerned.

"Not that I know of but we still need to talk."

Abe looked pensive through the rest of the meal and when they were done, he dutifully followed Bob out to his pickup. He climbed into the cab and Bob did the same.

"Abe I'm not your father or even a relative but I seem to be in a position to advise you sometimes. I can't order you to do anything, you're only a few days away from being an adult, legally, but someone has to do it and I was elected. What do you know about sex? Procreation? Babies, and so on?"

Abe visibly relaxed and smiled. "This is the father/son talk I never had with my dad, right?"

"I guess it is."

"If it makes you any less tense, I had sex education in high school and I've been with a few girls so I know what you're wanting to say."

"Probably you don't," said Bob. "I don't care how many girls you've been with, this has to do with pregnancy, STD's and emotional maturity. First, I hope you took precautions with the first two. An unwanted pregnancy at your age where you're expected to marry the mother, would throw a giant monkey wrench in your plans, don't you think? And giving someone, especially someone you care about, an STD is, at the least, embarrassing and gives rise to all kinds of bad feelings.

"Finally, the biggest one. I hope you're not the type who tells girls what you think they want to hear in order to get into their pants. There are a lot of guys like that and if you're one of them, let me know now so I can tell Rita to keep Meredith away from you. She's much too nice of a girl to have her heart broken by some asshole just looking to get laid. Meredith is one of those females who, given the right opportunity and relationship, can be the love your life. I'm not trying to sell you on her or anything like that, time will tell if you're right for each other, but she deserves to be treated with kindness and respect – as all women are. Some are just easier to be that way with and some make it very difficult. I'm hoping Rita is having a similar talk with Meredith because, thus far, you seem to be one of those kinds of guys who deserve the same treatment they give the woman, if that makes any sense.

"That's about all I have to say, as your Dutch Uncle. I think you're a pretty damned good guy, please don't disappoint me with Meredith."

Abe stared out the windshield for at least a minute. At last, he said, "Thank you for caring enough to have this talk. I think we can agree it would never have come from Uncle Raymond and sure wouldn't have been said the same way. I'd like to think I'm one of those guys you'd like me to be and I know I treat women with respect and kindness. My Aunt Beaulah is a good example of the woman you refer to. She just has really really bad taste in men and now she's stuck with that jerk. I don't plan to ever be like that, believe me. Meredith and I are taking it slow," he laughed. "We haven't slept together though under the present circumstances, you're making it awfully convenient to do so. We're old enough and smart enough to see what's going on and we both feel the same way toward each other. I hope you don't think I'm trying to tell you what you want to hear because I'm not. You've been incredibly good to me and believe me I appreciate it. I'm trying to be the guy you hope I'll be and I'll never let you down.

"Now why can't we go with you?"

"Ever heard the phrase 'need to know?'"

"Sure, the military hides behind it all the time."

"We're trying to keep the number of people who know about the Shrine to a manageable number. The old saying, words to the effect, 'Three may keep a secret if two are dead,' applies. I'm not saying Meredith can't keep a secret but anyone of us can slip up so why tempt fate any more than necessary? By the way, that phrase comes originally from *Poor Richard's Almanac* authored by Benjamin Franklin in the late 1700s. Even then people had trouble keeping a secret.

"We don't want this to turn to into a safari. We'd create a path with neon lights if we did that to start with, and equipping that many people and watching out for their safety just isn't practical for an excursion like this. I would have bowed out myself but neither Carlos nor Rita know anything about cameras and these photographs need to be at least adequate. Carlos obviously needs to go and Rita needs to see what she's going to be pitching to the President of the Navajo Nation."

"*She's* going to do that?" Abe exclaimed.

"From what you and Carlos tell me, finding this Shrine is like opening a sealed crypt in an Egyptian pyramid, it's that significant. We need to treat it right and take it to the people who can help preserve it; otherwise, it stays in the ground forever.

"Besides, you're going to have your hands full getting ready for school and by the time this all settles down, it will be darn near time to go to Tucson."

"Okay, I understand. Meredith will be disappointed that she's not in on it but she'll get over it. Can you think of anything we can do to help the cause?"

"Stay away from Bluff and Mexican Hat," said Bob. "I don't want those two hyenas to get you in a crossfire, okay?"

"You don't have to say it twice."

They got out of the pickup and walked over to where Carlos sat alone at a table on the veranda. "Where are the girls?" Abe asked.

"They are in Rita's car probably having the same discussion you two just had."

And they were.

"Meredith, if I know your mother, you two have already had the mother-daughter-sex-where-do-babies-come-from talk a long time ago. This isn't the same talk. I don't know how involved you have been with boys and it's none of my business to know. What I want to bring up – probably once again – how important taking precautions before having sex is. I'm sure you know single mothers your age or a little older and realize how an unexpected baby screws up your life. That's all I'm going to say other than be nice to Abe, I think he's a good one, and I don't want to see either of you hurt."

"Thank you, Aunt Rita, for not belaboring the point. I am *fully* educated, believe me, and I don't plan on messing up my life by being careless or reckless. I like Abe, a *lot*. We've talked about it and agreed that we want to take it slow. If it happens, it won't be a 'heat of the moment' wrestle in the back seat of a car like others have experienced. I want it to be right and so does he. But I can assure you, we'll be careful."

"That's all I can ask for, sweetheart. Your welfare, and Abe's are my chief concerns and I'd feel really bad if either one of you got hurt. We both know that sometimes that's unavoidable but let's try to be as gentle as possible, okay?"

"I understand. Now. Maybe I should have the same talk with you, after all you'll be very close to a nice-looking man and though I haven't seen the signs yet, I feel he's interested and we both know it's time for you to 'broaden your horizons.'"

"You know, I thought that the very first time I saw both of them. *These are good ones!* I won't push him away, but I don't think I'm quite ready to make the first move," said Rita with a smile.

"You're an intelligent, very attractive woman," said Meredith, "don't waste it. They walked back arm in arm to where Carlos was sitting. Abe and Bob were there and the three of them were laughing about something.

Abe gave Meredith a sheepish grin which she bounced back at him. "Okay," said Rita, "let's get this show on the road."

"Rita," said Bob, "what do you think of the kids using your SUV and us going up on the Mesa with the two pickups? I recall the road being very rough and rutted and I'd hate to ding up your SUV when the pickups can drive right over the rocks and ruts."

"I was going to suggest that," said Rita as she dug in her purse, retrieved her keys and handed them to Meredith. "It's full of gas and there's a gas credit card in the glove box if you need it. Just take care of my baby, I'm very fond of her!"

Meredith nodded then she and Abe shifted his gear over to the Highlander. With a wave, they were off, headed south toward Bluff then on to Montezuma Creek. Rita turned to Bob and said, "Since we both have to go into the town here, we might as well double up and kill two birds with one pickup."

Carlos stood up from the table and came down the steps into the parking lot. "Most of the gear we'll need is already in my pickup," he said, "but there's a man in Bluff who makes the best jerky around and I would like to take some along. I will meet you at the Twin Rocks Trading Post at noon. We can have lunch, then head for the Mesa."

The two pickups drove off in opposite directions. Bob's first stop was Clark's Market in Blanding. Instead of coming back for Rita, Bob went in with her and they did what grocery shopping was necessary. They were careful not to buy perishable food since there would be no way to keep it cold – Carlos had made it clear they were *not* packing in an ice chest!

From Clark's, they drove right to Cedar Breaks Trading Post and Bob contacted the same man from whom he had rented the drone. "Photographic equipment? We have a little, but nothing to brag about; people use their phones these days."

"Can you show me what you do have," asked Bob, a little let down.

The clerk led them into the back and pulled down two boxes from a shelf. "This is all I have, a decent DSLR and an older commercial quality digital video camera. I don't even know if the batteries are still good."

"Can we test them – the batteries in the video camera?"

"Yeah, sure. Let me just slip one into the camera. I'll be damned! It shows three quarters charged and this thing hasn't been out of here in eight months to a year. It comes with four long life lithium/ion batteries and I can be sure to charge them up before you need 'em."

Bob shook his head. "I need it all, like now. Can you test the others?"

The clerk nodded and went to work. "While I'm testing the others, I have the first one charging; it was the one in the camera."

To Bob and Rita's relief, the other three batteries were fully charged. "Let's go look at sporting goods while it charges," Rita suggested.

"What kind of sporting goods?" asked the clerk.

"We need a medium weight sleeping bag and a ground pad. I suppose we'll have to buy them?"

"Yeah, we don't rent stuff like that out – too personal. But I have a good variety and you're welcome to take a look while the battery charges." At Bob's nod, the clerk led them to shelves of backpacking equipment including all kinds of sleeping bags and pads.

The clerk immediately showed them a moderately-priced bag that he said would not be good for cold weather, but for the kind of weather they had been having it was a good fit. They took it and

Rita picked out a bright pink high-density foam ground pad that she thought would be adequate. They carried them up to the check stand then went to see how the battery was doing.

It was up over three-quarters. Bob asked, "What kind of data storage does the camera use?"

"Well, it's older and doesn't use the newer micro cards. I would recommend one hundred twenty-eight GB SD cards"

"Okay," said Bob, "we'll take four of them."

"Man, you must be planning on doing some serious shooting."

Bob smiled thinly, "You have no idea. I assume the video camera shoots quality digital stills as well as video?"

"Oh, yes, and on the same card if you want."

"What about lights. Do you have any battery-powered floods on tripods?" asked Bob, knowing the answer as soon as he asked.

"Can't help you there but I have an aftermarket flood for the video camera that I got so people could do weddings in the evening and such."

"How well does it work?"

"I've never shot in low light before but I'm told people need to squint when the light is too close. Luckily the camera has an excellent zoom feature and you can adjust the amount of light you want."

"And that attaches to the camera, in the shoe?"

"Yup. They work together like they were made for each other."

"You have a tripod for the camera?"

"Yup, three as a matter of fact, take your pick."

By the time they finished talking storage cards, lights and haggling over the price, the battery was topped off and ready to go."

Bob was glad to see that it all fit into a fairly small padded duffle bag.

When he finished paying for everything, he and Rita carried it out to the pickup and put it in the back seat.

Suddenly Rita stopped. "Uh oh. I forgot about freeze-dried meals. We'd better go back in and get some."

Bob grinned. "Carlos said he cached a lot of them and they don't expire until 2053."

"2053 huh? *That* should be interesting."

"Both he and Abe say they're pretty good; I guess we'll find out."

As they drove south toward Bluff, Bob said, "I hope the kids don't run into those two thugs that used to work for Robert Begay. I hate to think what might happen. I know Abe carries a knife all the time and it probably saved his hide one time that I saw. No one was cut but it wasn't because he wasn't willing. Henry Begay backed down or he would have died when he and that other yahoo kicked in Abe's door in Bluff."

"He's too young to have to deal with stuff like that," said Rita.

"I happen to agree with you, but the kids who are now joining the military and police forces are going to have to adjust. It's just the way of the world."

# CHAPTER 23

Carlos's pickup was already in the trading post lot when Bob and Rita arrived. They found him seated at a table inside sipping iced tea. "Were you successful?" he asked.

"I think so," said Bob. "At least on paper it looks like we are prepared to shoot pictures of half of Cedar Mesa. And you, did you find what you were looking for?"

"Yes. We are well-supplied now."

They ordered breakfast and as they waited, Rita said, "Carlos, do you think we should carry weapons?"

The Singer shook his head. "No, it is not necessary for we will see no one on this trip."

Rita just nodded, but Bob asked, "How can you know that?"

Carlos smiled. "My dreams told me," he said cryptically.

"Are they always right?" asked Bob.

"They are rarely in error."

"I guess that's good enough for me," said Bob as their food arrived.

There was little talk while they ate. When they finished, they all got up at the same time and Rita paid the bill. "We'll follow you up the hill, Carlos; you know the way better than I do," said Bob.

They set out for the Moki Dugway. Rita was excited about what she was finally going to witness. Bob was "up" more because

Rita was, but looked forward to the experience. She was on his mind a good portion of the time and he chastised himself and tried to keep his mind on the task at hand. All three kept watch for a green and white Ford pickup which was a no-show, much to their relief.

They passed through the Moki Dugway without saying much but when they got to the turn off to Harley's off Highway 261, Bob reminded Rita to cinch up her seat belt because the going would be a lot rougher. The track did not disappoint her as they followed Carlos into Harley Uskilith's camp. She thought it prudent that he asked her to note the latitude and longitude from his portable GPS receiver as they made each turn.

"I was thinking that Abe has only been to the Shrine once and his memory, though probably better than ours, might be affected by being around Meredith. A map can't hurt as long as we keep it safe."

They bounced and jostled to a stop at Harley's. He came out of his shelter and expressed relief that Carlos was alive and well. The story he had heard about the shootout at Millie Nez's place wasn't quite as accurate as Jim Campbell's, and he had been under the impression that Carlos was in the thick of things. Carlos corrected the misconceptions then turned to preparing to outfit them by extracting three large backpacks from the back seat and setting them up on the tailgate of his pickup. Bob and Rita laid out what they had acquired but let Carlos do the packing.

When he was satisfied, Carlos didn't wait around but donned his pack and looked expectantly at Bob and Rita. They did the same, said goodbye to Harley, and followed Carlos out of camp and down into the wash. Rita was an old hand at backpacking and fell right into a rhythm; this was all new to Bob, however, and though he was in pretty good shape, he would be using several muscles he rarely used.

The two hours to the first rest stop got Bob's attention, but he found that though he was sweating and puffing a bit, he was able to hold his own and keep the coordinate map up-to-date. He was grateful for the water stop, however, but ready to go when Carlos led off again. Carlos deliberately led a slower pace than he had with Abe. Bob and Rita were both unknown quantities to him and he didn't want them to overdo it. They rested once more after a couple more hours before entering the woods and the last mile to Carlos's cave.

When they arrived, Carlos explained about the spring and the necessity of keeping it uncontaminated. When he had things laid out, he brewed some tea and they all sat out on the "verandah" to discuss the next leg of their journey.

"The trails to the Shrine are much less defined than those we have been on so far. As a matter of fact, I think I created part of them when I was stomping around trying to find the Shrine in the first place. Dreams do not include latitude and longitude coordinates. I think your creating a map is a good thing as long as it stays secure. Where will you store it?"

"I thought to give it to you," said Bob. "Maybe a safe deposit box or something equally as secure?"

"Perhaps Rita would be a better custodian," said Carlos, "I'm just an old Singer and would not know about a safe deposit box or even a safe for that matter."

Rita smiled. "I'll do it Carlos," she said, patting his knee. What about copies?"

"I don't think there should be *any* copies. The less evidence of the Shrine's existence, the better," Bob opined.

"You are probably right," said Carlos. "Fewer things to steal." He changed the subject abruptly, "Is anyone hungry?"

"You know, now that you mention it," said Bob, "It *is* about time to eat."

"What sounds good? I have a pretty good selection."

"Just so it isn't liver or *menudo*."

Carlos went into the back of the cave and came out with three pouches. "Lasagna with meat sauce, chili mac with beef and buffalo style chicken mac and cheese. Who wants what?"

They made their choices and Carlos started water boiling. "Bob, you set the table – all three spoons. Rita, is there any tea left?" They were set up to eat on the "verandah" in the late afternoon sunshine.

Both Bob and Rita were pleasantly surprised at the flavor and quality of their freeze-dried meals and ate heartily. "I'm afraid I do not have anything for dessert," said Carlos with a smile.

"Doesn't matter," said Bob, "I've had plenty and it was pretty darn good too! Rita? How about you?"

"It was almost more than I could handle but I forced myself," she said. "Carlos, you are quite a cook."

"We can have more of these – breakfast versions – tomorrow, or just jerky and trail mix like Abe and I did."

"The latter sounds just fine to me," said Rita and Bob nodded in agreement.

By the time they finished, the sun was just about setting. Carlos brought out sleeping bags for himself and Bob, and Rita got the new bag with the sleeping pad. "You can spread the pad out anywhere you won't be walked on, but I suggest you stay in the cave instead of sleeping outside."

As they settled down as darkness fell, Bob asked, "How long is our hike tomorrow, Carlos?"

"Not quite as long as today," Carlos answered. "Everyone be sure to top off your canteen, there's no water where we're going."

As soon as everyone made themselves comfortable, they fell asleep – no tossing and turning after the day's hike.

Carlos was awake with the dawn and his rustlings soon had the others up and raring to go. They first had tea, jerky and trail mix, but were eager to be on the trail. Thirty minutes later they were skirting the talus slope headed toward the Shrine.

Carlos's estimate of the time to target was just a little slow since he was still favoring his hiking companions. They made it to the rim of the canyon without incident and carefully started down on what there was of a steep, treacherous trail. Forty-five minutes later they were standing on the ledge next to the piñon pine trees and

Carlos was explaining how they had to crawl in, pushing their packs ahead of them.

Bob was a little stouter than the two Navajos and had to struggle a little to get through the narrowest part before he could stand up. Both were speechless when they saw what Carlos had discovered.

"It's beyond words, Carlos," Rita exclaimed, "more even than what you described."

"That's a lot of work done down through the centuries by, presumably, the *Hatáli* caretakers," said Bob, examining some of the petroglyphs in the light of his flashlight. He set to work right away pulling out the tripod and the light to go with the camera. "Carlos, Rita? What do you think? Pan each grotto before zooming in on each panel of petroglyphs. Do you think they need to be so close you can see the depth of cut?"

"I would think these photographs and videos are going to be more for interpretation rather than technique," said Rita. "Just so long as every exposure isn't too dark or too light."

"Yes," said Carlos. "I had envisioned these photographs being analyzed by experts *and* being used for brochures, books and individual exposures. You're going to be famous, Bob."

"Hell, I don't care about being famous. I just want to be sure we do a good workmanlike job of photographing this place."

Bob experimented in the first grotto, trying different light intensities and zoom lens settings until he was satisfied he'd found the right combination. Rita was right there with him, moving his equipment as necessary and offering suggestions. Periodically they stopped to replay what had been shot and, as near as they could tell, the work product was excellent. There was more than a little flirting going on that amused Carlos who just stood back and watched, as there was little for him to do.

That first night they made little hills and valleys in the sand to cushion their bodies against the hard floor. They wrapped themselves in their space blankets and found that except for the moisture they generated inside the blanket, they were quite comfortable. The second morning Bob was mortified to find that, in his sleep, he had snuggled close to Rita – or *vice versa* – and she was spooned with her back up against his front. He woke with his arm curled around her torso and his hand cupping her breast.

When he tried to extricate himself, Rita awoke. "God I'm sorry, Rita, I was asleep, honestly."

As he tried to move his arm back, she clamped down on it with her own, halting his progress. "It's okay, really. I was wondering if you were *ever* going to make a move!" She turned her head around toward him and kissed him. "Not the most perfect setting for romance but it will do."

Carlos heard the whole exchange and just smiled in the dark.

It took them the day of their arrival, plus another full day to shoot the petroglyphs and pottery to everyone's satisfaction. They were down to their last battery but overestimated how much data storage they would need. All the extensive video and still photo work didn't quite fill up three of the data cards. Bob was relieved.

He didn't relish coming back to shoot what they couldn't fit on a memory card!

They were packed up and ready to go on the third morning and after a quick bite to eat, were crawling out of the tunnel to a bright sunny morning that blinded them for a bit. Once they could see, they began their climb back up to the rim, sometimes on all fours but always double checking foot placement and, when necessary, hand holds. They made it to the top without mishap and, after brushing the dust, dirt and detritus off, began their hike back to Carlos's cave. Bob had been double checking his map coordinates of their turns and was satisfied no errors had been made. He would continue checking them all the way to Harley's place.

The sun was just past its zenith when they arrived at Carlos's cave. They debated staying there overnight or continuing on but Carlos insisted they continue on. It meant another four or so hours of arduous hiking, but it also meant a hot shower, a hot meal and a soft bed! Carlos seemed quiet as they paused long enough to tidy up the cave and secure the caches. Carlos took extra care to be sure he was leaving nothing he might need or couldn't lose should someone or something invade the space.

They headed down Carlos's carefully constructed trail next to the talus slope until they reached the more level landscape of the forest. There the going was better and they made up some lost time. They stopped twice for water and a breather but each was feeling less apprehensive about the narrow trails the closer they made it to Harley's.

When they walked into Harley's camp, they found his ancient pickup gone and a note pinned to the door: *If you've come in early, I'm sorry I missed you. Had to go to town for supplies since no one will bring them to me now that you're gone.* Bob was gratified that Harley didn't name names, thus making the note's addressee more ambiguous.

Carlos and Bob retrieved their pickup keys from their packs and, after loading up their packs, headed back down toward the Moki Dugway. At the junction of Highway 261 and Highway 163, Carlos turned right. He wanted to confer with Adrian and maybe Adam Benally. Something was bothering him. Bob and Rita had estimated it would take them two or three days to edit the photographs and video then create a narrative to go along with them.

The moment Carlos was in the rearview mirror, Rita scooted over to the middle of the seat next to Bob. "I want to know how you plan to atone for groping me." said Rita in a husky voice, her eyes dancing.

"Well," said Bob with a grin, "since it isn't clear *who* snuggled up next to whom, I guess I'll bite the bullet and do the atoning. The question is where and how with the kids around?"

"Navajos are much more laid back and less hung up on matters of sex," said Rita. "How do you think Meredith and Abe would evaluate our talks of the other day if we tried to conceal the fact that we're attracted to each other and planned to take the next step in our relationship. When we get home – to Montezuma Creek – if we take both our packs into my bedroom, I think the situation will be pretty clear. If you slept in the other bedroom and tried to slip into my bedroom in the night or *vice versa,* they would probably conclude that we were ashamed of what we were doing and eventually that would have to be explained. They would also probably be confused about what we told them versus own actions. Let's just not tell them about your atoning for your previous misdeeds." With her last sentence, she laughed and put her hand on the inside of Bob's knee.

"I've been out of the dating or sex scene for so long, I don't know anything. I haven't been with a woman since Darby, my late wife, died fifteen years ago. I think I remember how it's supposed to go but the emotional part is alien. I never met a woman who measured up so I just kept to myself. Now, spending time with you seems almost disloyal but I know it isn't. I know she would not approve of the fact that I've been alone all these years. I guess I'm also asking you to bear with me."

"I'm no better off than you are, Bob. I haven't even looked at another man since my husband died and I know what you mean about maybe feeling disloyal. I say let's find out together what happens next. Whatever happens, as long as it's honest, the kids will adapt."

As they drove toward Bluff, Bob leaned over and kissed Rita. Not a passionate, even lingering kiss, but an honest, *I'm pretty sure I like you* kiss that made their conversation seem just right.

It was getting dark by the time they got to Bluff. "We probably ought to have dinner here, what do you think?"

299

Rita snuggled up closer to him and said, "Sounds about right to me."

They walked into the trading post restaurant and found it nearly empty. As the hostess approached, Rita asked, "Are we too late for dinner?"

"Not at all," said the new girl who had apparently replaced Meredith.

As she seated them, Bob asked, "We heard what happened to Mr. Begay. Who's running the place now?"

The girl looked around her before answering, "This place is a zoo. The rumor is that Mr. Begay was not only embezzling money from the store *and* the restaurant but he also was getting kickbacks from the suppliers. They're doing an audit and it doesn't look good for the assistant manager either, but you didn't hear that from me."

They both nodded as they ordered drinks and picked up their menus. "Well! That's hard to believe that a man as well off as Robert Begay would be tapping the till. Maybe that's *why* he was well off … that and selling drugs," said Rita with a grimace.

A waitress appeared and took their orders then they were left pretty much alone. "When Abe goes off to school, what are you going to do with yourself?" asked Rita.

"I'm not sure. I almost feel like a parent toward him since I don't think Carlos is up to filling that role. As such, I'm inclined to stay close to home or Tucson in case he needs something he can't handle himself, at least for this first semester. He seems a pretty self-reliant kid, and smart as a whip, but he lacks experience and confidence. That will come with socialization, something he's been short on most of his life I suspect. I figure he's worth the effort and, after all, what else can I do with my time? You'll be going back to school pretty soon too I assume?"

"I hate to say this because I'm afraid you'll think badly of me but yes, I'll be going back to teaching unless I get a better offer. This Shrine project will require quite a bit of time for a while depending on what the President decides to do about it. I want to be right in the middle of that because it deserves our best effort. What a magnificent find!"

"A better offer … as in a fulltime job working on the Shrine project or …?"

"Oh, I'm not hinting at a fulltime relationship with you," said Rita, "I figure that will take care of itself … after you atone, that is." She smiled as she said the last, rubbing Bob's shin under the table with her foot.

"What if I suggested you go with me on a grand tour of the red rock country? Could you do that or is it too soon to even contemplate?"

"Probably a little early, although I hate the idea of starting a new school year with my kids then leaving them part way through. I really get attached to some of them."

"I can imagine. I'm not asking yet. Hell, I'm not even contemplating that for myself though I *will* do it someday. I kind of like the idea of an RV full of my own stuff instead of someone else's motel room not knowing what happened in there the night before. It's pleasant food for thought so tuck that in the back of your head."

Their food came and their conversation died down as they ate. They finished, paid the check then headed out to Bob's pickup. "Time to go see what the kiddies are up to," said Bob with a grin. Rita's words about the Navajo attitude toward sex had dampened some of his apprehension about leaving Abe and Meredith by themselves. He guessed it was too late to worry about it now.

As he reached the pickup, his phone rang. It was Carlos. "Something is wrong … with the children," he said. "Henry Begay and Walter Bitsillie are involved and I think they have taken Meredith."

"My God," Bob exclaimed, alarming Rita. "We're in Bluff heading that way. Can you tell us any more? How did you find out?"

"It was a dream and it took me some time to make sense of it. I am on the way from Mexican Hat."

# CHAPTER 24

As she drove them away from the Twin Rocks Trading Post, Meredith asked Abe, "Do you want to go home and get settled or would you prefer to go shopping? You could do the shopping online but getting it here in time before you leave might be a problem."

"Yeah, I thought so too. Are there any places in Blanding? You must know it better than I do," Abe replied.

"There are a few stores not counting the trading posts that sell mostly touristy stuff. There's a WalMart in Cortez and that's about all for department stores."

"How far is Cortez?"

"Probably a little over an hour."

"Can we go to Cortez? This credit card is burning a hole in my pocket!" Abe joked.

"Oh, I can imagine. Okay, it's off to Cortez. We'll be going right through Montezuma Creek in case you want to stop."

"Nah, let's get this over with. Will you help me with colors and styles?"

"With pleasure," Meredith replied with a smile, patting his knee.

Neither noticed a green and white Ford pickup trailing just far enough back to not be spotted.

Meredith turned onto Highway 162 just out of Bluff. They drove through Montezuma Creek and Aneth before eventually making a left turn onto Highway 160. After one more turn, left onto Highway 491 they drove into Cortez.

"Do you need the address for the GPS?" asked Abe.

"Nope, Aunt Rita and I have been over here enough, I know the way." Soon they came to a massive parking lot surrounding a large WalMart super center and she found a parking space almost right in front. They walked in, hand in hand, grabbed a cart and began their search in earnest. They were clueless as to the presence of the green and white pickup which parked several lanes over, almost, but not quite out of sight.

Abe and Meredith spent most of the next hour finding and selecting everything from socks and underwear to jeans and shirts. Abe felt he had enough shoes but was eager to see what the store had in the way of laptop computers. They wound up in the electronics section and Abe set to work comparing the features of several models in the price range he had selected. He finally picked one and, at Meredith's suggestion chose an inexpensive printer and supplies to go with it. Storage media, paper and the usual assortment of necessary items were next and when it was all rung up, Abe was gobsmacked.

"I can't spend that much of Bob's money, especially when he's not here to approve it!" Abe protested.

"He gave you his credit card for a reason. He knows it's going to cost some money to get ready for college and he told you to buy what you needed, didn't he?" said Meredith.

"Well, yeah, but …."

"That's what you've been doing and you haven't been buying the most expensive stuff by a long shot. You got what you're going to need, so just sign the receipt and let's get going."

"I still feel bad about it," said Abe, "I'll find a way to pay him back."

"Whatever," sniffed Meredith, "If he hadn't expressly told you to get what you needed, I might look at this a little differently but I heard him say it."

They got everything loaded into the back of the Highlander and got in. "It's past time for lunch," said Meredith, "where do you want to go?"

"Oh, a burger is fine with me, you?"

"Okay. There's a Wendy's down the street. We can go in, sit down and eat. We're not in such a big of a hurry that we have to eat on the fly."

They walked in, ordered their food and found a table. "Can you think of anything else I need?" Abe asked.

"You still need some spiral notebooks or something in which to take notes. I hear there's a lot of that to do since just about all the time you're in class, the instructor is lecturing."

"Oh yeah! I forgot about that. I can probably get those just about anywhere."

Meredith nodded and smiled. "I think the computer case was a really good idea. Do you think your backpack will hold all your new clothes?"

"Oh yeah, it was pretty empty."

"So now we have at least three days with nothing to do but get us both packed. Got any ideas what we can do?" Meredith asked, a glint in her eye.

"Well, what do you say we head back to Montezuma Creek and start washing the contaminants out of these duds before I pack them?" asked Abe.

"Yes, and you need to set up that laptop and put in a password."

"Yeah, I forgot about that. That shouldn't take too long, just load some new software and get it arranged the way I'm used to."

"Considering your uncle, I'm surprised you had a computer."

"Oh, I didn't, it was issued by my school."

As they chattered, they walked up to the Highlander without seeing the green and white Ford pickup parked two blocks away under a juniper tree.

"Let's just go grab him!" growled Walter Bitsillie. "He ain't lookin' around or nothin'."

Surprisingly, since Robert Begay's death, without a mentor, Henry Begay had become more circumspect about their activities. "Nah, not in Blanding," Henry replied, we're wanted here and there are too many cops around. Once he gets out in the county away from town, we'll see what develops."

Walter sighed heavily in disgust but had to admit his partner was right. Outside the city, cops were few and far between. He popped the caps on a couple more beers.

They watched the Highlander pull away from the Wendy's parking lot and work its way south through town. Henry was driving and his poor old brain was working overtime trying to figure out the last part of an idea for a plan he was thinking about.

Meredith drove them back the way they had come, staying within speed limit and driving with caution. She particularly did not want to damage her aunt's pride-and-joy Highlander and took extra precautions. Abe had noticed but had, thus far, said nothing. They rode mostly in silence, each occupied with his or her own thoughts. They would have been surprised to know that each was thinking primarily about the other! It seemed to take an eternity to drive the sixty miles from Cortez to Montezuma Creek and both of them were tense and nervous when they arrived.

Meredith popped out first, then opened the back and retrieved Abe's clothing bags. Over her shoulder she told Abe to grab his laptop and peripherals. She was so tense, he wondered if she was mad at him or something.

By the time he made it into the house, Meredith had dropped her parcels on the couch and turned to face him. Before he could unload his packages, she had her arms around his neck and was kissing him passionately. Abe wanted to reciprocate in the worst way but he was encumbered by the computer and printer boxes and a few bags of supplies.

Finally he was able to shunt the cargo off onto a chair then took Meredith in his arms and returned her kisses just as passionately. Without breaking the embrace, they moved as one impassioned being through the small living room and down the hall to Meredith's bedroom.

"What are our kids going to say when they learn this is how mom and dad began?" he mumbled against her neck.

"I don't care," she breathed, pressing herself against him.

*The remainder of this encounter, dear Reader, must remain confidential for these two characters are only seventeen and this narrator does not want child pornography charges brought against him. Suffice it to say, it was a mutually satisfying experience for both of them, and for the next two days they didn't leave the house!*

"What the *hell* are they doing in there?" muttered Walter. "Are they even still there?"

"Oh," said Henry, "they're in there. You can't think what kids that age would be doing when no one else is around? You're dumber'n I thought."

"Huh! Never thought of that. They're just *kids!"*

"Tell that to their raging hormones."

"So how are we going to get him out of there?"

"I've been thinking about that and have concluded that it doesn't matter which one comes out first. We'll take whoever shows up. Having the girl will really motivate the kid, especially after what they've been doing. If we get to him first, the girl will raise hell, especially when the adults show up from wherever they've been."

"How long do we gotta wait?"

"Until our opportunity arrives."

Their opportunity arrived about an hour later. Meredith had come out of the house, headed to Bluff for take-out food. Henry instantly started the pickup and timed his approach to the Highlander just as Meredith reached the driver's door. He skidded to a stop behind the Highlander and yelled to Walter to pull his gun and hijack the vehicle and the girl. "Make her drive and follow me."

Meredith was already in the Highlander by the time Walter ripped open the front passenger door and climbed in, pointing the pistol at Meredith. "Just do as you're told and nobody has to get hurt," he said. "Follow the pickup and don't ask any questions."

Once Walter appeared to have control of the Highlander, Henry spun gravel as he went around the SUV and sped down the road. Abe had just appeared on the porch in response to the Ford's revving motor and the spinning gravel. He saw, in a glance, what was happening and jumped off the porch in pursuit of the departing Highlander but he was too late.

Abe dashed back into the house for his phone and, after fumbling the call twice, got through to the 911 operator. "911, what is your emergency?" a competent female voice asked.

"My girlfriend! She was just carjacked and the attacker is making her drive the car away!"

"Okay, calm down sir, I need to get some information. Do you live at 841 E. Fir in Montezuma Creek?"

"No, that's my girlfriend's address but it's where I'm calling from. Please get the cops after them; they're heading toward Bluff."

"What is your name, sir?"

"Who cares about that right now," yelled Abe into the phone.

"Calm down sir, we need that information."

"She's driving a silver Toyota Highlander and following an old green and white Ford pickup."

"Why is she following the pickup?"

"Because there's a guy in the Highlander with her and he has a gun. The guy in the Highlander is Walter Bitsillie and the driver of the pickup is Henry Begay. They're both wanted."

"Sir, are you following them?"

"No, I have no transportation."

"Okay, I have toned out the Sheriff's Office and the Highway Patrol. The closest unit is in Monticello."

"You don't have anyone any closer?" Abe shrieked.

"No sir, we're spread pretty thin."

"Can't you notify *someone?*" asked Abe, almost beside himself with frustration and disbelief.

"I'm sorry, sir, it's the best we can do. Now please calm down. I need your name."

"Abe Red Wolf."

"What is your address?"

"I don't have one. I'm in between. I'm starting college this fall at the University of Arizona but I don't know that address. Use the one here for now," he said sullenly.

"And your phone number is the one you're calling from?"

"Yes."

Just then Bob and Rita drove up. They were out of the pickup in a flash and went to Abe who was standing on the porch near tears. He had hung up with the dispatcher after being told to wait there for an officer.

"Abe? Are you okay?"

"Y... yeah. It's just that the cops are so far away they'll never catch those two before they go to ground. It was Henry Begay and Walter Bitsillie. They carjacked Meredith when she started to go to Bluff."

"Was she hurt?" asked Rita, holding her breath.

"No, I don't think so. She was driving and Walter had a gun on her."

"What do we need to do, Abe?" asked Bob.

"We can't go fast enough to chase after them, besides, we don't know where they're going."

"Maybe we'll get lucky and Carlos will spot them. He's on his way from Mexican Hat," said Bob.

"How did you guys know? For that matter, why aren't you still up on the Mesa?"

"Carlos insisted we not stop at his place but get to Harley's, so we came down a day early. He dreamed this was going to happen. I'll never doubt his dreams again!" said Bob.

"Bob?" asked Rita, "What can we do?"

"Not go all to pieces to begin with. We have to figure out where they've taken her. They'll be using her as pressure against Abe and therefore Carlos so they're bound to call."

Just then Bob's phone rang. "Hello," he said impatiently.

"Mr. Connelly? This is Detective Gene Whittaker. I understand we may be joining forces again?"

"It sounds like it," Bob replied. "Henry Begay and Walter Bitsillie have kidnapped Abe's girlfriend from in front of her house in Montezuma Creek. They got away; we have no idea where they might have taken her. We're very worried for her welfare, these are not nice men."

"Bad news, Bob, that's Navajo Nation, I have no jurisdiction. Is there a crime scene?"

"Not really. She drove away in it with Bitsillie holding a gun on her."

"Are there any witnesses?

"Just Abe, he saw them all drive away toward Bluff."

"Is he okay? Was he injured?"

"No. He chased them down the street on foot but you know how that ended up."

"Is he calmed down enough to where I can talk to him?"

"Sure, I'll put him on." Bob mouthed *Detective Whittaker* to Abe as he handed him the phone.

As Detective Whittaker spoke with Abe, Bob said to Rita, "I *HATE* crime scenes where there's nothing we can do. As soon as Abe is done talking to the detective, I'm going to have the detective run previous addresses for these two and we're going to check every one of them whether the occupants like it or not. Obviously this crime was committed on the Navajo Nation so the Sheriff's Office can't get involved. You doing okay?"

Rita shrugged. "Doesn't help much to go all to pieces, and I can see that everything that can be done is being done. I wish Carlos would get here, maybe there was more to his dream that might help."

"I'd go down to the place where the shootout occurred but Jim Campbell told me both the house and the barn were burned down to the ground by the warring cartels during the gunfight. Millie Nez died in the fire.

There's nothing left in which to hide her."

"I just hope they call soon," said Rita with a shudder. "They'd better not hurt that girl or their lives will be forfeit."

"I know what you mean and I'm with you a hundred percent. They've had all the breaks they're going to get."

Bob put his arms around Rita who snuggled in for comfort. They weren't lovers yet, due to happenstance, but from their conversation they might just as well be.

"Oh damn!" said Bob suddenly. "I should have called Carlos right away so he could keep an eye out for them. Can you call him? Do you know his number?"

Rita pulled back and reached in her purse and came out with her phone. "I have him in my phone book." She looked at Bob after she punched in the number. "I hope he pulls over first, I'm not sure he uses Bluetooth and this would be a lousy time to wreck his pickup." The phone rang and rang but Rita wasn't willing to hang up. If it went to voice mail, she would leave a message, but if he was just pulling over to answer; she wanted to be on the line.

Finally, "Yes, hello?" said Carlos.

"Carlos?"

"Yes."

"Bob needs to talk to you, here he is." She handed her phone to Bob.

"Carlos, where are you exactly?"

I am at Highway 163 where Highway 191 comes in."

"Begay and Bitsillie kidnapped Meredith in her aunt's silver Toyota Highlander. They're following Henry in that green and white Ford pickup. Have you seen it?"

"No and I would have noticed. Do you want me to start checking known places?"

"No, come on into Montezuma Creek, the address is …."

Bob looked at Rita, who said, "841 E Fir."

Bob repeated it to Carlos then asked, "Think you can find that?"

"Yes."

Carlos disconnected the call.

"Okay, thank you," said Abe as he disconnected the call with Detective Whittaker and handed the phone back to Bob.

"Damn," said Bob. "I was going to ask him to check known addresses."

"He's already doing it. If he finds anything, he'll let us know, said Abe."

"Good. Carlos is probably close to Bluff by now, heading this way."

"Let's go in the house," said Rita. Once in the living room, no one seemed to know what to do with him or herself. Finally, Rita asked if anyone wanted anything to drink. To give her something to do, Bob asked for coffee.

Henry Begay turned off the highway onto the road leading into the Valley of the Gods. Once he was out of sight of the highway, he stopped and Meredith pulled in behind him. Henry started to walk over to the passenger side of the SUV and Walter said, "Turn off the ignition and give me the keys. Don't try to run or you'll get hurt."

Meredith did as she was told. She was scared - the presence of the gun frightened her - but the whole thing was making her mad. She sat there fuming, waiting for a chance to unload on someone.

Walter had already rolled down the window as Henry walked up. "That went pretty smooth," said Henry with a grin.

"Yeah. But now what? Where we gonna stash her?"

"I have the perfect place," said Henry smugly. "They'll never think to look there."

"Where?"

"Just follow me, you'll see."

# CHAPTER 25

Carlos parked his pickup behind Bob's and Abe met him at the door. Abe told him what happened and that they were still waiting for a deputy to show up. "Carlos, can you think of anything else from your dream?"

"I've thought about nothing else since I learned what happened," said Carlos. "All I remember other than what I've told you is dark."

"As in no light at all?" asked Bob.

"There was not enough light to see where she was."

"Was there any sound? Like if she was in a closet she would hear house sounds."

"Absolutely quiet. Wait … it was cool. Not frosty but cooler than you'd be outside."

"Like maybe a basement?" asked Rita.

"It did not seem like a basement."

Just then there was a knock at the door and Rita let an officer from the Navajo Nation Police in. He took a report including the stolen vehicle and Rita gave him the license number and color. "I'll obtain the information on Begay's pickup from Blanding PD and get it and your car entered into the statewide and nationwide computer systems. Do you folks have any idea where to look for these two?"

"Believe me, if we did, we'd be there now!" Bob exclaimed.

"I have to advise you not to get involved in the investigation," said the officer. "Not only is it against the law, Obstruction of Justice, but you might wind up hindering the investigation and you don't want that."

"No," Bob said with a grim smile, "we don't want that."

"Wasn't the FBI notified already? I thought kidnapping was their jurisdiction," asked Rita.

"They were but, quite frankly, they're slow to respond, especially when locals, on the reservation are involved. I personally suspect they kind of drag their feet in hopes the matter will resolve itself."

"So essentially, this kidnapping and carjacking report gets the salient details, i.e. license numbers and suspects, entered in the nationwide computers but there really isn't any active investigation?" asked Rita, getting red-faced.

The officer could see the storm brewing. "Ms. Makespeace, if we knew where to look, or if you had information that we could use to track her down, we'd be all over it," said the officer. "If you have any suggestions at all how we can proceed further, you only have to tell us and we'll take action but we can't draw leads out of thin air."

Rita wilted. "I suppose not," she said with a deep sigh, leaning into Bob.

The officer left a card with a case number on it and left. "Now what?" asked Rita listlessly.

"We contact everyone who knows these two and try to come up with places they might go. They don't strike me as outdoorsy types so I would expect they'd hole up with friends, relatives or in abandoned places. I guess it's pretty much the same as when we were searching for Carlos except I doubt these two will be found in the wild."

Bob's phone rang. It was Adrian Tso. "You still lookin' for Henry and Walter?"

"More than ever. They kidnapped a young girl today and stole her aunt's car."

"You mean they're into sex trafficking now?" asked Adrian incredulously.

"No, they're not that smart and don't have the connections, why?"

"Well, I just saw them in Mexican Hat. They told me they would be leaving the country pretty soon … soon as they make one last big score. I have no idea what they meant but they seemed pretty smug."

"Any idea where they went?"

"None, but they were heading for the bridge onto Indian Country, two cars, the pickup and a silver SUV."

"Adrian, we're trying desperately to locate these two for the girl's sake. If you hear anything, *please* call, and spread the word. And thank you for calling, I owe you one."

"That was Adrian," said Bob. "The Dynamic Duo was just in Mexican Hat bragging about making a big score and blowing town."

"Let's get going!" cried Abe, "maybe we'll run into them!"

"Even those two aren't that stupid," said Bob. "They're already long gone out of town but it makes me wonder. Adrian said they headed across the river. What kind of contacts do they have between there and Kayenta besides the old lady's burned out place? Maybe we should spend the day wandering around down there and trying to find people who know them. Besides, I want another look at Millie Nez's place."

"You guys ready for dinner?" asked Rita.

"I am," said Abe.

"Please say you're not thinking of cooking after a day like today," said Bob.

"Well, we have to eat," she said.

"I know, we've probably worn out our welcome at Twin Rocks but let's let them do the cooking, at least for this evening. Okay?"

Over dinner they hashed and rehashed how they should go about finding Meredith. Over and over it came down to getting out there and beating the brush in the right area. Kayenta was at the top of everyone's list and they finally decided they'd just split up into two pairs and start knocking on doors. Someone *had* to know something.

319

That night, Abe took the room he had been using, and Carlos the other spare room. That left Bob either on the couch or in Rita's bed and even Abe could see how that was going to wind up. Abe didn't say a word but he was pleased that those two were getting involved, especially now, when Rita really needed someone to lean on.

They said their good nights and Bob followed Rita into her room. He was surprised to find his backpack already there. She turned and came into his arms.

"Thank you for insisting we eat out. I am so stressed worrying about Meredith I don't know which way is up. Do you mind if your "atonement" is delayed a bit longer? I want you here, in bed with me but I don't think I'd be much fun in the frolicking department."

Relieved, Bob said so. "We have plenty of time for that, but the timing needs to be right and this isn't it. Let's just try to get some sleep so we can function effectively tomorrow. Bob stripped down to his boxer shorts and Rita donned a short nightie. They clambered onto each side of the bed and immediately embraced in the middle.

"If something happens to that girl, I don't know how I'll face her parents. She's the oldest and, though they'd never say it out loud, the favorite. Losing her would be devastating – for the whole clan."

Bob kissed the tip of her nose and said, "Then we won't let anything bad happen. She's already got her hands full with school coming up and Abe."

Rita rolled over then wiggled backward until she was spooned up against Bob. "I'm *so* glad you're here," she sighed as she took his hand and cupped it around her breast. They maintained that position late into the night, neither wanting to break the mood. Finally one, then the other nodded off to sleep.

In spite of the late night, they both woke up refreshed and a shower together didn't hurt, but the time of atonement had not yet arrived. Abe had taken it upon himself to get up early and had driven into Blanding for bagels and cream cheese to go with their coffee.

Over breakfast, they divided Kayenta in half and agreed on how they would proceed. Abe and Carlos took the southern half and left the rest to Bob and Rita. They set off shortly thereafter.

Bob stopped at the driveway into the late Millie Nez's place. It was forlorn with only a couple of very small closet-sized structures still standing. Bob discovered the gate into the property closed and chained with a new padlock. A new "No Trespassing" sign was mounted on the gate and both made Bob wonder. It would be a good question to ask during their canvass: who would put up a sign and lock the gate? He supposed it could be someone who didn't want newsies and looters wandering around but what was left to steal?

They began their interviews at the city limits where Highway 163 entered the town. They tried businesses and private homes until one of the residents called the Navajo Nation Police Department and reported them as suspicious persons. When the officer responding contacted them, Bob explained what they were doing and why. The officer had not even heard about the kidnapping! Bob gave him all the pertinent data and asked that he broadcast it to other units. The officer checked them out rather thoroughly then turned them loose.

It was a time-consuming effort and many residents reacted with suspicion because Bob was a *Bilagaana*. Rita started taking over the contacts, speaking in Navajo and she was received much more cordially but wasn't any more successful. At noon, they met Abe and Carlos at a café in town and compared notes. Either the town was very tight-lipped or Henry Begay and Walter Bitsillie were not well known or people just didn't want to get involved which was what Bob suspected.

By the end of the day, both pairs of interviewers were getting close to believing that the two suspects spent very little time in Kayenta. They decided to try the same technique in Mexican Hat the following day.

Bob still wanted a look at the Nez property but didn't know who to call. The city employees suggested he go to Window Rock and make inquiries there. They were less than helpful, again, probably because he was a *Bilagaana,* and they even viewed Rita with distrust.

They were tired when they halted their efforts at about 6:00 PM. Abe and Carlos had not had any better luck than Bob and Rita, and all were disgusted with the response they were getting. Very few people claimed to have heard of the kidnapping and of those who did, few seemed to know anything.

They had dinner at the same café in Kayenta then headed the eighty-one miles back to Montezuma Creek. Bob and Rita went to bed that night bone tired and discouraged. On the way home she had voiced her concern about no call from the suspects and Bob agreed. "I've had that on my mind all day and I'm wondering if it means something or if they're just trying to build up their courage. They didn't strike me as the patient types. Have you talked to Carlos about what he should say when they call?"

"No, I thought it would be better coming from you considering your background."

Bob sighed. "I suppose you're right. I'd better do it tonight." It turned out to be a four-person discussion. All four of them had been thinking about what to say to the suspects.

Carlos was first with an opinion. "We cannot tell them the truth, the Shrine is sacrosanct, it must not be jeopardized. It also occurred to me that they simply might not have my phone number."

"I wondered that too," said Bob. "I keep swinging back and forth about how to treat these guys. They're not very smart, but if they put the lock on the gate then legitimized it with a no trespassing sign, it shows a certain amount of cunning. But why? What are they trying to keep people away from on the property? There's nothing left!"

"I think they'll find a way to communicate even if it's a rock with a note on it thrown through one of Rita's windows," Abe speculated. Rita winced, and Abe apologized, "Sorry Rita, but that might be the way they think."

323

Rita was the last to speak. "If Carlos convinces them the only thing he has found out in the desert is the wrecked plane, then maybe they'll simply ask for money. Unless someone is holding out, I don't think we have the means to pay a 'big score.' I just want that terrified little girl to come home."

"I suggest," said Bob, looking at Carlos, "that you stick with the plane wreck story. We've been consistent so far and they'll jump on any variation as proof that we're lying. If they switch to Plan Two and just demand money, delay, buy time. Maybe the Navajo Nation would be willing to pay a ransom. Tell them we don't have any money and would need time to get what we have together. But most important," Bob emphasized, "insist on proof of life. It'll put them on the defensive, if only for a little while and buy us some time. But tell them they have to prove that Meredith is okay and the only satisfactory way is for one of us to talk to her."

Everyone woke up with their motivation renewed and ready to do another day of knocking on doors and asking questions. Abe, predictably, suggested they stop for breakfast in Bluff since they were going that way anyway. That changed in an instant when Carlos found a note tucked under the windshield wiper of his pickup:

*If you want to see the girl alive again, Carlos Greyhawk must meet us*

*alone at Sand Island at 11:00 AM today. Do not get the cops involved or*

*she dies.*

"My God," Rita exclaimed, "that's only two hours from now!"

"Take it easy, Rita," soothed Bob. "If push came to shove, they'd wait, but I don't think we want to deliver Carlos into their hands alone – at least I don't. They'd get everything they wanted without a guarantee of giving up anything, and God help Carlos! No, I suggest I go down to Sand Island and pin a note on the bulletin board with Carlos's name and phone number on it, or meet them and talk in person."

"Why you," asked Abe.

"I'm the only one of us carrying a gun that I know of," Bob replied.

"Do you think they're smart enough to look on the bulletin board if I don't show up?" asked Carlos.

"Good point," said Abe.

"Well, if they're not," Bob said, "we're going to have to dumb up our communication with them."

"What do you mean by that?"

"We'll have to start giving them express directions on what to do next, i.e. *explain* things to them as we go along. Look, no negotiation I've ever been involved in is done on the first sally. That's why they call it negotiation. They demand, we counter. They'll stick around because Meredith represents their big score and they don't want to lose the opportunity to get rich."

"Why don't we go down there and hide then follow them?" asked Rita.

"It's impossible to follow anyone out here without a plane, that should have been made clear when they followed us over Cedar Mesa, they couldn't hide behind us for fear of losing us and there weren't enough places to hide and let us pass. We couldn't do much better than they did."

"Then, when they show up at Sand Island, why don't we just grab them and beat Meredith's location out of them?"

"If they have a brain in their head at all, only one will show up. Then we have a problem."

"So we must play the game their way," mused Carlos.

"To a point. They'll start not getting their way when I leave the note – which reminds me, I'd better get going, no sense in tweaking the tiger's nose unnecessarily. Carlos, why don't you write your name and phone number in BIG letters on a sheet of notebook paper so they'll be sure to see it?"

Rita and Carlos went back into the house to get the paper. Abe said, "I wish I could go with you."

"Too many people at once will scare them off. I think we have a good chance of getting Meredith back unharmed as long as we don't take any unnecessary liberties during the negotiations or take them for granted. I believe in overestimating my adversary, even ones like these two. And I'm not going to wait around for them, that might be pushing it a little far."

"I just wish I could *do* something!"

"I understand. Just hang in there, and we'll all get through this."

They came back out with the piece of paper, a bright pink notebook-sized sheet with the name and number printed clearly in black felt pen.

"That do?" asked Rita.

"Nicely," said Bob.

Before he left, Rita, on tiptoes, stuck her head in the pickup and gave him a kiss, "For luck," she whispered.

He was back in a little over an hour and reported no activity at the park. The bulletin board was prominently situated and he was confident they'd get the message.

Until they called, all the group could do was wait.

Carlos had been coached to answer his phone and immediately put it on speaker phone so they could all hear. Adrian Tso called to tell him no one he had talked to had seen hide nor hair of the Dynamic Duo since the day before. Adrian's opinion was that Henry and Walter were roughing it since no one in Mexican Hat would let them stay.

Meredith had pretty much gotten over being scared of the Dynamic Duo. They had shoved her, hands still bound, into some kind of underground bunker with dirt walls and a dirt floor. It was a little chilly but she was okay with that; the temperature didn't vary much with the time of the day. They had given her a blanket and a couple of bales of straw to lay on off the dirt floor and one or the other of them was bringing her water and what they laughingly called cold McHamburgers and McFries periodically. They wouldn't talk to her, telling her to shut up and threatening her if she got out of line.

The bunker appeared to be mostly below ground except for the half door. It swung outward and she had been forced to duck to get in but once in, was able to stand upright in the eight feet by ten feet space with a five-gallon plastic bucket in one corner. Very little light filtered in through the weathered cracks in the door but she could see evidence of a burned out building about a hundred feet away. Occasionally she could hear cars or trucks passing but they were too far away to hear her yells or her pounding on the surprisingly substantial door.

Meredith spent most of her time on the straw bales, fearful of what might be on the floor. She had been able to tell when Henry brought her food and water that there were no snakes or four-legged critters in her bunker but she feared the crawly kind more. She kept telling them that Carlos had found the drug plane and that was all, but they insisted there was something else but wouldn't tell her how they knew. She was fed up with this treatment and planned to tell them so.

# CHAPTER 26

The call they had all been waiting for finally came in just after 3:00 PM. It was Henry Begay and he sounded angry and full of beer. "Old man, if you don' start doing what yer told this little girl is going to die and it's gonna be your fault. We ain't kiddin' around here and we're not patient men so you better get with the program. You been talking to that cop friend, haven't you? He's behind all this bullshit. You better quit listening to him and do what yer told."

Bob signaled for Carlos to be silent, then said, "Henry, this is Bob Connelly, that cop you were talking about. What do we have to do to convince you the valuable thing Carlos found was the plane full of dope?"

"You asshole! Why don' you just butt out and let me and Carlos do our bidness?"

"Your business involves the life of a young, innocent girl, all for an imagined score that doesn't exist!" said Bob. "There is no other valuable thing and if you harm that girl, it will be forever on your conscience. What do you think this mythical score is worth, anyway?"

"What do you mean?" asked a semi-addled Henry.

"I mean, how much did you expect to get out of this score?"

There was silence, then Bob could hear Henry talking to someone in the background but he had muffled the phone so Bob and the others couldn't understand what he was saying. He heard Henry's voice suddenly get louder as if he was angry.

He came back on the phone. "I'll call you back. We have to discuss … this."

"The worst possible circumstances!" Bob exclaimed. "Trying to negotiate with a drunk! We can't possibly make any kind of headway with the way his brain is muddled. If he calls back, I'm going to tell him to sober up then call back."

"But he'll get mad and do something to Meredith if you do that!" cried Abe.

"I do not think so, Abe," said Carlos. "Drunks are stubborn, that's true, and do not listen to reason, but Henry knows what is at stake here and I believe he will listen and not go off on a tangent."

"I wish I could be as sure as Carlos," was all Rita said.

"I'm sure he'll never listen to reason given the shape he's in. He's belligerent but he's still listening, that's a good sign. I'll plant the seed about a ransom and then let him think about it overnight."

Henry called back about an hour and a half later. Now his words were so slurred, he was hard to understand. Bob took the initiative and asked, "Henry, if this is about ransom, how much do you want?"

Again there was silence on the phone and then discussion in the background.

"Henry?" Bob asked sharply and loudly. "Henry, listen to me. You are way too drunk to negotiate. Call us back in the

330

morning when you're sober." With that, Bob hung up on Henry Begay amid worried eyes.

"You could not negotiate with him," said Carlos, "he was too drunk, but he did not sound belligerent. I am guessing that Walter is in no better condition. I did not hear music or other people so perhaps they are settled in for the night, not in a bar, and will not be driving. They could kill themselves on the highway and that would leave us no way to get to Meredith."

"Yeah," said Abe. "In the shape he was in when he called back, we could not have reasoned with him or negotiate anything he would remember."

"I just hope Meredith is safe and unharmed," whispered Rita, more to herself than anyone else.

No one wanted to cook so Bob volunteered to drive to Blanding for dinner. It was a solemn meal, no one had much to say and any attempt to start a conversation quickly petered out. Back in Montezuma Creek, everyone drifted off to bed early without saying much. Rita spooned up against Bob and wrapped his arm around her but said little. He was worried about what he had done, but he knew in his heart there had been no other choice. He lay awake long into the night second guessing himself. He knew Rita was awake but they didn't talk.

The next morning Abe was again up early and went to Bluff for baked goods for breakfast. When he returned, everyone was up but it was a quiet group with not much said as they waited, hopefully, for a phone call.

The call didn't come until noon. Henry sounded a little rocky on the phone but he seemed to have his wits about him. "What do you mean ransom?" he asked right away.

"Isn't that what you're after? Money to set the girl free? Does it matter where it comes from?"

"No, no I guess not."

"How much?"

"We need enough to get out of here and start a life somewhere else. At least $20,000 each."

"Henry, we don't have that kind of money among us. But maybe we can appeal to the Navajo Nation for help."

"Yeah. Yeah, that's a good idea. Let the Nation pay the ransom."

"Henry, there is something that has to be done before we go any further. Have you ever heard the phrase 'proof of life?'"

"No, what does it mean?"

"It means that we have to be convinced that the girl is still alive, preferably by talking to her on the phone."

"She's okay! We haven't done nothing to her."

"I don't doubt you for a minute, but I can't see the Nation accepting anyone's word that she's okay. We need to tell them we talked to her and she's alright. Can you arrange that?"

"Yeah, I suppose so. When?"

"That's up to you, you're in the driver's seat."

"Maybe later this afternoon?  We need to feed her and bring her water so when we do that, I'll call then put her on the phone so someone can verify she's okay.  Is that what you want?"

"Yes, exactly.  Once we do that, we can go to the Nation for help."

"Okay.  It's about noon now.  Say around 2:30?"

"We'll be waiting.  And thank you Henry."

There was a click as Henry disconnected the call.

"Well," said Rita, "I feel better.  It doesn't sound like they've harmed her but talking to her on the phone will ease my mind *a lot!"*

Everyone seemed relieved, it really sounded like the girl was unharmed.  Bob gave Rita a hug and bumped fists with Abe.  He smiled and offered his hand to Carlos.  "Now all we have to do is come up with $40,000" he said ruefully.

Henry told Walter about the arrangement and Walter was all enthused.  "This sounds good.  We'll be out of here with money in our pockets and no one the wiser.  Let's go over to *Shimasani's* place, feed and water the girl and, depending on how she behaves, maybe we'll tell her we're working on getting her released."

He reached into a duffle bag and extracted three McBurgers, a large McFries and a liter of water then headed for the Highlander.  "I'll be glad to be over doing this too," he muttered to himself.

They decided to celebrate with lunch in Mexican Hat but Henry didn't have enough money nor did Walter.  They just bought a couple of candy bars each and headed toward Kayenta and the late Millie Nez's place.

When they got there, Henry was leading and stopped to check the chain and lock on the gate. It had been his idea to lock the gate and post the no trespassing sign just to keep curious people away. Nothing appeared tampered with so he unlocked the lock and swung the gate wide open so Walter could come in too. They'd lock it on the way out.

They both parked to the side of what had been the barn and walked toward a root cellar behind it. Walter split off, grabbed a hoe leaning against the root cellar, and walked through the ashes of the barn to where he thought the drugs had been.

"What are you doing?" asked Henry.

"From what I hear, that was a lot of meth. Maybe a kilo or two down near the bottom survived. That would be a nice way to finish up this little project. He started running the hoe through the debris and ashes hoping to find something.

Henry rattled the locked door on the root cellar then yelled, "Hey! Anybody home? Are you decent? I'm coming in with McLunch."

He unlocked the padlock securing chain and pulled open the door to illuminate the dark interior. After his eyes adjusted, he saw Meredith sitting on one of the straw bales. She glared malevolently at him but said nothing. She stood up as he entered the small space. She didn't want him to pin her to the bales and do something to her. He hadn't done anything yet but she could tell he wanted to.

Henry sat the food and water on the bales and said, "You'll be happy to know we're working on freeing you. I've talked to that

Bob guy and he wants me to call him from here so he can talk to you and be convinced you're okay. It's called proof of life and they need it before they can go any further. You're okay, aren't you?"

She nodded but said nothing.

He walked over next to her and produced a cell phone. He punched in a number, put it on speaker and Bob answered right away, "Hello."

"This is Henry Begay. You wanted to talk to the girl, here she is." He handed her the phone.

"Meredith? This is Bob, you're on speaker and everyone can hear. Are you okay, honey?"

"Yes, I'm okay, but they won't let me go."

"We're working on that, believe me. Rita is here, so is Abe and Carlos. Want to say hi?"

"Hi, you guys. Everything is okay so far, but please get me out of here!"

"See?" said Henry, "I told you she was okay but that's enough talk until maybe next time."

As she handed the phone back to him, Henry reached out with his other hand, cupped, then squeezed Meredith's breast. She jerked back a step and yelled at him to leave her alone. Suddenly it all crystallized: the rough treatment, bad food and, worst of all, not knowing what was going on. This was just the last straw. She reared back and kicked him directly in, what she later described as the McNuggets. Henry didn't say anything, just doubled over with his hands in his crotch and slowly sank to his knees on the dirt floor.

Meredith, stunned by his reaction to her kick, didn't know what to do but quickly decided the best thing to do was run. She ran to the door and spotted Walter dragging through the barn's ashes. She noticed her aunt's Highlander parked close by and ran for it. She was a third of the way there before Walter saw her, dropped the hoe and gave chase. She reached the SUV and yanked open the driver's door. Walter slowed a step and called, "Are you looking for these, sweetheart?" He jingled the keys in his hand.

Walter misunderstood Meredith's actions and it cost him his life. Meredith bent down into the car, intent on the center console when Walter reached her and put an arm around her waist. He started to yank her back out of the car saying, "It's time you were taught a little respect. He pulled her rear end up against his crotch as he tried to wrestle her from the vehicle. Meredith desperately pawed through the console until her hand finally found what she was looking for. She grabbed it and started to turn then pulled the trigger. Nothing happened!

The safety! She had forgotten the safety and quickly snapped it off while Walter pulled her around to face him and groped her breasts with his free hand. "Mmm, been wanting to do this for a while," he murmured as he began to nuzzle her neck. Meredith brought Rita's .380 up against the big man's chest and emptied the magazine. Walter stiffened then sort of slithered down the car door onto the ground.

Meredith grabbed the keys off the ground where Walter had dropped them, got in the SUV and started it. She looked around for

Henry but didn't see him and wasn't going to give him time to respond. She put it in gear, did a spinning u-turn around Henry's pickup and headed for the highway. She wished she had had enough presence of mind to grab Henry's cell phone but it was enough that she was free of them and on her way home. Her greatest fear now was that Henry would catch up to her and force her off the road like he had Carlos. Her fear would prove to be unwarranted, Henry was suffering from two testicular ruptures.

After driving for what seemed like hours in the unfamiliar country, Meredith, came to Mexican Hat. She wasn't sure she was even on the right road, but continued on, hoping she had made the correct turn back in Kayenta. Not many miles past Mexican Hat she spotted a junction sign, one sign pointed to the left and said "Moki Dugway," the other fork led to Bluff. At last, familiar country! Relieved, she headed to Bluff and safety. Her only decision now was should she drive all the way to Montezuma Creek or stop and call home in Bluff? She opted for stopping in Bluff; she didn't want Henry to get away if there was a chance to catch him at the burned out farm.

Her arrival at Twin Rocks Trading Post caused a stir. The staff knew she had been kidnapped and when she appeared at the entrance with blood all over her jeans and sweatshirt, some of the folks went into panic mode. Meredith got them calmed down enough that she could get to a phone.

"Hello?" answered Abe.

337

"Abe, this is Meredith. I'm free and I'm okay. I'm at the Twin Rocks Trading Post. Can you come here? Abe, I think I killed Walter and I'm pretty sure I injured Henry but I left them there, got in the Highlander and ran. I thought about just coming all the way home but I don't want Henry to get away."

"Meredith, oh thank heavens! Just a minute, let me get the others up and going and we'll be right there but don't hang up! You're alright, you're not hurt or anything?"

"I'm okay, Abe. I'm about to lose it with these people mobbing me. I didn't realize I was all bloody until I walked into the trading post. They thought I was hurt and called the ambulance and everything. I keep telling them I'm fine but the EMTs want to check me out."

"Tell them *firmly* that you are not injured and do not need medical assistance. You don't have to let them do anything. How did you … I mean … how did you get away from those guys? No, wait. You can tell us all when we get there; we're on the way now, about fifteen minutes. I've been so worried about you, Meredith! Your being abducted made me realize how much you mean to me." His words caused a glow in Meredith that even the people trying to "help" her couldn't erase.

"I know what you mean, Abe. For a while I thought I was never going to see you again and when they put me in that root cellar, I was afraid I was going to die."

"Root cellar? What root cellar?"

338

"That's where they imprisoned me, in a root cellar with dirt walls and a dirt floor. It was a long long way from Mexican Hat and the buildings that had been on the farm looked like they had just burned down."

"You were at Milllie Nez's old place!" Abe exclaimed. "I don't know how many times we drove by that place and Bob really wanted to stop to look around but there was a lock on the gate and a no trespassing sign."

"Well, it's open now, I just drove through the open gate less than two hours ago."

"Henry and Walter are still there?"

"I know Walter will still be there but I'm not sure about Henry. I kicked him in the you-know-whats and he doubled over like he was really in pain."

"Good for you! He better hope I never see him one on one."

"That's over with now, Abe. Now we can think about going to school and being together."

"We just stopped at 191, be there in less than two minutes."

Both pickups came blazing into the trading post's parking lot and skidded to a stop near the Highlander. Abe and Rita were out of the pickups and running for the entrance before Bob and Carlos could shift their vehicles into park.

As Bob walked in, he said, "I called the Navajo Nation Police in Kayenta and told them what happened. They're going to take a crime scene crew out to the Nez place and go to work. They would like Meredith – when she's up to it – to come back out there

339

and walk their detective through the scene. I told them I'd check with her and Rita and get back to them. The sooner you do that, honey, the better, before your memory starts playing tricks on you. Henry and Walter won't be there." A frown of concern was erased from Meredith's face at Bob's last words. "As much as I'm sure you'd like to freshen up, probably letting them photograph you in the clothes you have on is far more telling than hearing someone talk about them."

Meredith considered what Bob said for just a moment before nodding her head and saying, "Okay, let's go, as long as *they* won't be there."

As she and Abe walked out toward the pickups, Rita said to Bob, "You know this is going to hit her pretty soon, and she's probably going to go all to pieces."

"Maybe, she already has the telling out and maybe she won't feel the need to re-live it. Anyway, all the more reason to get this over with before she does, so she doesn't have to re-live it over and over again."

"I need to call her mother and fill her in. She might want Meredith to come home right away."

"All you can do is assure her that Meredith is safe and well-looked after. If she wants her home, we'll take her home but she'll be spending a week in Many Farms very shortly." While Bob drove, Rita called her sister, Meredith's mother. She explained everything and the mother wanted to speak to her daughter right away.

Abe and Meredith had hopped into the back seat of the Highlander, and Rita immediately handed her the phone and explained who it was and why she was on the phone.

"Hi Mom," said Meredith in her chirpiest voice.

"Meredith, my sister has told me what happened. Are you alright? Were you injured in any way?"

"No, Mom," she replied. "It was an awful experience but I survived and am with Aunt Rita and her friend, Bob. Did Aunt Rita tell you I have a boyfriend I met up here?"

"She did not mention that but I can hardly blame her for all that you have been through. Are you sure you don't need to come home now instead of next week? Will you bring your boyfriend so I can meet him?"

"I don't know if he'll have time. He's going to be going to the University of Arizona too. He graduated a year early from high school, he's really smart." Meredith rolled her eyes at Abe and smiled.

"Well, that's fine. Is he working?"

"No, not right now. He's also studying to become an *Hatáli* like his grandfather."

"I like him already!"

"His name is Abe Red Wolf and he's from Shiprock."

"Well, tell him I look forward to meeting him when possible."

"Okay, I'll tell him. I have to go, good talking with you."

"You too, daughter, be careful!"

341

Assuming the police would want photos of the vehicle since it was involved in the case, Rita motioned Bob to drive and got into the front passenger seat. Bob stopped for a moment, got out and went over to Carlos who was sitting in his pickup.

"Do you know the place we're talking about?"

"I think so. Even though I was there not long ago, I did not pay attention to how it looked from the front, so it is best I follow you."

It was late afternoon by the time the motorcade arrived. The gate was still open and Bob could see Henry's pickup, a forensics van, a detective's car and a patrol car whose occupant was guarding the gate. Bob made contact with the gate guard and explained why they were there. The officer got on his portable to someone at the crime scene who gave instructions where *not* to park.

A man in coveralls walked over as Bob's party emerged from the Highlander. "I'm Detective Sergeant George Peshlakai. Thank you for coming out so promptly, you're saving the department a lot of overtime. This must be Ms. Twin Feather," he said after glancing at Meredith's bloody clothes. Meredith nodded and stepped forward to shake the detective's hand.

Sergeant Peshlakai said, "Mr. Begay was still here, slumped over the straw bales in the root cellar. He couldn't or wouldn't talk and we sent him, under guard, to the ER at the Kayenta Health Center. I haven't heard anything from the officer who accompanied him.

"Ms. Twin Feather, may I call you Meredith?" Peshlakai asked and Meredith nodded. "I know that this isn't what you want to do, but you're greatly assisting us by walking us through the scene, it helps so much in reconstructing what happened and making sense of the evidence."

"Would you say the best place to start would be in the root cellar?" During her re-enactment, one of the forensic technicians would record both video and audio of her statement. Inasmuch as her parents were not present, Rita gave consent.

Meredith nodded and headed that way, doing a wide detour around the blood-soaked gravel and weeds where Walter died. She walked Sergeant Peshlakai through everything she could remember about the events with Henry inside the cellar. She pointed out the McBurgers and McFries and explained that both Henry and Walter thought it was hilarious calling them that and it was why she said she kicked him in the McNuggets.

She described the race to the SUV and the mauling by Walter and her desperate effort to get to her aunt's gun.

"Yes, we found that, locked open, next to the body."

"Locked open?" asked Meredith.

"The slide was locked in the open position. It's what semi-automatic handguns do when the ammunition is exhausted." Meredith nodded in understanding.

She described Walter falling and her frantic attempt to get away. "What was Walter doing out in the ashes?" she asked.

Peshlakai grunted. "We think he was hoping to find some of the kilos of dope that had been stored there. Ironically, not a foot and a half from where he dropped the hoe, one of my technicians found three undamaged packages."

"What next?" asked Meredith.

"You've given us pretty much all we need until Mr. Begay can or will speak with us and the forensics people finish up. Once he can be released, Mr. Begay will be lodged in the jail here in Kayenta on a no bail warrant, and a hold from San Juan County for the crimes he has pending.

It was hard to believe it was all over! No more threats or kidnappings or fears. Meredith and Abe could now go on with their lives and take on the next objective – the University of Arizona.

But for some, the effort was just starting: what to do with the Shrine of the Ancients?

# CHAPTER 27

Sleeping arrangements were in chaos that night until Meredith put her foot down and announced she was sleeping with Abe no matter what. Bob and Rita sort of followed her lead which left Carlos with a bed to himself.

The next morning, Meredith and Abe arose early and cooked breakfast for everyone. Carlos announced that he was going to Shiprock to re-connect with family but would be in touch. Inasmuch as they were leaving for Tucson in less than two weeks and Meredith was going home for a week before that, the kids had many last-minute errands to run and were in and out of the house all day. Bob and Rita, after checking with Carlos, began work on the photos and video of the Shrine in an effort to mold them into some kind of organization that the President of the Navajo Nation could understand, without overwhelming him.

They were having just a little difficulty concentrating, considering Bob's "night of atonement" was just past. Better said, they were having trouble keeping their hands off each other. Their night had been everything from tumultuous to tender and both were eager for more.

As they sat at the table over a second cup of coffee, making eyes at each other, Rita said; out of the blue, "PowerPoint! That's how we should organize the Shrine's material for Enid Yazzie. It's audio/video so he doesn't have to read pagers and pages of stuff which will quickly bore him. This way we'll hold his attention for a little while longer and see if we're just wishful thinking hoping the Nation will adopt this project."

"If they say no," said Bob, "I guess the Shrine will languish as it is for a few more centuries."

"That's too far away for my mind to reach," said Rita as she re-filled both their coffee cups and trailed a caressing hand over Bob's shoulders as she put the pot back. "I'm just glad the material is digital, it won't deteriorate like film would."

"That's not necessarily true," warned Bob. "The first thing we ought to do is make at least four copies of everything for the time being. I remember reading recently that digital media is best saved in the cloud, since current hardware and media may be obsolete in just a few years. I'm a dinosaur, and don't yet trust the cloud, especially with all the hackers around. The next best thing is probably external hard drives but even they should be upgraded at least every ten years. By then, what we shot will be in someone else's hands so thumb drives should be good enough for a while considering USB drives aren't going away anytime soon."

"So USB instead of SD cards?" asked Rita.

"The SD cards are good, but you can plug a flash drive into any USB port whereas you're limited to hardware with a card reader for SD cards."

"So you bought USB instead of SD," Rita observed. "Before, we didn't have much choice considering the camera was set up for an SD card, but we'll store on flash drives. If memory serves, we were using 128 GB SD cards and pretty much used up three of them, so the half terabyte flash drives there should have enough room for everything. Then we can put one with the map in the safe deposit box, give Carlos one if he wants one and, gulp, give Enid Yazzie one. I doubt Abe would want one so long as he has access and we'll hold on to the last one."

Bob called Abe to borrow his new laptop and Rita brought hers out of the bedroom and brought with her a fairly short USB cable with a small box in the middle.

"This is a data transfer cable," she said. "I use it to transfer files from one computer to another and it's much faster than just doing a few files on a flash drive at a time. We could even slave one laptop to the other if we needed to but I don't think that will be necessary. Why don't you go get the SD cards? First we can make the copies onto the half terabyte flash drives, then we'll transfer the photos and video over to the computers Then we can massage it any way we want.

"My laptop has only a five hundred gigabyte hard drive and there's a lot of stuff on there. Maybe it would be better if we eventually loaded everything on Abe's laptop since it's so new and has a terabyte hard drive," said Rita. "By downloading files onto two computers, we can screen it that much faster, then combine what we want to show. We can review what we have then decide what to put into the presentation."

After that, they downloaded the massive amount of data onto the two laptops. As they worked, they chatted about what should go into the presentation. Bob thought the panning video of the petroglyph panels one at a time would be best to give a scale to what the project was. They could intersperse photographs of close-ups now and then to emphasize what they were showing.

Rita, who was the PowerPoint expert, liked Bob's idea and added that they could dub voice in certain areas to explain to the viewers what they were seeing. Reviewing what was on the cards before downloading the files was mind-numbing work, it was a *lot* of data and certainly most of it would not be in the presentation. Rita thought that due to the exciting content, they might be able to hold the President's interest for thirty minutes, no more. But first they had to go through *all* the material and rough out what they thought should go into the final draft. Then they would transfer the draft files to one computer then go over the files there over and over until it was just right. After all, they would only have one shot at impressing the Navajo President!

Suddenly Rita noticed the sun was setting and they had worked through lunch. "My God, look at the time!" she exclaimed. "How about I call the kids and see if they want to meet somewhere for dinner?"

"Yeah," said Bob, "I've had about enough of this for one day and, now that you mention it, I'm hungry."

The kids had already had dinner so Bob and Rita opted for the good ol' Twin Rocks Trading Post mainly because it was closer.

Speaking of closer, the two couldn't get much closer to each other. Bob's hand was on Rita's leg just above the knee and Rita's left arm was draped around Bob's shoulders as he drove. Neither knew where this would wind up, but they were enjoying each other immensely now and planned on making the most of it for as long as it lasted.

Abe and Meredith were home when Bob and Rita returned. They were already in Meredith's room with the door closed when Bob and Rita came in. Rita paused at the door for a moment before continuing down the hall.

"Are we doing the right thing allowing them to sleep together?" Rita asked.

"The way I look at is if they want to have sex, they'll find a way. I guess it's kind of like drinking. I'd rather they be home instead of in the back seat of a car in the dark where someone could cause trouble and endanger them."

Rita sighed. "I suppose, but it's a long ways from how I was raised."

"Yeah, me too, but that was a generation ago and I know kidnappers were never after me, and probably not you either. Besides, they're both so close to eighteen, it's not even worth debating."

"Are we setting a bad example?" Rita asked. "I mean what I hear and read says that sex is okay on the third date. That sounds awfully soon, and casual to me. I always thought love entered into it but now it's just hooking up and they hardly know each other."

"We've known each other about the same amount of time as the kids have though we haven't spent nearly as much time together – something I'd like to rectify – so why should we be any different?"

"But we're adults and both of us 'have been there and done that.'"

"Not sure that applies anymore to their generation. I know it does to me and, I hope, to you, but we can't compare ourselves to them. There are a lot of years of life experience behind us and before them. Besides, we both had *the talk* with them so if they screw up, they can't say they weren't warned."

"I can only imagine what Meredith's mother would say."

"Well," said Bob with a smile, "come to bed. We have a lot more work to do tomorrow. From the pictures we've screened out so far, it looks like we're on the same page more-or-less for the vision in our heads of what this project should look like."

"I thought the same thing and, frankly, was relieved."

"Me too." said Bob then pulled Rita close and kissed her.

The kids were finishing up their breakfast dishes when Bob and Rita came down the hall into the dining room. "Good morning," said Bob and they both turned and smiled. "What's on your agenda for today?"

"We have to be in Kayenta at the police station at 11:00 to meet with the FBI," said Meredith. "According to the Navajo National Police investigator who interviewed me that day, the feds are finally responding but probably won't do much since the matter is resolved."

"Do you want us to go with you?" asked Rita.

"The detective expected the interview to be perfunctory, mainly because we did the video. They may have more questions but nothing to worry about," Meredith replied. "So, what are *you* going to do today?" asked Meredith with mischief in her eyes.

"Work on this project to present to the President," said Rita, catching Meredith's innuendo and ignoring it.

"Will I ever get to know what it's about?" asked the teenager almost plaintively.

"Yes," said Bob, "and soon. Matter of fact we might have you view the PowerPoint presentation for a critique before we show it to the President."

"That would be awesome, how soon?"

"As soon as we're satisfied we have a solid product," Bob said with a sigh. "This is taking a *lot* of time; I hope it will be worth it."

"It will," said Rita and Abe at the same time.

"Call us if you need us," said Rita. "We'll be here and the phone will be on and close."

"C'mon, we ought to get going. Don't want to keep the big dogs waiting," said Abe as he held out Meredith's jacket. He helped her into it and they left out the front door.

"Now," said Rita, "where were we?"

"About to decide about breakfast," said Bob. "Cereal and coffee will suit me fine, then we can get back to work. Well, almost

…." whispered Bob as Rita tucked his hand inside her robe and he came in contact with warm, soft flesh and smiling soft lips.

Later, when they were sitting side by side at the table engrossed in sorting photos, reviewing video and making notes, Rita said, "This really isn't what you had planned when you left Santa Fe to tour the red rock country, is it?"

"Nope, and I'm missing out on a lot of lonely nights between sightseeing tours," he said in mock indignation. "I'm not complaining, mind you, hanging out with and sleeping with a beautiful woman and helping, in a small way, to make Navajo history isn't all that bad. I don't mind suffering in silence as long as everyone knows about it."

Rita laughed and gave him a playful shove. "I seem to remember your saying something about looking for adventure too. I guess you've missed out on that too, huh?"

"Absolutely. One boring day after another, what's a guy to do?"

"This guy better get back to work!"

"Yes'm," said Bob quickly and looked back at his computer screen.

"Tell you what, Connelly, to make up for all your inconvenience, I'll take you out to McDonalds for a McBurger. How does that sound."

"Hold the McNuggets!" Bob said hastily and they both laughed.

Two days later they finished the first screening of the material. They had pared down almost fourteen hours of filming to two and now they had to fine tune it down to about thirty minutes. Rita was in her element, she had done this very type of thing several times over her career with the Nation and the only difficulty lay with what material to discard.

They transferred the remaining "keepers" onto Abe's bigger hard drive and now sat side by side reviewing and weeding them out. It was slow going, but remarkably, they were in agreement about most of the choices. They finally decided on a ten-minute eye-catching spliced video of the whole Shrine to get the viewers' attention, then shift to individual close-up slides of some of the more graphic petroglyphs from different periods and the pottery. They would conclude the presentation with another short video. All the while, Rita would be describing and explaining what it was her audience was seeing, and what they were after. Hopefully, she could shift the responsibility for the Shrine onto the President's staff.

That evening – the last evening before Meredith was to go home to Many Farms for a week – Rita and Bob showed the presentation to Meredith and Abe on Rita's big screen television. Both kids sat on the couch together spellbound, until the presentation concluded.

They stared wide-eyed at the television even after the presentation ended. "It was like going back in time," gushed Meredith. "Talk about bringing history to life! That was fantastic."

Pensive, Abe sat there quiet for several moments after Meredith's statement. "That makes me so proud to be Diné," he said, finally.

"Was it clear we believe some of the petroglyphs predate the Navajo and maybe even the Ancestral Puebloans?"

"The historical line is clear," said Abe. "You have created something that should be shown in every Navajo classroom and chapter meeting."

"Criticisms?" asked Rita.

"Only that it was too short," Abe commented.

"There's a reason for that," said Rita. "The president is a very busy man and his time is valuable. We didn't want to take up too much of it or cause him to lose interest."

"These pictures belong in every Navajo museum in the southwest. After seeing it I realize it fills a gap in our history that heretofore was a question mark," said Abe.

"We still have to figure out what to do with the physical Shrine," said Bob. "Right now it's on BLM land and buried so no one who doesn't know where it is can molest it, but once it's made public, people are going to want to see it and scholars are going to want to study it in detail."

"Couldn't the Nation trade parcels of land for where the Shrine is?" asked Meredith.

"It's right in the middle of Cedar Mesa which is in the southern part of Bear's Ears National Monument. Coming up with a trade might be difficult but not as difficult as making the Shrine available to people. It is underground and, right now, only four people know where it is, which guarantees its safety but people will encroach once its existence is known," said Abe.

"It's a question far greater than what we can address," said Bob. "That's why Rita is arranging to show the presentation to the President of the Navajo Nation."

"Then what's holding you up?" asked Meredith with a smile. "Let's get this show on the road!"

The next morning, Rita and Meredith set out for Many Farms. Rita wasn't sure just how much of Meredith's summer adventures would be made known to her parents but Rita would try to put them in the best light. In her mind, all in all, Meredith had grown enormously from her experiences and was no longer the little naïve girl that came to Rita in early June.

Abe decided he wanted to spend that same week with Carlos in Shiprock. He called and Carlos told him yes, he could get some *Hatáli* training during that time and he had a place for him to stay before Abe headed for Tucson. Carlos even agreed to come get him.

That night Abe and Bob had a long conversation about Abe's future. Abe was adamant he wanted Bob to take him to Tucson, and to be his surrogate father. Bob was touched and surprised by the depth of emotion Abe's desire engendered. They came to an agreement that ended in a (manly) hug.

After Carlos had picked up Abe, Bob helped Rita fine-tune the Shrine presentation and Rita finally called the President's office and asked for an appointment. The staffer asked what it was in regard to and Rita resorted to *stafferese* in her response, "I'm afraid it's confidential until the President decides otherwise. I am Rita Makespeace and I am his former executive assistant. I know that the President will be vitally interested in seeing and hearing what I have to present. We would require about forty-five minutes though I will be surprised if it doesn't go longer than that. The President may wish to spend more time and we are certainly open to that."

The staffer hemmed and hawed about such a long appointment but finally gave in and scheduled her and Carlos for the following Wednesday at 4:00 PM. The aide thought that by scheduling the appointment late, if it ran over, they wouldn't infringe on someone else's time.

In the interim Rita and Bob practiced and practiced until the presentation was second nature. They were determined that if this project was shot down, it wouldn't be because the delivery was flawed. The more they rehearsed the more they believed that the Nation could not turn its back on such a historical treasure.

They heard from Meredith. She was disappointed in how "immature" her former school friends were. She chose not to confide in them about her kidnapping and the shooting of Walter Bitsillie. She was sure they would not believe her and sometimes she wondered if she believed it herself. All they seemed to want to talk about was sex and boys. Meredith felt she had outgrown that infatuation stage of childhood and was now looking forward to a mature relationship with Abe whom she talked to every day.

Carlos was working Abe's tail off to make up for all the tutelage time he had lost due to the Robert Begay fiasco and the subsequent discovery of the Shrine of the Ancients. Carlos kept Abe busy making packets of herbs and other components for the *Jish*. He was picking it up quickly but he had a lot of ground to make up. He had not even participated in a Blessingway Ceremony yet mainly because Carlos was not taking appointments yet. What free time Carlos allowed Abe was taken up learning the songs and chants that were the essence of a Singer. Abe thrived on the workload but was daunted by the idea of keeping up this pace, having a girlfriend and tackling school too.

# CHAPTER 28

Wednesday afternoon at 3:45 found Rita and Carlos sitting in the waiting area outside the President's suite of offices. Rita had wanted Bob to come too, but Bob declined, saying the issue was strictly Navajo business, and having a *Biligaana* there would only be an impediment.

Indignant, Rita said, "That's not right. You've been part of this - sometimes the *backbone* of it - since the beginning! You did all the photography, saved Abe from being kidnapped and helped rescue Carlos. We could not have done this without you."

Bob held up his hands, palms out in an effort to calm her outburst. "I know, you're right, I'm a hero, but not to the President and we don't want him distracted from the main topic which is all-important."

She finally relented though unhappy about it. She had had to plead with Carlos to come with her and finally won him over by telling him his status as an *Hatáli* was critical in convincing the President that this was a worthwhile project that affected every man, woman and child of the Navajo Nation.

Bless his heart, Carlos even came dressed for the part in *clean,* unscuffed Tony Lamas, pressed Levis, a plaid conservative western long-sleeve snap button shirt sporting a bolo tie with a clasp of silver and turquoise.  His belt buckle matched the clasp and he had his hair tied back in a Navajo bun.

Rita was stunning in a light tan buckskin ankle-length skirt bearing Navajo-patterned designs in turquoise beads.  She wore dark brown suede boots and a dark green Navajo rug-design silk blouse gathered at the waist by a silver conch belt with inlaid turquoise.  She wore the requisite squash-blossom turquoise and silver necklace and had her hair in a Navajo bun traditionally tied with strands of white wool.  She wore little makeup as she was striking without it.

At precisely 4:00 PM, the door into the inner offices opened and a young Navajo man in a business suit appeared.  "Ms. Makespeace?" he asked politely.

"Yes," said Rita, standing and gathering up her briefcase and computer valise.

"The President will see you now."  Carlos stood up also and the young man asked, "And this is?"

"*Hatáli* Grey Hawk," said Rita walking past the young man with Carlos following right behind.

The young functionary rushed past them, knocked, then opened a door marked "President Enid Yazzie" and announced them, "Mr. President?  Ms. Makespeace and *Hatáli* Grey Hawk."  Yazzi was a man in his fifties, medium build wearing Levis, a western shirt and cowboy boots.  There was a cowboy hat with a silver conch and turquoise hatband hanging from a hat rack off to his left.

Enid Yazzi exclaimed "Rita, *yá'át'ééh!*"  With a big smile he came around his desk to shake her hand then give her a hug.  "It is good see you, the place just hasn't been the same without you. Who is your friend?"

"This is *Hatáli* Carlos Grey Hawk from Shiprock. He is the man who discovered what we've come here to show you."

"Show me? By all means. What kind of equipment do you need?"

"It's a PowerPoint presentation so we'll need a pretty good-sized television so you can see the slides."

The President nodded to the young man who left but was back in less than five minutes pushing a big-screen television on a cart. He waited expectantly to help connect Rita's computer but when she did it herself, he just stood there waiting.

"Um, Mr. President? As I said when I made this appointment, we consider this confidential until you say differently. Can he wait outside?"

The President nodded and the young man left the room after dimming the lights and closing the drapes at Rita's request. Rita started right in with an introduction then turned on the television and synched it with the laptop.

For the next twenty-six minutes thirty seconds, President Yazzie said nothing, keeping his eyes glued to the television while he sat at the front of his chair with his hands folded in his lap. When Rita finished, he sat back in his chair with a stunned look on his face. Rita turned up the lights and opened the drapes. She shut down the computer and television and handed the flash drive to the President.

"There are four complete copies besides the original on SD cards," she told him. "This is one plus a copy of the PowerPoint presentation," she said, nodding at his hand. "I have one, Bob Connelly has one and one is in a safe deposit box along with a map of how to find the cave and the SD cards. We have tried very hard to keep this quiet for fear someone would loot the Shrine."

"Unbelievable! What an incredible windfall for the Navajo Nation," President Yazzie blurted when he quit staring in thought at the television. "There is no way to make this place accessible to the public?"

"Carlos, why don't you describe how to get to the cave from the rim of the canyon?"

With extreme deliberate calm, Carlos described climbing/crawling backward down the "trail" on all fours then crawling under the trees. He then rendered a mental image of going into the narrow neck of the cave and pushing his pack ahead of him to barely squeeze through.

When Carlos finished, the President asked, "So there is no way to cut an access into the cave beyond the narrow passage?"

"I can't see how, Mr. President, and we might risk bringing the whole rim down into the cave and burying it forever," Carlos replied.

"There is something else," said Rita. "The Shrine lies several miles north of the south boundary of Cedar Mesa in the Bear's Ears National Monument. It is not even close to being on Navajo land."

The President frowned then sighed. "We would play hell – excuse the language – trying to swap land for that piece after all the controversy surrounding the establishment of the Monument," he said pensively.

"Mr. Grey Hawk, how did you *find* this to begin with?" the President asked suddenly.

"Sometimes my dreams direct me to places or to people," Carlos replied. "Finding this place took many trials and errors before I found the path clear in my dreams but it was so strong and so recurrent I could not ignore it."

"I'm very glad you didn't. Rita, you say you and, ah, Bob shot a lot of still and video?"

"Yes. We filled up three 128GB SD cards and used just a small fraction of it for this presentation. As I said, we have transferred the data onto flash drives since it is less likely to deteriorate and the USB drives will still be around after SD cards, DVDs and external hard drives are obsolete. I should tell you, the average lifespan for data on flash drives is about ten years so we can't tuck it away and forget about it or we'll lose it."

"I can see the Navajo Nation Museum getting involved in the study of the petroglyphs and pottery but it seems they'll have to rely on the photographs and video to do so," said President Yazzie. "Other archeology types from all over will want in on the action too," he mused. "I suppose, at some point, the pottery should be extracted for study and for display.

"Well, it's a sweet and sour gift you have given the people, you two. Why isn't Mr. Connelly with you?"

"He thought he'd be in the way of a strictly Navajo matter. I suppose, in a way, he's right, but he has a great mind for the big picture and is as honest as anyone I've ever met," said Rita, hoping she wasn't laying it on too thick.

"Well, at some point, the Nation will officially thank him for his efforts on our behalf, but like you said, this should remain confidential for now."

"Mr. President," said Carlos, "in my dreams I learned that through the centuries, one *Hatáli* held the secret of the Shrine's location and was responsible for its upkeep and carving the petroglyphs that represent that era. The last *Hatáli* before me was killed in battle and was not able to pass on the information of the Shrine to his successor. I learned in my dream that I had been designated the present caretaker of the Shrine of the Ancients until such time as I pass it on to my successor which, in this case, is my grandson who is currently serving his apprenticeship."

"I see no reason for that to change, do you?" Both Carlos and Rita shook their heads.

"I still do not know how Robert Begay heard what he heard."

"There was a leak?" the President asked, raising his eyebrows.

"Indirectly," said Rita. For thirty minutes, she explained how Robert Begay had confused Carlos's "something valuable" with the wrecked aircraft full of dope the Singer had found, and Begay's attempts to coerce the location out of Carlos. She explained Abe's attempted kidnapping and Carlos's abduction and subsequent escape. She described the shootout with the drug cartels and, finally, Meredith's kidnapping and escape from her abductors.

"My Lord, Rita, this sounds like this should all be on the big screen, but it happened in real life. How many lives were lost?"

"Over thirty if you count the members of Begay's group and those from the two drug cartels. Millie Nez, from Kayenta, who helped Carlos escape, died when one of the cartels set her house on fire. She was the only innocent victim."

"I remember being briefed about the shootout, but I didn't know you were involved or your friends."

"We were a long way away from the shooting, Mr. President. The DEA pretty much handled that and the survivors not in the hospital are still in jail on multiple federal charges."

"How much dope?"

"We figured about half a ton, perhaps two million dollar's worth depending on who values it and how."

"You've been a busy girl, Rita, and so have your friends. They all came out unscathed, out of danger and facing no legal problems?"

"Yes. Carlos's grandson, Abe, and my niece, Meredith, will be going to the University of Arizona this fall. Carlos here has returned to Shiprock after his hiatus on Cedar Mesa, and plans to return to Singing."

"What about you, Rita?" asked the President.

364

"I would like to return to Montezuma Creek and resume my duties as a teacher and dealing with whatever administrative issues arise for the community."

"I don't suppose there's any way to tempt you to come back here?"

"I'm afraid not. My weaving has been sadly neglected and I prefer that to politics, but thank you anyway."

"Had to ask. Now, what do you think we ought to do about the Shrine of the Ancients?"

"I think we are in agreement about keeping its location secret and those who know about it under the radar so they aren't pestered to death. The site has been there for hundreds of years and is as safe there as it can be. I would like to see the photographic evidence in the hands of those who can study and learn from it; after all, it might be the Rosetta Stone for petroglyphs for at least the southwest. Finally, is there any chance a display at one or more of the museums of the photos and videos would be possible? As you said, this is a windfall for all the native people of the southwestern U.S., living or dead, and those living would be enriched by seeing it. It is part of their heritage."

"That is the very least that will be done. If there are revelations to be gleaned from those petroglyphs, shame on us if we don't put our very best minds to work on them. But I see a problem on the horizon. And this isn't my underhanded way to get you back on my team, Rita, but someone familiar with the project and familiar with the publicizing of it is going to be hard to find. You fit the bill perfectly and we can create a temporary consultancy position for you for the time it would take to accomplish and maintain your duties.

"*Hatáli* Grey Hawk, like a polite senior Navajo, you have been mostly silent as Rita and I discussed the Shrine of the Ancients. I would appreciate your input and your concerns about what we have discussed," said President Yazzie.

"Mr. President, most of what you have discussed is beyond my purview. I am just a Navajo Singer unfamiliar with the ways of government. I was satisfied when you announced that you agree we should keep the Shrine's location secret. Beyond that, I am gratified that you wish to share it with the Diné and believe that Ms. Makespeace is uniquely suited to fill the coordinator role."

"No fair ganging up on me, Carlos!" said Rita with a smile. To President Yazzie, she said, "I will give your offer some serious thought and if I decide to decline, I stand ready to help train someone to fill the position."

The President stood, concluding the meeting. "That is all I can ask," he said to Rita. "This project deserves top notch people and that is why I thought of you." He held out his hand to Carlos who shook it. "*Yá'át'ééh, Hatáli* Grey Hawk, for following your dream and bringing such a treasure to the Navajo people." Carlos nodded but did not speak.

"Rita? What can I say? It was wonderful to see you again and thank you for bringing the Shrine of the Ancients to my attention. I won't drop the ball, I promise."

Rita shook the President's hand warmly then gave him a hug. "I'll get back to you in no longer than a week, is that okay?" she asked.

"Take as long as you need, those petroglyphs have waited a long time to surface." He escorted them to the door and opened it for them. His assistant was waiting and looking none too pleased that over two hours of the President's valuable time had been consumed by something he was not privy to.

President Yazzie patted him on the shoulder. "It is okay, Leonard, you will eventually learn all about this meeting, but whatever you learn must be kept confidential until Ms. Makespeace or I say otherwise."

Rita walked Carlos to his pickup. "Yá'át'ééh, Carlos. Don't be a stranger. I'm hopeful your disappearing days are over and you will come see me once in a while."

"Yá'át'ééh, Rita. You are a good woman, have done a good thing and I appreciate it."

It was getting dark by the time Rita drove the one hundred forty-five miles home to Montezuma Creek. Bob met her at the door with a hug, a kiss, and a frosty glass of iced tea. "Welcome home. Are you hungry? I have dinner all ready if you are and if you are not, I'll put it in the refrigerator."

"I'm starved, but let me change clothes first, I don't want to get anything on these clothes, especially the skirt."

"Too bad you have to shuck 'em, you look terrific in them. Then again, you look terrific *out* of them too." She chuckled and kissed him for the complement.

As Rita changed, Bob laid out a dinner of marinated barbecued chicken breasts, green salad and stir fried rice. She was so surprised when she saw the repast she was speechless.

"Are you secretly a chef and didn't tell anyone? This is wonderful and so appreciated," said Rita.

"Glad you're hungry and believe me I'm no kind of closet chef. I just thought you'd like to eat something other than takeout or Mcburgers."

"You could have fooled me about being a chef, this tastes great."

"So, how did the meeting with the President go?"

"Oh, Bob, he reacted just like the kids did – speechless, and then he was overwhelmed after Carlos and I told him the story – all of it. He had heard about the shootout but he had no idea we were involved. I was quick to point out we weren't anywhere nearby when the shooting started but we did have knowledge of the circumstances."

"What is he going to do?"

"I expected him to think about it for at least a few days but he was in agreement with us on every point, the main one being the Shrine's location remains secret and he wants to help disseminate the photography. He wondered why you weren't there too but I explained what you told me and he was okay with that. The only fly in the ointment is that he wants me to coordinate the release of the photos and video to the Navajo Nation Museum and to whomever else shows interest that is qualified to study them.

"I can see where it will get very hectic for a while once the word gets out. I mean, this is a *big* deal, archeologically speaking. I told him I'd think about it and if I declined, I'd help get someone up to speed."

"Are you going to take it?"

"Right now the answer is no since school starts in late August and I won't have time to do that, help Meredith and Abe get settled and see to Montezuma Creek business too."

"You've been doing a pretty good job of juggling so far."

"I've been just skimming through the mail, dealing with the important stuff but the rest of it needs to be addressed too. It isn't a big workload but it has built up since this matter of the Shrine came up."

"Okay, do I fit in there anywhere?"

"Only if you want to, Bob. If I had the only say, the answer would be a resounding yes, but you're half of this equation and I don't want you to feel obligated to stay when you're actually getting restless."

"Well, I *am* getting restless. I want to finish my red rock tour through southern Utah … and I want you to come with me. I realize it's Wednesday, and we have to get the kids and get them to Tucson by next Tuesday. That doesn't leave a lot of time but I'd sure like to take you up to see Bryce Canyon and Zion and Capitol Reef just to

369

name a few places.   Seeing the red rock is secondary, you understand, having you all to myself is  the main objective."

"When you put it like that, how can a girl refuse?  Let's go!"

Terry L. Shaffer grew up near Oregon City, Oregon, graduated from Oregon City High School and Clackamas Community College before moving on to Portland State University. Between high school and college, Terry spent four years in the United States Navy, working primarily in intelligence billets.

While at Portland State, Terry joined the Clackamas County Sheriff's Department where he was assigned a variety of positions including patrol, detectives and narcotics. He retired in 2000 after twenty-five years' service. After writing thousands of pages of police reports and search warrant affidavits, he likes to say that he has twenty-five years' experience writing in the true crime genre.

Terry began his writing career in fiction shortly before he retired and has been at it ever since. He lives full time in his motor home and divides his time between his small acreage in Colton, Oregon, and various locations in the American Southwest, where he spends his time writing and exploring. Terry enjoys off-roading, photography, reading and, of course, writing.

He welcomes feedback and may be reached at jbugley@gmail.com.

Made in United States
Troutdale, OR
09/29/2024

23143754R00216